ZANE PRESENTS

THE TRUTH IS IN THE WINE

A NOVEL

Dear Reader:

Everyone knows that when alcohol goes in, the truth usually comes out. In his latest novel, *The Truth Is In The Wine*, *Essence* bestselling author, Curtis Bunn, puts that theory to task. When a couple struggling to decide whether to remain married or not decides to take their dream vacation to the Napa Valley in California, along with both of their mothers who cannot stand to breathe the same air, anything is likely to happen…and it does.

Happiness and pain in a marriage are often interchangeable and when two people truly love each other, things can change in the blink of an eye…or a roll in the hay. This novel could be a much-needed therapeutic aide for a lot of couples trying to make a decision about whether to stick it out with each other or part ways. It is an intense at times, humorous at times, portrayal of why family and love trump everything else. I am sure that readers will be engaged in the characters and storyline from the first page. Bunn is a prolific author who never tells the same story twice, a godsend in today's literary climate.

As always, thanks for supporting the authors of Strebor Books. We always try to bring you groundbreaking, innovative stories that will entertain and enlighten. For a list of complete titles, please visit www.zanestore.com and I can be located at www.facebook.com/AuthorZane or reached via email at Zane@eroticanoir.com.

Blessings,

Zane

Zane
Publisher
Strebor Books
www.simonandschuster.com

ZANE PRESENTS

THE
TRUTH
IS IN
THE WINE

A NOVEL

CURTIS BUNN

SBI

STREBOR BOOKS

NEW YORK LONDON TORONTO SYDNEY

Strebor Books
P.O. Box 6505
Largo, MD 20792
http://www.streborbooks.com

This book is a work of fiction. Names, characters, places and incidents are products of the author's imagination or are used fictitiously. Any resemblance to actual events or locales or persons, living or dead, is entirely coincidental.

ISBN 978-1-59309-503-1
ISBN 978-1-4767-1146-1 (ebook)
LCCN 2013933667

First Strebor Books trade paperback edition October 2013

Cover design: www.mariondesigns.com
Cover photograph: © Keith Saunders/Marion Designs

10 9 8 7 6 5 4 3 2 1

Manufactured in the United States of America

For information regarding special discounts for bulk purchases,
please contact Simon & Schuster Special Sales at 1-866-506-1949
or business@simonandschuster.com

The Simon & Schuster Speakers Bureau can bring authors to your live event. For more information or to book an event, contact the Simon & Schuster Speakers Bureau at 1-866-248-3049 or visit our website at www.simonspeakers.com.

For my Felita, who is sweeter than any wine.
And that's the truth.

ACKNOWLEDGMENTS

Always, I give honor and praise to God for his unlimited blessings. He certainly carried me through this book. Thank you, Lord.

My family, which I love so much, remains to the core: my late father, Edward Earl Bunn, Sr.; he was not much of a wine-drinker, as I recall. Scotch was his drink of choice; my mother, Julia Bunn, who is simply wonderful; my brothers, Billy and Eddie and my sister, Tammy. My grandmother, Nettie Royster, remains our spiritual foundation.

Curtis, Jr. and Gwendolyn (Bunny) are my children, my life-blood, my heartbeats. My nephew, Gordon, has always been like a second son. And my niece, Tamayah (Bink Bink) and nephew Eddie, Jr. are blessings that I love so much. My cousins, Greg Agnew and Warren Eggleston, are like my brothers, as well as my brother-in-law, Deryk. And I am grateful for cousin Carolyn Keener and uncle Al and aunts Thelma and Barbara and Ms. Brenda Brown, who has been like an aunt/second mom much of my life.

Additionally, Felita Sisco Rascoe is my wife-to-be, foundation, heart and soul, super-duper closest friend and beacon of hope.

Again, Zane, Charmaine Roberts Parker and the entire Strebor Books/ Atria/Simon & Schuster family have been great, and I am eternally grateful for you. I'm proud to be a part of the wonderful, talented Strebor family.

I enjoy listing by name the supporters because you all mean so much to me: My ace, Trevor Nigel Lawrence, Keith (Blind) Gibson, Kerry Muldrow, Randy Brown, Sam Myers, Ronnie Bagley, Tony Starks, Darryl Washington, Darryl (DJ) Johnson, Lyle Harris, Monya Bunch, Tony (Kilroy) Hall, Marc Davenport, Tami Rice-Mitchell, Brad Corbin, William Mitchell, J.B. Hill, Bob White, Kent Davis, Wayne Ferguson, Tony & Erika Sisco, Betty Roby, Kathy Brown, Venus Chapman, Nicole McDowell, Tara Ford, Flecia Brown, Christine Beatty, Greg Willis, Al Whitney, Brian White, Ronnie Akers, Jacques Walden, Dennis Wade, Julian Jackson, Mark Webb, Kelvin Lloyd, Frank Nelson, Hayward Horton, Mark Bartlett, Marvin Burch, Derrick (Nick Lambert), Gerald Mason, Charles E. Johnson, Harry Sykes, Kim Mosley, Ed (Bat) Lewis, Shelia Harrison, David A. Brown, Leslie LeGrande, Rev. Hank Davis, Susan Davis-Wigenton, Donna Richardson, Sheila Wilson, Curtis West, Bruce Lee, Val Guilford, Derek T. Dingle, Ramona Palmer, Joi Edwards, Warren Jones, Deberah (Sparkle) Williams, Leon H. Carter, Zack Withers, Kevin Davis, Sybil & Leroy Savage, Avis Easley, Demetress Graves, Anna Burch, Natalie Crawford, Najah Aziz, George Hughes, Monica Harris Wade, Yetta Gipson, Mary Knatt, Serena Knight, Sonya Perry, Denise Taylor, Diana Joseph, Derrick (Tinee) Muldrow, Rick Eley, Marty McNeal, D.L. Cummings, Rob Parker, Cliff Brown, D. Orlando Ledbetter, Garry Howard, Stephen A. Smith, Clifford Benton, Len Burnett, Lesley Hanesworth, Sherline Tavenier, Jeri Byrom, E. Franklin Dudley, Skip Grimes, Carla Griffin, Jeff Stevenson, Angela Norwood, Lateefah Aziz, Billy Robinson, Jay Nichols, Ralph Howard, Paul Spencer, Jai Wilson, Garry Raines, Glen Robinson, Dwayne Gray, Jessica Ferguson, Carolyn Glover, David R. Squires, Kim Royster, Keela Starr, Mike Dean, Veda McNeal, Dexter Santos,

John Hughes, Mark Lassiter, Tony Carter, Kimberly Frelow, Michele Ship, Michelle Lemon, Zain, Tammy Thompson, Karen Shepherd, Carmen Carter, Erin Sherrod, Tawana Turner-Green, Sheryl Williams-Jones, Vonda Henderson, Danny Anderson, Keisha Hutchinson, Olivia Alston, John Hollis, Dorothy (Dot) Harrell, Aggie Nteta, LaKesha Williams, Ursula Renee, Carrie Haley, Anita Wilson, Tim Lewis, Sandra Velazquez, Patricia Hale, Pam Cooper, Michelle Hixon, Regina Troy, Denise Thomas, Andre Aldridge, Brenda O'Bryant, Ron Thomas, Pargeet Wright, Laurie Hunt, Deborah Sharpe, Mike Christian, Sid Tutani, Tracie Andrews, Toni Tyrell, Tanecia Raphael, Tammy Grier, Roland Louis, April Tarver, Penny Payne, Cynthia Fields, TaToya Tokley, Dr. Yvonne Sanders-Butler, Alicia Guice, Clara LeRoy, Denise Bethea, Hadjii Hand, Petey Franklin, Sibyl Johnson, Shauna Tisdale and The Osagyefuo Amoatia Ofori Panin, King of Akyem Abuakwa, Eastern Region of Ghana, West Africa.

Special thanks and love to my great alma mater, Norfolk State University (Class of 1983); the brothers of Alpha Phi Alpha (especially the Notorious E Pi of Norfolk State); Ballou High School (Class of '79), ALL of Washington, D.C., especially Southeast and the team at www.atlantablackstar.com.

I am also grateful to all the readers and book clubs that have supported my work over the years and to my many literary friends Nathan McCall, Carol Mackey, Linda Duggins, Terrie Williams, Kimberla Lawson Roby, Walter Mosley.

I'm sure I left off some names; I ask your forgiveness. If you know me you know it is an error of the head, not the heart. :-) I appreciate and I am grateful for you.

Peace and blessings,
CURTIS

In vino veritas (in vee-noh ver-i-tas) *Latin*. In wine, there is truth. A Latin expression that suggests people are more likely to say what they really feel under the influence of alcohol.

CHAPTER 1
CONFLICTING EMOTIONS

The pain shot up Ginger Wall's left arm, a jolt that rendered half of her body immobile. Her heartbeat was rapid, even though it felt like her chest was collapsing. Breathing was a chore. She was sure she was going to die.

No one was around to help her. No one was around because there was no one in her life. Her husband was her husband, but pretty much in name only; their marriage was on a spectacular descent. And he was in the house, anyway. Her daughter, whom she had smothered like a blanket, was just off to college. The few friends she maintained were kept at a distance. She was alone, and that thought pushed her to the edge of death.

Unable to move and desperate for air, Ginger resigned herself to dying—right there behind the wheel of her Lexus coupe in the garage of her modest townhouse near downtown Atlanta.

Seconds went by, then minutes, and finally she passed out. When she came to a few minutes later, the pain was gone. She could breathe easily. There was relief of the pressure she felt on her chest.

It almost seemed like a dream, like she pulled into the garage and passed out from exhaustion, and that scary moment came to her in her sleep. The reality was that the thought of entering a loveless house paralyzed her with anxiety and fear. She knew it was not a dream because her face was damp with tears.

Ginger had recently returned from dropping off her only child, Helena, at college. Paul, her husband, said his goodbyes to his baby girl at the airport, a fear of flying keeping him from making the trip to Washington, D.C.

But not her mom. Helena had become Ginger's everything. Right around the time Paul was laid off from his job as a heating and air conditioning repair specialist was when their marriage turned into an eighteen-wheeler going downhill with no brakes. He lost his self-esteem and she, eventually, lost interest. The combination made for a mundane existence and rapid fall over an eleven-month period.

This was not easy to accept for Ginger. She was crushed, crestfallen. It was if someone had died. As if *she* had died.

Only she hadn't. She was alive, but not living. To breathe, Ginger threw what was left of herself into Helena, serving as mother, chef, security, fan, chauffeur and anything else that kept her occupied and gave her some sense of fulfillment. That was why she pleaded with her child to attend a local college; her going away was akin to pulling the plug on the activity in Ginger's life.

"Mom, you know I love you and I'm going to miss you," Helena said when she decided to attend college in Washington, D.C. "But I've got to get away. Not from you, but from Atlanta. You are the one who told me when I turned fifteen that I should go to school out of town, that it would help me to grow up and be responsible. Ever since then that has been my goal. Plus, you have Dad."

Somehow, through the strife, they managed to shield Helena, to, indeed, fool her. She thought her parents were in a fulfilling relationship. If she had taken the time to *really* pay attention, she would have noticed that all the cheery conversation around the house was between her and her mom or her and her dad. There was only token dialogue between her parents, and none of it loving.

But she was merely seventeen when the downturn began; *her* life was the focal point of *her* existence. She simply did not notice.

One night while Helena was at a school play, the troubles in the marriage reached a crescendo.

"I thought about it. I thought about it a lot," Paul said, rising from the dinner table with Ginger. "I've got to go."

Ginger had a forkful of risotto headed toward her mouth when he said that. She dropped it into her plate below. He said it so casually, as one would reveal it was raining outside. The words registered with Ginger instantly, but for a nanosecond, though, she thought he meant he had to leave the dining room because there was a game on television he had to see. Or that he was tired and needed to go to bed early. Or that he wanted something from the store and had to go and get it. It could *not* have meant what it really sounded like he meant. It was not what he said; it was the *way* he said it that clued her in.

So, she did what anyone would do: She asked for confirmation. "What do you mean?"

Paul continued toward the kitchen. He did not bother to turn around.

"Divorce, Ginger," he said, again so nonchalantly that it was staggering. "Divorce."

Ginger reached for her glass of homemade tea and knocked it over, spilling its contents across the table and onto the hardwood floor. She was frozen there, unable to move until her emotions switched from confusion to anger. It was not April Fool's Day and Paul was not a joking kind of man. He, in fact, had become so serious, that Ginger and Helena privately called him "Heart Attack," as in "Serious as a heart attack."

Her anger allowed her to rise from the table and storm her way to the kitchen, where Paul was uncorking a second bottle of Malbec from the vast collection of wines he coveted like rare coins. He did not share the first bottle with his wife.

Ginger was five-foot-six, but appeared smaller when side-by-side with Paul, who was eight inches taller.

Looking up at him, she demanded: "What are you talking about, Paul?"

Ginger raised her voice when her husband did not answer. "Paul, what the hell are you talking about?"

"Don't act like this is some surprise," he said, finally. There was an edge to his voice—and a coldness, too. "This has been building for a while now. I'm fifty years old. You're only forty-seven. And—"

"Are you drunk? I'm forty-three," Ginger interrupted.

"No, I'm not drunk. And, okay, you're forty-three," Paul went on. "Anyway, we have some time to live still. Face it: We're not good together anymore."

"And this is the result?" Ginger asked. "You making a decision for both of us? No discussion about it? No counseling? Nothing? And what about our daughter, Paul? What about her?"

"Helena is a smart girl and she's strong," he said. "She will adjust. She'll be fine."

Ginger was not so sure about that. She and her daughter were close, but she was a daddy's girl. This news would rock her.

"Well, you tell her why you're breaking up this family," Ginger said. "You tell her that she and I are not good enough for you."

"This is not about Helena," Paul said, and a chill ran through Ginger's body despite how heated she was.

"So, it's about me? You don't want *me* anymore?" she asked. It was a rhetorical question because she knew the answer. But Paul answered anyway.

"I'm simply not sure about this marriage anymore," he said. He sipped his wine. "I'm sorry. I really am. I can't make you happy. And you don't try to make me happy. We've had sex one time in the last nine months. One time, a few weeks ago. And that was because we both were drunk.

"So why should we stay in a marriage for appearance sake? Or even for Helena? It wouldn't be teaching her the right thing."

"And it's teaching her the right thing by breaking up her family?" Ginger asked. She wanted to continue, but it suddenly hit her that going back and forth with Paul would give him the impression she was trying to convince him to stay, which she did not want to do. No doubt, she was devastated and hurt; she had built her life around her family. But she was prideful, too, and somewhere in their back-and-forth she decided, "Fuck him."

"I only ask that you do two things for me," she said. "Pick up your daughter from school and explain this to her."

"I will talk to Helena," Paul said. "But not tonight."

"You bastard," Ginger fired back. "You had it all planned out, huh? So who's your woman? Who's your side chick?"

Paul studied his wife, scanned her from head-to-toe and back again. There was a time looking at her smooth skin and full, pouty lips and dark eyes would mesmerize him. Not anymore. He held animus toward her that he did not bother to explain.

"Believe it or not," he said as calmly as one would give driving directions, "it's not about being with someone else. It's about being away from you."

And as tranquil as Paul was, Ginger turned equally irate. "I have done nothing but love you and be here for you and provide a nice home for you," she said. "You're such an egomaniac to try to belittle me. That's very hateful of you. But it shows you don't deserve me. You have been depressed since losing your job and I have been supportive and encouraging. Since we're being honest about everything, let me tell you this: You're a selfish pig. All you've ever thought about was yourself. You never considered how hard this whole thing has been for me. And that makes you a selfish pig.

"I'm woman enough to admit that I'm hurt by all of this. But the more I talk the more strength I get. I don't mean to call you names, but you're a loser. And whatever God has in store for you, well, good luck with that because He does not reward selfish pigs."

"Yeah, that's really mature, Ginger," Paul said. "You wishing bad on me. I won't stoop that low."

"You'd have to cut off your legs to get any lower than you are," Ginger said.

"I could say something, but I'm not," Paul responded. "But I will say this: You call being a nasty, mean, cold person supportive of me? That's all you have been. And that's not supportive."

Paul looked at Ginger with a strange expression. "I'm going to pick up Helena," he said. "I'll explain everything to her, but not now. She's happy. I will, though, in due time."

"Yeah, right," Ginger said. "You'll explain what you want to explain—not the truth, I'm sure."

Paul finished his wine, corked the bottle and placed it in its proper place among the alphabetized collection. He looked at his wife, who could not detect the pain that engulfed him. He hid it well, but inside he cried. Finally, before tears seeped from his eyes, he turned and walked away.

Ginger was left standing there to struggle with an influx of emotions that came crashing down. She waited until she heard the garage close, indicating Paul had gone.

It was then that she was overcome with a confluence of pain, shock, hurt, disappointment and failure. She cried. She laughed. She perspired—all over a three- or four-minute span. Ginger thought she was having a breakdown. "I'm OK," she said aloud. "I'm OK."

But she wasn't.

CHAPTER 2
SAVING
GRACE

A s Ginger sat in the garage that evening, fearful that she was dying, Paul stood in the house, perhaps fifty feet away, feeling as alive as ever, as if he were starting a new life. His hands shook, but not from some kind of breakdown. It was from the possibilities, from relief, from joy, from amazement. While his wife fretted coming into the loveless house she shared with a man who wanted out, Paul held in his unsteady possession a lottery ticket that represented $8 million.

A whole new world was now his, one that suddenly had boundless possibilities.

Processing it all jolted him. He played the Georgia State Lottery because it seemed the thing to do. "You have to play to win," its slogan said. And yet he never expected to actually have the prized numbers.

In one sense, it was liberating: financial concerns, concerns that overwhelmed him and robbed him of his dignity, no longer existed. In another sense, there was trepidation: What to do? Where to begin? And in still another way there was a true dilemma: What to do about his wife?

He had $4 million or so coming to him after taxes, but it was not enough to bring him total joy. The reality was that he still loved Ginger. Yes, he told her he wanted out of the marriage, but he did not mean it. Not really. He was frustrated, almost depressed and did not see any other way to spare *her* life.

He wanted her love, *needed* her love. Before he lost his job, Paul was devoted and loving. He was not the most light-hearted guy, but Ginger could rely on him to love her and be there for her and their daughter. Losing his job changed him. He became distant and evil. His self-esteem evaporated. He felt no sense of self-worth. His changed disposition led to a troubled marriage.

Winning the money instantly turned Paul into the Paul of old. He felt totally rejuvenated. But he needed Ginger's love. Other than Diana, his high-school girlfriend, Ginger was the only woman he loved. And he wanted her love back. But he wanted her back on genuine terms; not because he became a millionaire.

After his outburst a few weeks earlier, when he told her he wanted a divorce, their "marriage" really leveled off. They spoke pleasantly enough to each other around their daughter, but that was it. Ginger gathered herself and displayed a lack of interest in Paul, a disregard for their marriage and a disinterest in trying to save it.

Paul was troubled. He had no idea he would get a financial windfall. When he did, still feeling like his life was incomplete told him something significant: He needed Ginger. Buying back her love was akin to prostitution, and Paul viewed prostitution as an act against God.

Rather, he wanted to earn his wife's love and admiration, something he once possessed. The early years of their eighteen-year marriage were idyllic. It was a union that was nearly story-book in their joy and commitment to each other. When they learned they could not conceive a child, they adopted Helena, who was eight days old at the time. He was thirty-three and she was twenty-six, and having their daughter brought Paul and

Ginger even closer, as they threw their love into making the child feel loved. And she did.

They did not have a lot of money but they had love and two salaries and they made it work—right up until around the time Paul was laid off his job. Over that nearly year of unemployment, his self-esteem plummeted like the economy and his weight increased by about fifteen unflattering pounds, all seemingly in his midsection and face.

Their marriage was not on the rocks; it was *under* the rocks. The getaway road trips to Miami and New Orleans ceased. The affection they showed each other—affection that at one time made other couples uncomfortable and envious at the same time—vanished like the rabbit in the magician's hat.

In the month after he told Ginger he wanted a divorce, they only seemed to tolerate each other while uttering nary a loving word between them. Paul was mum because he was depressed and she was displeased because her man no longer was the provider and comforter he had been. And he blamed her for his woes.

Her displeasure manifested itself in more and more time away with Helena and away from Paul—anything to not be around her husband whose manhood was assaulted with unemployment.

But Paul loved his wife and he believed she still loved him. At least, he wanted to believe that. Circumstances got in the way, he told himself. Looking down at that lottery ticket shaking in his hand, he believed he had the elixir to their toxic union.

The fix was not directly in how the money would influence his wife, however. It was in how it would impact *him*. The swagger, confidence, self-assuredness returned, and so he was immediately extracted from the doldrums. His renewed vim and vigor would be the keys to Ginger feeling better about him and, consequently, rescue their marriage. That was his hope.

However, to make sure she would return to the loving woman he admired for the right reasons, he almost immediately determined he could not tell her of his winnings. Surely she would at least act as if she were back on board knowing the new extent of his bank account. If she was coming back, he wanted it to be on his merits, not his luck.

As his wife, she was entitled to half of the jackpot. He was not trying to avoid giving it to her—$2 million surely would be enough to live a cherished life, he reasoned. But he really needed to see if he could repair the damage that wrecked their marriage and restore the love from Ginger he used as fuel.

His shaking stopped as he worked his brain to conjure up something he could tell her that would at least minimize the questions of his sudden fat pockets.

Paul could claim the money at any time, but decided he would wait a few weeks. He wanted the attention around the drawing to diminish before he contacted the lottery office. Paul liked to play the numbers, but Ginger berated him about doing so, saying, "That's an ignorant way to waste money."

But Paul continued to play, only he did so in silence; Ginger had no idea. And neither she nor anyone knew about his winning numbers. He had no formula. There were no birthdays or license plate numbers or addresses. He selected random numbers that popped into his head for no particular reason.

Of all the things that could have been overwhelming his brain— where to travel, what to buy, how to celebrate, never having to work again—Paul's thoughts centered on saving his marriage. He considered Ginger his "wholemate," saying "You make me whole" in reciting his vows at their wedding. Ginger was it for him, from the first time they met at the quaint bar at Aria restaurant in the Buckhead section of Atlanta.

Ginger was with friends celebrating a birthday. When she went to the bar to order a bottle of wine, Paul—after observing her alluring presence—volunteered his expertise.

"That bottle of wine you ordered will have the effect you want; it will get you drunk," he said, smiling. "But if you want to have a great-tasting wine that also will get you where you want to get, I would recommend this."

He pointed to a sixty-five-dollar bottle of Palmeri Riesling. Ginger took his advice and later came back to thank him for the suggestion. She loved it. Paul was happy she came back to the bar, where he sat alone, sipping wine.

"You should let me be your sommelier," he said.

"Maybe I would if I knew what that was," Ginger answered. "You might be trying to set me up."

They laughed. "A sommelier is basically a wine steward, someone who knows and understands wines and can recommend the right one for the right meal, right occasion, right mood," he said.

"OK, I get it," she answered. "And you'll be my personal sommelier? How did I get so lucky?"

"You obviously are a lucky person," he said with a no-nonsense look on his face. Then he smiled.

He had her then. Ginger was intrigued, soon in love and less than two years later they were married. And now Paul, in an instant, was an unlikely millionaire, married to a woman he loved despite having told her he wanted a divorce.

Because he was so down about himself, he did not know how to change the course of his marriage. If only he could get a job, it would do something toward his self-esteem and therefore bring out the person she fell in love with, instead of the person that became mired in so much self-pity.

Well, he came up better than finding a job. He hit the lottery, and his self-esteem rushed back to him as if injected into his bloodstream.

Paul did not have any siblings and was not sure when he would tell his mother, although he would take care of her in every way she desired. Alvin, meanwhile, was the ace among his plethora of friends, his Super Glue-tight "dog" of twenty-two years. When Paul got the trembling out of his system, he screamed so loudly his head hurt. Then he shed joyous tears. Then he called Alvin, whom he referred to as Big Al.

"Get over here right now. I don't care what you're doing; please, get here now," Paul said.

He alarmed Big Al. "What's wrong, boy? Talk to me."

"Can't. Not over the phone. Just get here," Paul said. "Big news."

"Twenty minutes," Big Al said.

The news was so big that Big Al could not contain his glee. He knew Paul being a millionaire meant he was one, too. His life as he knew it also had changed. That's how tight they were.

And so he leaped around Paul's as if on a pogo stick. Paul sat there watching and laughing. He never let the ticket out of his hands.

"I'd rather not have her than have her back because I have money," Paul told Big Al.

"Why do you want her back at all?" Alvin shot back. "You know how I feel about Ginger. She's cool with me. But there's a new world out there for you. You can do anything you want and acquire anything you want. I mean, seriously. You're telling me you have four million dollars coming to you and you want to stay with a woman who has basically turned her back on you when stuff got tight? Let me tell you something: If I were *happily* married and hit the lottery for four mil, I'd get a divorce. Ain't nothing one woman could do for me with that kinda money."

"You would say that, Big Al," Paul said. "But then you don't have your 'wholemate.' I do. All you have are 'whoremates.' It went bad for us, yeah. But now we can get it back."

"You think she won't get inspired to act like she's happy with all that money?" Big Al wanted to know.

"That's why I said I'm not telling her—at least not right now," Paul said. "I'm going to act like everything is the same."

"How can you have that money and act like everything is the same? Are you crazy?" Big Al said.

"Discipline," Paul answered. "This is important. This is my life. This is my wife. I recognize where her head is: she's disappointed that I'm not contributing to the household as I have, as I promised, as I'm supposed to. I told her a few weeks ago that I wanted a divorce. I didn't want to hold her back. So, I need to know where Gin's heart is. I haven't been able to find out before now because my head has been messed up. An out-of-work man is a man with a burden that only another out-of-work man can understand. I'm fifty years old. Been working since I was fourteen—that's thirty-six years straight where I earned a living.

"To be out of work for almost year took something out of me. I couldn't really convey it to her. I fell into a funk and she into a funk about me. I don't like it, but I can't blame her. I was supposed to be the man for her, to provide. Not working drained some of my manhood, in her eyes."

"It's not like you weren't trying to get employed," Big Al said. "Or that you quit your job. You got downsized. Millions of guys have been downsized. And since then you have been hitting the bricks, interviewing, trying to get on. It's a bad time in the country, no matter how hard President Obama tries. Seems like if you were trying to get work she would understand and not simply check out on you.

"But, hey, that's just me. Anyway, so what's your plan? Anyone else gets rich, they act like they just got rich. You...you're gonna act like nothing changed? I gotta see this."

"Well, not exactly," he said. "I was part of a major class action suit against a bank that was overcharging on overdraft fees for twenty years. Ginger knows about it. I'm gonna tell her I got a settlement check of five thousand for that and that my income tax check came from last year—a little more money.

"Then I'm going to take her on a trip we both said we really wanted to go on before I lost my job—to the Napa Valley in California, to the wine country. We never went because I don't like to fly. But I'm going to for this.

"Al, this is my chance to get my life back the way I want it, but even better because we'll have each other and no more financial issues. Truth be told, I don't want anyone else. I want Ginger."

"Well, good luck, my brother," Al said. "I gotta get home. But when you're ready to start really spending that money, hit me up."

"You know I got you, man," Paul said. "First thing to do is line up your bills. We're gonna pay all them off and go from there. I'll have some nice cash for you."

They shook hands and slapped each other on the back.

"Tomorrow!" Paul yelled to Al as he walked toward his car.

An hour later, after he had pinched himself and the reality of the money set it, he heard the garage door open, indicating Ginger was home. The timing for the money was ideal; they had wiped out their savings for their daughter's first year of college. Paying for her education no longer would be a worry.

It seemed his only worry was if his wife would embrace him trying to mend their broken marriage.

CHAPTER 3
PICKING UP
THE PIECES

Paul got concerned when he realized Ginger had been in the car about fifteen minutes after he heard the garage door go up. He went to the refrigerator and pulled out a bottle of Viognier and two glasses.

Before he could go check on Ginger, she emerged, moving slowly, with her head down. She was down about her daughter being off to college and scared about the panic attack she had.

"Hey," Paul said with a level of concern in his voice—something Ginger had not heard in some time, "You OK?"

Ginger was stunned by his concern. She had heard no caring inflection in his voice for months, not toward her, anyway. She lifted her head and looked at him. Paul looked different, she noticed right away. He stood more upright and his eyes were bright, not sullen.

"Do you care, Paul?" she said, walking past him to the living room, where she sat on the couch.

Paul did not answer. He went to the kitchen and retrieved the wine and the glasses. He placed it on the coffee table in front of Ginger. She was confused. He had not offered her any of his precious wine in months.

"Ginger," he said, "I do care."

"Since when?" she asked.

Paul poured wine into the glasses. He picked up one and handed it to Ginger. She looked at the glass for several seconds, looked at her husband and finally reached for the glass.

"I have always cared, Gin," he said. "I just…"

"You just what, Paul?"

"I just lost who I was," he said.

Ginger did not respond. She sat back on the couch, wine in hand.

Paul went on. "I want you to realize that I'm sorry."

"You said you want a divorce, Paul," she shot out.

"I know and I didn't mean it," he said.

"So why would you say something so hurtful?" Ginger said. "You said you wanted to get away from me. You think that didn't hurt me, hurt my feelings?"

"I didn't mean it," he said. "Listen, I was depressed. I was miserable. You won't believe this, but I thought I would be doing the right thing by letting you move on. I didn't see anything getting better and…I…I don't know where that came from—divorce—but I just said it."

"You don't just say you want a divorce, Paul," she said.

"I just said it," he responded. "I don't want a divorce, Gin. I want us to get back to where we used to be. I really do."

"Why? Why would you want that after how bad it has been?" she asked.

"Please taste your wine," Paul said. "It's good."

"Paul," Ginger said, exasperated.

"OK, I'm just saying," he said. He sipped his wine and added: "Anyway, think about it: Our baby is off to college. It's only you and me. This is the perfect time for us to find what we used to have."

Ginger finally tasted the wine. It was good—clean, light, fresh, floral.

"I don't know how to respond to this, Paul," she said. "I was in the car just now and I felt like I was dying. I dreaded coming in here and dealing with your attitude and total disregard for me. I literally was in the car crying. I couldn't breathe."

"What?"

"Yes, I'm serious," she said. "I felt like there was nothing for me to come into this house to, no love. So, for you to tell me you didn't mean all the awful things you said to me, the way you have treated me the last few weeks....I don't know."

"You're supposed to be skeptical," Paul said. "I understand it. I'm not asking you to do anything except have an open mind. I want to work this thing out. It's very important to me."

Ginger took a big gulp of the wine, and it went straight to her head. She sipped more, and she could feel a change coming over her from it. When that happened, she became audacious.

"So, what's this about? You want sex?" she said. "All of a sudden you're serving me wine and you want to work it out? Look at you. You're all shaven and even have on cologne. What's going on? I don't get it. It was bad before, but the last three weeks have been terrible.

"And now you want to work it out? That's hard to believe. I don't care what you say."

Paul knew his wife and he knew that the wine was kicking in. He also knew that challenging her would result in her getting more and more combative, especially after she finished her glass and immediately poured herself another.

There were times when he would challenge her. But this was not one of them.

"You will see over time," he said. "Ginger, let's make this work."

"How do you propose we do this, Mr. I Want A Divorce?" she said.

Paul smiled.

"What's so funny?" she wanted to know. "You laughing at me?"

"No. I was thinking we should take a trip," he said.

"A trip?" Ginger cracked. "To where? Fantasy Island?"

"I was thinking the trip we have been talking about for years—to Napa Valley," Paul said.

"Napa? You want to drive across country?"

"No," he said. "Let's fly."

"You wanna fly?" Ginger said. "Now I'm sure something's up. You're the same man who two days ago would not fly to see your daughter off at college. Now, you wanna fly to California with me to the wine country? Nah, something's going on. What's going on?"

"I regret not flying with you and Helena to D.C.," Paul said. "I do. I don't like flying, but I should have made the trip anyway for my daughter. I regret that. But I will fly up there and fly back with her when she comes home for the first time. I have to do that for her.

"But in the meantime, I think we should go to Napa and enjoy the wine and see if we can't bring this marriage back together."

Ginger remained confused. The idea sounded good to her. No matter how bad things had gotten, Paul was still her husband and she silently prayed for their marriage to be saved.

But her rational mind would not push aside obvious questions.

"How we gonna pay for this?" she asked. "The mortgage is due and we barely got Helena into college. You think we should borrow money to go on a vacation? I know you're not saying that."

"I'm not saying that at all," Paul said, sipping the last of his wine. "Something happened today. I got a call about the class-action suit. I have some money coming to me next week: seven thousand dollars.

"We can pay the mortgage and still have more than enough to go out there. Not long. Maybe three days. Enough to hit some vineyards and talk and see where we really are."

"So you got some money coming in for the first time in almost a year and you want to spend it all?" Ginger asked. "What about saving some? Bills come around every month, you know? Or did you forget?"

Paul was insulted but he did not let it show. It was not easy for him to hold back, but he did.

"Let's not forget that I have been providing some money for the longest here," he said calmly. "I worked with Eric cutting grass. I drove a cab. I worked at Home Depot. Don't act like I sat around here and did nothing. I'm not gonna let you put that out there like you might believe it's true. I have tried."

"You did, Paul," she conceded. "I won't deny that. But—"

"There is no but, Gin," he jumped in. "I have been through hell this year. You don't know what it's like to work all of your life and then one day, out of the blue, someone tells you that you can't work anymore. You can't provide for your family.

"That's not a small thing, Gin. It hurt. It changed me. And now I have some money coming my way; I deserve to take a vacation. You do, too."

He ain't never lied, she thought to herself. Ginger was emotionally spent. Between her daughter being off to college and the drama Paul inflicted—and now his one hundred eighty degrees in attitude change—she thought she was in a bad dream. Going away with anyone would be an elixir to her doldrums. And to Napa Valley, the one place she and Paul talked about really wanting to visit?

"You really want me to go?" Ginger asked.

"Yes," he answered.

"Well, if you really do, then you'd do this one thing for me," she said.

"What's that?" Paul wanted to know.

"Take my mother with us," she said.

It was such an out-of-left-field request that Paul spat the wine in his mouth out onto the coffee table and a little on Ginger.

"Damn, Paul. That's disgusting," she said, using a napkin to wipe off her arm.

"I'm sorry," he said. "You surprised me with that."

Madeline Price, Ginger's mother, lost her husband of 34 years about ten months prior, to a heart attack. He was working in the yard of their small ranch home near downtown Decatur, near Atlanta, with his wife, who went inside to fetch them some lemonade. When Madeline got back, her husband was facedown in the rose bushes, dead.

Her grieving was enormous and understandable. Theirs was a marriage the antithesis of most.

"I actually didn't heard my parents argue or speak of arguing in their last twenty years together," Ginger said. "If they were hiding it, they hid it well. You have seen them together—they were happy, like a fairy tale.

"So, taking her with us to the Wine Country would be really great for her. It hasn't been that long since my dad passed and she's done nothing but stay in the house. She needs to get away."

"We need to get away, too, Ginger," Paul said. "We really need this time. You think we can have the same experience with your mother there?"

"My mother being there won't interfere with anything between us," she said.

Ginger never took her eyes off of her husband and he never blinked. They were locked in, which was an advantage to Ginger, and she knew it. Paul melted at his wife's eyes and her desires. At least he used to.

"OK," he said. "OK. We'll work it out. It'll be good."

Ginger got up from the couch and hugged Paul, a show of affection so rare that he closed his eyes as they embraced, so as to savor the moment.

Then he opened them suddenly and pulled away from Ginger.

"What if I invite my mom, too?" he said. "She and your mom can keep each other company, finally get to know each other and maybe even end up liking each other. And that would give us some space to do something by ourselves."

Ginger was surprised; their parents were not close. They were not friends. There was no obvious dislike, but there was obvious unspoken discord.

"You didn't get that much money and now you're looking to spend it all on one trip?" she said.

"You weren't concerned about money when you asked about bringing your mom," Paul said.

"That's not the point," Ginger shot back.

"No, actually, it's exactly the point," Paul said. "I want my mom to come and suddenly you're worried about the money I spend? Well, if your mom is going, my mom should, too. She needs to get away as much as any of us."

Paul's point made Ginger think—and soften her stance. She was at Brenda Wall's the day after she told her husband when he came home from a round of golf: "I'm sorry. I'm moving out. I don't want to be married anymore."

And by the next morning, most of her belongings were in her new apartment in downtown Atlanta. She was that decisive. It was such a shocking move that she did not even get emotional about it.

"You're right," Ginger said. "Your mom and my mom both need to go someplace like Napa and clear their heads. It will be good for them. When?"

"I was thinking in a few weeks or so," Paul said. "I want to research where we should stay, what vineyards to see and so on and so forth."

"Paul, I don't think we should tell them about the trip yet," Ginger said. "Right now, I am agreeing to it, but I'm still not one hundred percent. I don't know. A lot of stuff has happened and I can't say I'm really over it."

"I'm sure you're not over it," he responded. "But life is too short to not get over it. This is a start, Gin. You know you want to go. You talk about how much I love wine, but you love it, too. To go there would be awesome. Listen, I'm willing to get on an airplane to do it. That's telling you how much I think we should do this."

Ginger simply stared at him, so he went on.

"Think about it: We need this. Think of how picturesque it is, how peaceful. Think of the great wines we will have. Think of how close we all will become because of this."

She took a deep breath. Almost an hour before she was in her garage, thinking she was about to die. Now, she had an invitation to live out a dream. How could she pass it up? How could she accept it, coming from a man who made her feel so bad about herself?

"Let me think about it, Paul," she said. "But I don't know if I should go with you. There's a lot of water under the bridge."

"I understand," Paul said. "I understand. But we're going. This is too good an idea to pass up. And think about your mother and how much she needs this trip. In the meantime, I'm going to do some research."

CHAPTER 4
WHAT'S IN A NAME?

His mother named him Paul. She liked the name because it went nicely, she thought, with their last name, which was Wall. She especially liked that in The Bible, Paul was a man who faithfully spread the word of God throughout the nations.

Not that she was a religious zealot or anything. Simply, she believed in the power of God and she wanted her son to have a name that was at least associated with the Almighty.

And so, that made the nickname she gave her only child all the more perplexing.

"Vino," she called him.

Unlike most who picked up nicknames as kids that followed them through adulthood, Paul was labeled "Vino" when he was twenty-one—the legal age to drink alcohol. It was then that he became a wine lover of extraordinary measure.

After dropping out of college one year before graduation, he celebrated by going out alone for a drink. As he had not consumed an alcoholic beverage to that point, the bartender at the Capital Grille in Atlanta recommended he try a glass of Cabernet Sauvignon.

"Start slowly," the man said.

He poured Paul some in a wide-rimmed, elegant glass that felt like a delicate instrument. The bartender, Jimmy, explained that the circumference of the glass allowed the wine to breath.

Paul started to ask, "Why does wine need to breathe?" but thought better of it. Instead, he admired it for a while, analyzed it. It was deep and rich in color, like blood, only darker. He had seen someone in a movie smell wine and swish it around in a glass before tasting it, and so he did that. The bartender stood there watching, curious about his reaction.

"This is a small part of history—your first drink," he said.

He swished the wine around his mouth as one would Listerine, but not as violently. He closed his eyes and finally swallowed. When he opened his eyes, the bartender was staring and smiling.

"Well...," he said.

Paul's response shocked the man. He talked of the wine's texture and its "oaky taste" and "smoky smell."

"It has a floral sense to it, too. I taste something like berries or dark cherries. And it was clean. I thought it would be chilled. But if it were chilled I think the taste of it would be different, not as powerful."

Jimmy, the bartender, stared at him. "So you were lying to me, huh?" he finally asked.

"Lying? No," Paul answered. "About what?"

"Then how could you come up with that kind of analysis? Someone who never had wine couldn't possibly figure all that out," Jimmy said. "Even if you were wrong, it would be outrageous to think someone with no experience drinking would be able to come up with anything close to those thoughts. *And* it's the right analysis."

"I don't know," Paul said.

"Well, that makes you some kind of wine genius because I

don't hear people who claim they appreciate and love wine give that kind of insight."

Paul did not know what to think. But he finished off the glass and then another, savoring each sip as a death row inmate would a last meal.

That night, he took his mother out to dinner. He broke the news that he quit school. "I tried it and realized, finally, it wasn't for me, Ma," he said. "No need to waste another year doing something I don't want to do."

His mom was stunned...in a bad way. "I had more dreams for you than becoming a dropout," she said.

Unfazed, Paul told her: "That's not how I look at it. I understand how you see it, though. But I see it as me waking up so I can finally start doing what I want to do," he said.

She was afraid to even ask what that might be, so she didn't. Instead, she sought the waiter.

"I will have a big, tall glass of bourbon," she said. "I don't care what brand. Straight."

"No," Paul told the waiter. "We'll have two glasses of wine. Pinot Noir."

She looked at her son as he gave detailed instructions.

"Since when do you drink?" she said. "And how do you know about wine?"

"Since this afternoon," he said. "I don't know a lot, but I know I like wine...a lot."

The Pinot arrived and he raised his glass. "This, Ma, is to following your dreams," he said, and they tapped glasses.

His mom sucked hers down as if it was Gatorade and she was stranded in the Arizona desert.

Paul was appalled. "That's not how you drink wine," he said. He then explained that wine was to be "pampered and savored, nurtured and seduced. Hold the glass by the stem; if you hold it by the glass your body temperature will warm it up."

"What's going on with you?" she said. "I don't understand any of this."

"It's easy to understand," Paul started. "I have taken back over my life. I'm twenty-one and I'm going to figure out exactly what I want to do. But it's going to be something I really want to do. Not some job to make money. I want to be happy to go to work."

His mother did not bother to challenge that logic, although she argued that having a college degree was a pedigree that could only help in whatever he wanted to do. After all, she knew her son. Paul had a passion for golf and playing Scrabble and watching *Jeopardy* on television. He enjoyed card games, especially "I Declare War," and "Tonk." Brenda Wall did not see a career in any of that.

Paul convinced her to let him dream outside of *her* dreams and work toward whatever career he developed an interest. His mom relented, but she was surprised that her son went through years of searching—painting, cooking, furniture-making—before he settled in on something that really resonated with him: working on heaters and air conditioners.

"I love it because I get to work with my hands and I get to figure out a problem and solve it," Paul explained. "It's not glamorous, but it's needed and I actually enjoy it."

He went to technical school for two years to get certified and he was on his way.

So he was at a good place. He identified his life's work and his love for wine increased.

For nearly two decades he dreamed of a vacation in the United States' finest region for wine: Napa Valley in northern California.

One thing or another—getting married, an Achilles injury, lack of money—prevented him from fulfilling that ambition.

And after losing his job, it seemed he might not fulfill his dream any time soon but the lottery changed all that.

They decided to do something totally different: to visit Napa Valley for Thanksgiving. It was Ginger's idea. She woke up one morning with the feeling that if she was going on the trip, she'd rather it be in the Ffall and for the holiday. She had always wanted a destination Thanksgiving where she did not have to cook and clean, where she could enjoy the food and sit back like everyone else.

Even when she went to her mom's for Thanksgiving or to her mother-in-law's, she always was obligated to help with the food and clean up. She did not want to do that again, especially with so much drama swirling around her marriage.

Helena, their daughter, went to Columbia, Maryland for the holiday with her college roommate and her family. Paul and Ginger were not happy about it, but they liked her roommate and family and were really glad their daughter had gained a true friend. So, the adults took to the journey across country.

Traveling there was relatively uneventful, if you discount Paul's panic attack, Ginger's frustration with her mother, Brenda Wall's unhappiness with the passenger sitting next to her and Madeline Price's displeasure about her daughter questioning her drinking on the plane. Other than that, it was all smooth.

And it all started so well. All parties gathered at Paul and Ginger's at seven o'clock Thanksgiving morning; flights were cheaper leaving on the holiday. Although Paul clearly could afford it, he went with the program so as to not arouse suspicion.

Ginger prepared a light breakfast of muffins, turkey bacon and fruit. Paul surprised everyone by arranging for a limousine to take them to the airport. They enjoyed the early meal and the luxurious ride to the airport without incident. Paul chalked it up to the early-morning hour. *They must be sleepy*, he thought to himself about the ladies.

Ginger had rebuffed all but one of Paul's sexual advances after he won the money. They had consumed two bottles of Fairfield Viognier from South Africa while watching the Presidential returns on November 6th. And when Barack Obama was reelected, all inhibitions came tumbling down in the celebration and relief.

It was an intense session, one that reminded Ginger of their early days together and made her forget their recent troubled times. Paul believed that night signaled they were on their way back to something significant.

But the next morning, Ginger was lukewarm, almost distant. It was almost as if the night before had not happened. When Paul tried to kiss her before leaving to go to "work," she moved away.

"What's wrong?" he said.

"You think everything is all right because we slept together, Paul?" she answered. "That changes nothing. We have problems and they are serious."

Paul was dumbfounded, but not deterred. "I understand," he said. "There's no need to act like it didn't happen because it did. So let's build on it and not take away from it."

Ginger knew he was right but her pride and stubbornness would not allow her to fall all the way back into the marriage after he so severely hurt her. "People think that as long as the man doesn't cheat on you, it's OK," she told her closest friend, Serena, a sweet and honest woman.

"I know," Serena said, "Like he should get credit for doing something he's supposed to do anyway."

"Right," Ginger said. "I'm glad he didn't cheat; don't get me wrong. But you can really hurt someone with your words and attitude. Paul sat at our dining room table and told me he didn't want me anymore. And he acted like it. And I'm supposed to simply melt when he says he didn't mean it? I don't think so."

"You're right, Ginger," Serena told her. "But don't be so caught up in what he said then. You know him better than anyone. You should be able to determine if he's sincere or not. And I'm not saying run back into his arms. But he is your husband and you do love him. If you can put your marriage back together, why wouldn't you?"

Then she added: "Never let him forget his words that hurt you. Don't use them against him. But if he needs to be reminded that he disappointed you..."

"That's why you're my girl," Ginger said, and they laughed.

Serena's words helped Ginger at least let down her guard enough to observe Paul and his actions with an objective eye, not a tainted one. And that allowed her to agree to the trip and to go with an open mind to enjoy it.

She did quietly wonder how three-and-a-half days with her mother and her mother-in-law would pass without someone looking to pull out someone's hair. But she was up to the challenge because the trip very well could be the turning point in her marriage, which she wanted to get back on track.

Paul wanted that, too, and he was in a good place in his life, finally. He was with his beloved wife on their dream trip, even as she remained suspect about him. He had lost ten pounds since receiving the lottery check and discarded the cloud that hung over him. He was rich. And, above all, he had hope.

He did have a bit of drama, though: the way he saw it, his wife had not totally fallen back in line; indeed, she carried a bit of an attitude with her to California. But he could work on that. His mom and Ginger's mom represented a different story. They had not seen each other in months and that time apart did not temper their issues.

From the start, they did not agree that their children should marry. Brenda Wall saw Ginger as an overly emotional weakling who only sought a husband, not a true mate.

"I don't trust her," she told Paul at the time. "There's something about her that is sneaky and underhanded. And you told me she can't have children, right? So, why would you want to marry someone who cannot bear your children?"

"Because I love her, Ma," Paul said. "Because I am better with her than without her. Because we match and enjoy each other and have the same ideas about life. I'm almost ashamed that you're telling me to not marry someone I love because she can't have children, like that's all there is to life and happiness."

Brenda accepted her son's position, but she never agreed with it. And so, she treated Ginger with disdain or disregard, albeit not overtly. When they adopted Helena, the new grandmother said at a gathering of family and friends: "I'm so proud of you, Paul. You're going to be a great parent and instill all the character in this child that she needs."

She did not mention Ginger, and Ginger's mom was incensed. She told her daughter in the kitchen, when they were alone and away from the guests: "This woman is sick. How dare her ignore your role in your baby's life. I don't have a problem with Paul. But that mother of his…going around talking about God this and God that. In reality, she's Lucifer. Let her disrespect you like that again and I'm—"

"You're gonna what, Ma? Fight her?" Ginger asked. "That's not happening. You're too old to be even talking about something like that. She might have a problem with me, but we're gonna take the high road. Momma, I'm a mother. I have a baby. We shouldn't even be talking about that woman right now."

And the talk ended there, but the animosity did not. They were around each other for special occasions like Helena's graduation from high school, and they had token conversation. This would have to change over the trip, and neither Paul nor Ginger knew in what way.

A sense of what was to come occurred at the Atlanta airport. Ginger's mother, Madeline, was a bit taken aback by the Southwest Airlines boarding procedure—first-come-first served—and complained about it to her daughter for twenty minutes. Finally, Ginger told her: "Mother, we're gonna get on the plane and that's it. It's Thanksgiving morning. Let's be thankful for this.

"Plus," she added, "you're a senior. You can board before everyone else."

That logic brought down Madeline's emotions. "It could be worse," she said. "I could be sitting next to Brenda."

"Momma," Ginger said, "you're sharing a room with her in Napa. So, what's wrong with sitting next to her on the flight? We're not gonna have any nonsense on this trip. Right? *Right?*"

Madeline reluctantly nodded her heard.

"This is an important trip," Ginger said. "We're going to a beautiful place. We're a family. Let's enjoy it and not mess it up with petty stuff. I don't get along that great with Mrs. Wall, either. But I don't let it bother me. I do what I believe is the right thing and keep it moving. You should adopt the same attitude."

"Yeah, well, we'll see," Madeline said. "She thinks her son is all that, that he's too good for you. And here he is, he can't even keep a job."

"Mother," Ginger jumped in. She found herself defending her

husband, which was not the plan. Her position was more about altering her mother's attitude than taking up for Paul.

"Paul has worked all his life," she said. "He got laid off. It's been a tough economy lately. But he still worked hard to provide for us. You need to stop looking at him as a failure. He could have given up or sat back and collected unemployment. But he didn't. It hasn't been easy for him. But he's hung there."

She said all that and yet she at times felt about Paul exactly as her mom did. But the wife in her would not allow anyone, not even her mother, to bad-mouth her husband.

"If you say so," Madeline allowed.

"Momma, you can get on the plane now," Ginger said. "I'm in Group B, so I will be on later. Why don't you sit with Mrs. Hall?"

"What?" Madeline said. "No way. She left to go to the little store over there and didn't even ask if I wanted anything. She only cares about herself."

"Momma, you were in the bathroom when she went to the store; so how could she ask you if you wanted something?" Ginger said. "And why can't you walk over there and get something if you want something? See, this is what I'm talking about, Momma. This is unnecessary drama you're trying to create and that's not good."

"Well, I'm still not sitting next to her," she said. "I will hold a seat for you."

"Momma, what about Paul?"

"What about him? He can sit with his mother," Madeline said.

In the store, as they sought reading material for the flight, Brenda Wall said, "This is a long flight; I hope you plan to sit with me."

"Why you say that, Ma?" Paul asked.

"Because I don't want to sit next to a stranger; you never know who those people are," she said. "I don't want to have to fake small talk with someone I'll never see again."

"Then read and go to sleep," Paul said. "No one said you have to talk to anyone. And why don't you sit with Ms. Price anyway?"

"No way," she snapped. "I'd rather sit on the wing."

"Ma, I have enough anxiety already; I hate to fly," he said. "I haven't been on a plane in ten years and I'm not that excited about getting back on one now. And you're complaining about sitting beside strangers? Sit with Ms. Price and you'll see she's not nearly as bad as you think."

"She's a borderline alcoholic who would go anywhere alcohol is being served," Brenda said. "And you want me to sit with her as she drinks for five hours?"

"Yes," Paul said, "I do. I want you to and I need you to at least try to get along with her. I bet you'll find that you all hate the same things."

"Is that supposed to be funny?" she said, while purchasing a fashion magazine. "What are you saying? That I'm negative? That I'm like her?"

"All I'm saying is that you probably have similar interests and could probably at least learn a little more about each other. Maybe that will help you all act more like family toward each other."

As it would turn out, with Southwest's open seating policy, the in-laws were unable to sit together, even if they wanted. But that did not mean it was a smooth flight for any of them.

CHAPTER 5
UP, UP
AND AWAY

Minutes before the doors were shut on the plane, Paul went to the men's room and splashed his face with water. He took some Dramamine and talked to himself about enjoying the experience of flying as opposed to fearing it. He read something on the Internet about that approach.

And it worked. He stepped onto the plane feeling at ease and confident. Paul chewed the gum in his mouth at a furious pace, but it helped calm him. There were no seats near the front, so he managed his way near the back, where he found a center seat between a young man who seemed to be hung over and an older woman who was working on a crossword puzzle.

He thought, *This guy is sleeping and this lady is doing a word game—it's going to be fine.*

And it was—for a while. Paul's heart pounded as the jet picked up speed on the runway. He held on to the armrests with a death grip. His body constricted and his breathing was impaired. He began to sweat. And he even started to feel nauseous.

The guy and senior on either side of him did not notice his issues. And when the plane elevated from the ground, Paul began to feel more and more at ease. He looked around and only he seemed uptight about the take off. Many passengers were already asleep; others seemed totally unconcerned.

Finally, Paul calmed all the way down to where he eventually dozed off. He felt accomplished. He had conquered his fear. He was flying to California. When he woke up, he looked around and found Ginger across the aisle two rows in front of him. He didn't even notice her as he entered the plane; he was so wound up with anxiety.

He waved at her and she nodded her head in a reassuring way. She wanted to take Serena's advice and embrace reconciliation. But it was not easy. Being stubborn and prideful remained a part of her disposition. But she fought her instincts.

Ginger got up from her seat and came over to Paul's row. "How you feeling?" she asked. She said it in a loving way, a way Paul had not heard from her in some time. It made him feel like his wife was coming back to him. She cared.

"I'm not on the floor curled up in the fetal position, so I guess I'm OK," he said.

Ginger laughed, and Paul's world lit up. When he was in his rational mind, he loved to make her laugh; it made both of them feel good. He had forgotten how much he enjoyed that because he had not heard her laugh in months.

"Good," she said. "Get some rest. That'll make the trip shorter."

She went back to her seat and checked on her mom, who was sitting directly in front of her, on the aisle. Ginger leaned forward and her mom leaned back so her ear could meet her daughter's mouth.

"Is that alcohol I smell on your breath?" Ginger whispered. "How can that be? They haven't even started the beverage service yet?"

"Why I have to wait on them?" Madeline Price said, showing Ginger a small plastic bottle in her purse. "It's legal. It's the right size to take as a carryon. And who are you anyway? I'm the mother."

"Well, it would be nice if you acted like it," Ginger said.

"What did I do now?" Madeline asked.

"Why can't you wait until they bring you drinks?" Ginger said. "Do you have to bring drinks with you? It's not even eleven o'clock and you're drinking. We're going to Napa Valley, for Christ's sakes."

"Don't you get snappy with me, girl," her mother responded, almost turning completely around in her chair. "You watch your mouth with me. If I want to drink now, I will drink now. I don't need your permission or anyone else's."

She then reached into her purse, pulled out her little stash and took a swig. Ginger dropped back in her seat, frustrated and angry and was not sure which emotion was more prominent.

Maybe we should have left her at home, she thought to herself.

At the same time, Brenda Wall was seething. She had a window seat, but the man next to her smelled of some kind of vinegar, from his mouth and pores. And he would not stop talking.

"I live in the South because the people are nicer," he said to Brenda. "You said you're going to Napa. You're gonna love it. I would start off slow. That's where first-timers make the mistake. They come in so excited that they shoot their whole wad at the first winery. Big mistake.

"You have to pace yourself. Enjoy wherever you go first, but realize that's only the first one. You don't have to try to get drunk on your first visit. There is nothing out there if there isn't wine. So, it's not like they're going to run out of it, you know?

"I like the smaller vineyards over the big ones. Small ones like—you want me to write this down for you?—Black Coyote and Brown are very underrated. But the big ones aren't overrated. Mondavi, Beringer, Mumm's...they are all good. Really, you can't go wrong out there. I realize you've probably done your research. You look like a woman who plans things out thoroughly, to every detail.

"Am I right?"

Before Brenda could answer, he jumped in and went on.

"Of course, I'm right. But, still, when you're going somewhere you don't know, local knowledge is very important. So be sure to contact the concierge of your hotel and anyone you run into who lives out there. They'll really give you someplace that will be nice…"

He went on for another five minutes before taking a breath. She had long since stopped hearing what he was saying and was seething that he would besiege her with chatter—and an aroma that insulted her senses. When he took that pause, she finally jumped in.

"Thanks for all that info," she said as politely as she could. "I will put it to good use. Now I'm going to get some sleep so I can have some energy when we get there."

She was relieved to get that out, but it did not stop her neighbor.

"Sleeping on planes is overrated," he said. "You're not comfortable, you're probably going to get a stiff neck and that doesn't feel good. Plus, sleep on a plane is fake sleep; it only fools you to believe you are rested when you really are not. So, pretty soon after you get off the plane, you'll crash.

"I make sure I get my rest before my flight, no matter how early it is. That way, I don't have to worry about sleeping or being rested when I get to the other end. You get what I'm saying?

"Now, some people—and you might be one of them—can sleep on a plane as they do in their beds. Not me. My arm goes to sleep. My knees get achy. My head is jerking all over the place. Me, I like to sit here and meet nice people and talk and learn something and take in the view and enjoy a great experience that way…"

Brenda was beside herself. She told the man she wanted to go to sleep and he ignored her and continued to talk—and shoot that disgusting smell in her direction. She did not know what to do. At an earlier time in her life, she would have stopped the man in mid-sentence and let him know he was annoying her. But as she got older and seriously involved in the church, she softened a little.

So, instead of humiliating the man, she pretended to fall asleep as he rambled. She slowly closed her eyes and even let her head drift forward. She had to hold back laughing at herself. Still, while it was funny to her, to the guy it was another reason for him to talk.

"Hey, watch it," he said. "You're falling asleep. That's what I'm talking about. Your head jerked, you were kind of suspended. Any minute you were going to be slobbering all over yourself. And that wouldn't have been pretty. See what I'm saying?

"One time I saw this man snore on a plane. He had stuff dripping out of his mouth. He was a mess. And when he woke up, guess what he said: That he was tired. All that snoring and everything and he still felt sluggish. Best thing to do is to get some rest and a light meal for the flight and you'll be fine. You won't need to try to go to sleep in this tight little space.

"The best thing—"

Brenda couldn't take it anymore. She stopped him in the middle of another monologue. "Excuse me," she said. "I have to go to the bathroom."

Even with that, the man continued to talk. "Good luck in that little space in there," he started. "I have heard of a case where a particularly large person got stuck in there. It took two flight attendants and a passenger to pull him out."

"Excuse me," Brenda said again, sounding exasperated as she unbuckled her seat belt. "I've really got to go."

Finally, she was free, and when she reached the aisle, she let out a sigh of relief. Oddly enough, there was but one free seat on the plane—next to her son's mother-in-law, Madeline. It was a center seat that became vacant just as she got up from her seat, as that woman moved to the only other open seat on the plane, a few rows up near a friend.

So Brenda had a choice: to return to sit next to stinky mouth-all-mighty or to sit next to Madeline, who she did not like. It was a tough choice. Before she decided, though, she asked Ginger if she wanted to take the seat next to her mother, which would give Brenda Ginger's seat.

"No, thank you," Ginger said without hesitation. "It's all yours."

Damn, Brenda thought. *Her own daughter doesn't want to sit next to her. Why should I?*

She went a couple rows back to check on Paul, who was sleeping. That relieved her because she was concerned about his paranoia around flying. After the bathroom visit, she decided she could not bear another few hours next to the loquacious man. So she swallowed hard and asked Madeline to allow her past so she could take the now-empty center seat next to her.

Madeline was shocked, but obliged. As she stood up to let Brenda into the aisle, Paul woke up. The women were face to face in the cramped aisle, and to Paul it looked like a confrontation. And he panicked.

"No," he yelled, and everyone turned to him. "Stop. Stop."

"Paul," Brenda said.

"No, I don't want to hear it," Paul answered. He unbuckled his seat belt and climbed over the sleepy-headed guy next to him and stumbled into the aisle, bumping into a seated passenger.

He hurried over to his mother and mother-in-law and separated them. "Why can't you just simply get along?" he said. "This is silly. You're fighting on a plane?"

"Paul," Ginger said, pulling him by the arm. "No one is fighting."

"I saw it; they were in each other's face," he said. "And I heard them yelling."

"Honey," his wife said, "you were dreaming. They weren't fighting."

"Is there a problem?" a flight attendant asked.

Paul looked around confused. "Maybe I was dreaming," he said. "I'm sorry. I think I dreamed that you all were fighting and then I woke up and there you were, in each other's face… I'm sorry."

Before he could ask for a cup of water, the plane hit some turbulence and rocked. Right away, Paul was panicked again, only worse—and Ginger knew it. She could see it in his eyes, which darted back and forth.

"Come on, sit back down," she said, guiding Paul back to his seat.

"What's going on?" he said. "What was that?"

"A little turbulence, that's all," the flight attendant said.

"But why? Why is the plane shaking?" he asked.

The flight attendant got him secure in his seat before answering. "It's just that we're going through some clouds or some wind bursts," she said. "Nothing big."

"Dude, you gonna be OK? You ain't gon' throw up on me, are you?" the sleepy guy next to him said. Paul did not answer.

The captain came over the intercom. "Folks, please strap yourselves in. We have some rough spots up ahead that will make it a little bumpy. But we'll be fine. It should only last about five minutes."

Those five minutes seemed much longer to Paul. All the good feelings he mustered up diminished. He reached up to open the air vent above his seat; he was getting hot, sweating profusely and he felt as if the cabin was shrinking around him.

In his panic, he wondered how the lady to his right could continue to fiddle with the puzzle and how the guy next to him fell right back to sleep. The plane not only was jumping, but it was spinning, too, at least in his mind. He felt like he was drunk off of two bottles of Shiraz, but was also fiercely scared.

Paul decided he would close his eyes and hold on. He started reciting a poem he memorized called "Invictus," by William Ernest Henley:

Out of the night that covers me,
Black as the Pit from pole to pole,
I thank whatever gods may be
For my unconquerable soul.
In the fell clutch of circumstance
I have not winced nor cried aloud.
Under the bludgeonings of chance
My head is bloody, but unbowed.
Beyond this place of wrath and tears
Looms but the Horror of the shade,
And yet the menace of the years
Finds, and shall find, me unafraid.
It matters not how strait the gate,
How charged with punishments the scroll.
I am the master of my fate:
I am the captain of my soul.

In focusing on the words, Paul's attention was off the turbulence. And while he was far from comfortable, he did stop sweating.

He recited the poem over and over until, finally, the plane stabilized; they were out of the turbulent area. Paul did not open his eyes, though. He kept them closed, hoping that he would drift off to sleep so he wouldn't have to deal with anything else that could come.

And there was more to come. His mother and mother in-law, sitting side-by-side, got along like a mongoose and a snake.

"What's wrong with him?" Madeline asked Brenda, which was not a good thing to ask.

"What's wrong with *you*?" Brenda replied. "You smell like a bottle of Scotch."

"Actually, it's cognac," Madeline said. "You know the last time I was on vacation? Do you know what's been going on in my life? And do you know that I am sixty-four years old? I can drink whatever I want, whenever I want."

"Who said you couldn't?" Brenda asked. "I wanted to know if you have a drinking problem. We're going to the wine country. I mean, we will be drinking a lot."

"I have always been respectful of you, and I don't want to not be respectful now," Madeline said. "But I really don't give a damn what you think. I lost my husband of forty-four years less than a year ago. Do you have any idea what that is like?"

"Actually, I do, sort of," Brenda said. "I lost my second husband—my first marriage lasted a year; we were both too young. I woke up one morning and said I didn't want to be married anymore. And just like that, it was over. So, yeah, I understand exactly what you mean. My husband didn't die, but he might as well had. Shit, I wish he were dead because I feel like I wasted a lot of years with him."

Madeline laughed. It was one of the few times they shared a laugh in the twenty years they knew each other. She then twisted the lid off her stash of Remy Martin and handed it to Brenda.

"Go ahead," Madeline said. "You could use it."

Brenda stared at it for a few seconds, reached over and took a swig. She curled up her face. "This is too strong for me," she said. "But it did warm me up."

They laughed again. And whatever animosity they held for each other subsided with each turn they took downing the alcohol.

Ginger sat a row behind them, watching in disbelief. She did not know what to think, how to feel. She thought: *Wow, it is great to see them actually talking and laughing. But is my mother corrupting Ms. Wall? This is crazy.*

She shook her head. She was in a crossfire of drama. To her right and two rows behind her was her husband with his eyes closed reciting a poem. In front of her were her mom and mother-in-law getting drunk.

This is gonna be some trip, she said to herself.

CHAPTER 6
TOUCH DOWN

It was a rough landing. The wind off the San Francisco Bay rocked the plane on its approach to the landing strip. Paul closed his eyes tighter and recited the poem louder.

And when the pilot got it on the ground, it was as if it were dropped from the sky.

Boom!

So hard was the landing that an overhead bin opened up on impact. None of this made Paul feel good about the prospect of having to fly back home in a few days.

People clapped that the plane was safely on the runway, and Paul was confused. "They're clapping for *that* landing. I damn near got whiplash," he said aloud.

"No, dude," the guy that had slept nearly the entire flight said. "We're clapping for being safe. You never flew before?"

"Long time ago, when I was a kid and didn't know any better," he said.

"Don't sweat it, man," the guy said. "Go to sleep. It shortens the trip."

"Up in the air is not the place to be," Paul said. "But I hear you."

His and Ginger's eyes met, and she offered him a reassuring smile that said, "You did it."

He smiled back—and then looked right ahead of Ginger and

noticed his mom and Madeline chatting as if they were old, close friends.

"Well, I'll be damned," he said. "Gin?…"

His wife looked at him, shook her head and hunched her shoulders. Then she did the motion with her hand toward her mouth to indicate they had been drinking. Paul rolled his eyes and grew concerned. The impact of alcohol could take it one of two ways, and one of them was not good.

But to see them getting along made Ginger and Paul feel good—even if it was alcohol-induced.

"I see we're gonna have to keep them drunk to make sure this is a good trip," Ginger said to Paul when they exited the plane.

"Maybe I should get drunk before the flight back," he said.

"You did good," Ginger responded. "It was a little rough for you in the beginning, but it got better. I'm proud of you. How do you feel?"

"Not as good as them," he said, looking at Brenda and Madeline. "You're right; gotta keep them drunk."

"That shouldn't be hard considering where we're going," Ginger said.

They walked over to their parents, who were giggling like schoolgirls.

"How's it going?" Paul asked.

"Great," the parents said in unison.

Paul and Ginger looked at each other and smiled.

"Let's pick up the bags and then go rent the car," Paul said.

"I need to go to the bathroom," Madeline said.

"I'll go with you," Brenda said, and off they went.

"Am I in the Twilight Zone or something?" Ginger said.

"Hey, let's ride it out. It might not last," Paul said.

Paul was right. By the time they picked up the luggage and

started up the 101 Freeway toward San Francisco, it started to change.

"It's about ninety minutes to get to Napa," Brenda said. "We should stop in San Francisco and find someplace to watch the game."

"The game?" Madeline asked. "What game?"

"The Redskins are playing the Cowboys," Brenda answered. "We are Redskins fans in my house."

"That's not a bad idea, Ma," Paul said. "And we can get something to eat, too."

"Aren't we having Thanksgiving dinner at the hotel?" Madeline said.

"Yes, but it's only two o'clock now," Brenda said. "Dinner is at eight-thirty."

"At eight-thirty?" Madeline said. "That's eleven-thirty East Coast time. That's too late."

"So you want to have Thanksgiving dinner now?" Brenda asked.

And back and forth they went for another two minutes, the dialogue increasing in contention as they went on. Paul glanced over at Ginger, who closed her eyes and shook her head.

"Mother," Ginger chimed in, "what's wrong with stopping in San Francisco and having lunch? You have never been to San Francisco. I haven't either. It'll be a shame to drive past it without at least stopping for a short time."

"Look," Madeline said, pointing to the dramatic skyline of San Francisco off in the distance. "There. You've seen it. Let's get to where we came out here to visit."

"Don't worry," Brenda said, "I'm sure there is alcohol in San Francisco, too."

And it went from contentious to ugly in warp speed.

All the chumminess developed on the end of the flight was

crushed. Madeline was irate. It didn't help that she still had a slight buzz from the drinking. It heightened her emotions.

"You have some nerve, Brenda," Madeline said. "You sat there and drank most of my stash and had two—wait—three other drinks. That's just like an alcoholic to try to point attention at someone else."

"Alcoholic? I was only drinking so you wouldn't drink that whole thing by yourself and get crazy behind it," Brenda said. "And I didn't drink most of that cheap liquor you had. Tasted like spoiled Witch Hazel."

Madeline was ready to go "ham," as the kids say, when Ginger jumped in. "OK, OK," she said. "Not in front of the children."

Paul burst into laughter, hoping his action would charge the parents to calm down, at least a little. It worked. Well, sort of. They stopped bickering but stopped talking altogether.

They moved away from each other, up against the back doors of the rented Monte Carlo.

"Mrs. Price, I hope you don't mind if we do stop in the city," Paul said. "I'd like to see the game and I'm hungry. Aren't you? It's Thanksgiving afternoon, but we should be able to find someplace where we can eat and watch the game."

"I think we're all probably a little irritable because we're hungry," Ginger chimed in. "And I don't particularly care to watch the game. But I'd like to see San Francisco. Let's go down to Union Square. I read about it. We should be able to find a place to eat with some TVs, too."

The parents in the backseat did not say a word. They looked out of their respective windows, seething.

Paul and Ginger were disappointed that the harmony did not last an hour. Ginger turned on the radio and searched for songs that would promote a good mood.

They hit near-standstill traffic about five miles from down-town—surprising for Thanksgiving afternoon. "Can you believe this?" Paul asked, looking over his shoulder at the in-laws. Neither responded.

It was then that Ginger, ironically enough, found a song on the radio that fit the occasion: "We Are Family" by Sister Sledge.

She turned up the volume on the song and started to sing along with it. So did Paul.

The parents looked at their kids with disdain.

When the song ended, Paul decided to give the seniors a speech for them to consider.

"That song came on at the right time," he said. "We are supposed to be reminded that we are a family. Like it or not, that's what we are. And we're doing something most families don't get a chance to do.

"We're taking a trip together as a family. In the end, that's all we have. We are the people we should be able to rely on. And we shouldn't be at each other's throats. Especially today. How can we, on Thanksgiving, sit up here and listen to our parents go at it like enemies? That's not right."

"I cannot believe it, to be honest," Ginger contributed. "Although we are adults, parents never stop teaching and being parents. This is a bad example. Helena will get married one day and I hope to God Paul and I do not behave with her in-laws as you are. It doesn't make any sense. We respect you so much. But this is disappointing."

The women felt foolish, but did not respond.

Paul waited a few minutes before saying anything else. They had arrived in downtown San Francisco. They maneuvered up and down the hilly streets toward Union Square. Instead of piling it on, he decided his place was to leave it alone and show his mother respect. Under any circumstance, he would honor his mom.

"Welcome to San Francisco," he said. "I can't believe I am here. I heard so much about it, seen it on TV. To be here…"

"It's very nice," Ginger added.

Paul decided to park in a lot right in Union Square, across from Macy's. A prodigious Christmas tree with big, colorful bulbs rested in the center of the square, adjacent to an ice-skating rink.

The mild weather—temperatures in the mid-sixties—promoted walking, and there were many people out on Thanksgiving afternoon milling about.

Paul walked from the underground lot with his arm around his mother's shoulder and Ginger locked arms with Madeline.

"Ma, we're in San Francisco," Paul said. "How awesome is this?"

"It is beautiful," she said. "I didn't tell you earlier, but I will say it now, son. I'm proud of you to get on that plane. I read all about people who have a fear of flying. Do you know most of them never conquer it? But you have. I'm proud of you."

"Thanks, Ma," Paul said. "It wasn't easy. I hated it, to be honest. But I did it."

Behind them, Madeline said to her daughter: "See what I mean? She thinks she's better than us, trying to talk about my drinking when she probably had more than me."

"Mother, it doesn't even matter," Ginger said. "Like you told me, you are grown and can drink what you want. We don't need her approval. I simply don't want you to let something she—or anyone, for that matter—says influence your trip. This is supposed to be a great trip."

"You're right, honey, and that's what it will be," Madeline said. "People make me shake my head."

They walked around the square and up the hill, past an Italian restaurant, Scoma's, which was closed. The doorman at the small hotel suggested a diner on the corner, a small spot across the street or an Italian restaurant around the corner. But Ginger spotted a Marriott.

"They should have a bar and restaurant, right?" she said.

"Let's try it out," her mother said.

Not only that, but they had the Redskins game on, too.

"Ma, this is perfect, right?" Paul said.

That comment annoyed Ginger. It was as if he was still seeking his mother's approval.

"Perfect," his mom said. "Things have a way of working out."

They took a table near the bar and the server distributed menus.

"Can I take the liberty and ordering something to drink for everyone?" Paul asked.

No one contested, so he ordered a bottle of St. Supery Chardonnay, 2009. "It's buttery and has a citrus taste, but not sweet," Paul explained. "They have a winery in Napa. We have to check it out."

"Sounds like it will go well with a burger," his mom said.

"See, you're trying to be funny, but it actually does go well with beef," Paul said. "Usually I'd go with a red wine with beef. But this chardonnay will work because for me, it's really—it's about what tastes good."

"What do you think, Mother?" Ginger asked. "When is the last time you had a burger?"

"Probably when you were a baby," she answered. "Maybe a burger would be good."

"How about it?" Paul asked his mother.

"Fine," Brenda said.

And so, they all ordered burgers. The wine came and Paul poured and then made a toast as everyone lifted a glass.

"Happy Thanksgiving," he started. "To love and family and happiness."

"That's it?" Ginger asked.

"Isn't that enough?" he answered.

"You know what? You're right," she said, and they all tapped glasses, even Madeline and Brenda.

Paul and Brenda were into the football game on the TV in front of their table like two buddies would be. The mother was as passionate about the Redskins as the son, making commentary with every play and hanging on to every action on the field.

When a commercial came, Paul noticed that it was still awkward with the in-laws not speaking to each other. At the same time, the more they sipped, the more the wine began to take a toll.

"Y'all need to keep some of that noise down," Madeline finally said to Paul and Brenda.

"Are we loud?" Paul asked. He had not eaten in ten hours, so the wine went straight to his head. All of them, in fact, were buzzing.

"Yeah, you are, a little," Ginger said.

"Well, when you watch a football game, you can't sit here all quiet," Brenda said. "And there's hardly anyone in here. We're not bothering anybody."

"Well, you're bothering me," Madeline said.

"Oh, I'm sorry," Brenda said. "I didn't realize your ears were so sensitive."

"Well, they are," Madeline said.

"Perhaps you should go on the other side—there's no one over there," Brenda said. "It's perfectly quiet. You won't be missed."

"Wait," Ginger said before her mom responded. "On the plane, you all were laughing and talking and getting along. What were you talking about? What was so funny?"

Her questions stumped them. They wanted to remember, but couldn't. The wine had them going. They looked at each other and laughed.

"You don't remember?" Brenda asked.

"Well, I think… Weren't we talking about… Didn't you say…" Madeline said, unable to complete a thought.

"Oh, I remember one thing," Brenda said. "You said your husband died and I said I wished mine had died."

"Oh, yeah," Madeline said, laughing.

"Paul, pour us some more wine," Brenda told her son.

"Ma, you said you wish Dad was dead?" Paul asked. He was serious. He maintained a close relationship with his father, who retired to Palm Beach, Florida. He had planned to remarry in the next year.

"He is dead to me," Brenda said. She reached for the bottle, but it was empty. The server was standing there to alert them the food would arrive shortly.

"Bring us another bottle of this," Brenda to the server.

"He's dead to you is different from wishing he were dead," Paul said.

"I don't wish no harm on the man," she said. "Not anymore."

Which led Paul to ask the question he not dare ask sober.

"So, Ma, why did you really get a divorce?" he said. "I mean, thirty-something, forty years, whatever it was. What could be that bad? Did he cheat on you? I asked him that and he said he didn't? Did you cheat on him? He said you didn't. So what was it?"

Brenda Wall wanted to tell her son the truth but had not. The wine made it easier for the truth to flow out of her mouth.

"I didn't love him," she said. "I had stopped loving your dad probably ten, twelve years ago."

"What?" Ginger said. She was feeling bold, too, and jumped into the conversation. "How can that be? How can you stay married to someone that long and not love him? I don't understand."

"Some things aren't meant for you to understand," Brenda said. "I hope you don't ever understand. If you do, then that would mean you don't love my son, because the only way to really understand is to be in a situation like I was. That's the only way."

"Ma, I was around you guys all my life," Paul said. "I didn't see anything that made me feel like you all didn't love each other."

"We did love each other," Brenda explained. "But we were not *in* love. That ended a long time ago. It faded away, like smoke, into the air. Gone. And I believe it hit both of us around the same time. There was no spark, no magic."

The second bottle of wine came and Paul refilled the glasses. Brenda went on.

"We stayed together for one reason: loyalty. We were best friends at one time and we saw each other through some serious issues that brought us closer together."

"Like what, Ma?" Paul said. "This is blowing my mind and I'm trying to understand."

Brenda Wall sipped her wine and closed her eyes. The room was rotating and she was trying to stop it—and her tongue. It didn't work.

She sat back in her chair and took a deep breath. "When you were a baby, too young to even understand what was happening," Brenda explained, "I was very sick. Doctors didn't know what was wrong with me, but I couldn't keep any food down and I lost weight like crazy and was tired all the time.

"Finally, I went to the hospital; stayed there for eleven days. They ran all kinds of tests, but couldn't find anything. They thought it might be lupus at one point. They tried all the experimental drugs on me.

"Your father was right there with me, in the hospital, taking care of you. He was totally positive; he kept my head up. If he hadn't, I think I would have died. Seriously. Altogether, I was sick for about three weeks. I mean, really sick. When they sent me home, your father carried me from the bed to the bathroom. He cleaned up after me. He did everything. And he never complained.

"The doctors finally put me on some kind of steroids, and I finally started feeling better. Do you know what it's like to feel like you're going to die? To feel like you're fading away? Here I was with a precious little boy and I was dying. That's what I believed. And I cried my eyes out every night. And your father held me in his arms every night—until, finally, the steroids, did something to right the ship."

"He did that out of love, Ms. Wall," Ginger said. "That's beautiful."

"It was beautiful," Brenda said. "But over time, it all faded. Why? How? Because, really, being totally honest, he wasn't the man for me."

"What do you mean, Ma?"

"I mean…" Brenda said, taking a deep breath, "when I was pregnant with you, I wasn't sure your father was your father."

"What? What do you mean?" Paul said.

"I mean that I was dating someone else, in love with someone else, when I got pregnant by your dad," Brenda said. Suddenly, she became almost sullen. She sipped more wine and spewed more truths, truths she never thought she would share with her son.

"The man I was in love with was special to me," she explained. "We were young and in love and used to talk all the time about the life we would have. But he got drafted into the Army and before I knew it, he was gone.

"He wrote me and I wrote him, but he wasn't sure when he was going to come back home. Finally, he did come back home, and nothing changed. He was fun and exciting and he loved me. We had fun for about a week before he had to go back.

"He was stationed in North Carolina but was going overseas somewhere, Germany, I think. We were barely twenty years old. I was mad that he left and, at a most vulnerable point, I met your father. He was the friend of a coworker. He was outside our building when we got off work, waiting for his friend, who I was walking with.

"He invited me to go out with them, and I did. And it grew from there.

"A little while later—about a month or two—I realized I didn't have my regular cycle. And that's where the confusion came in. But when the doctors told me how long I had been pregnant, I knew it was James' baby."

"Why is it I never heard this before?" Paul asked.

"I don't know," his mother said. "It's not a good story, really. When he came back home, I was eight months pregnant and it broke his heart when I told him he wasn't the father. And it broke my heart, too. I should have waited on him, but I really didn't think I would see him again. My friends were telling me, 'Brenda, he's going to travel the world and you think he's coming back to you?' And after hearing it enough, I started to believe it."

"Where is he now?" Madeline asked.

"I don't know," Brenda said. "After I told him I was pregnant, he still wanted to marry me. That's the kind of man he was. But I had already made plans to marry James and I thought it wouldn't be fair to you, Paul, to not have your father in your life. My friend understood, but he had tears in his eyes when he left me. And I cried."

Brenda actually developed tears in her eyes as she told the story. And Paul noticed.

"You still love him, don't you, Ma?" he asked.

She wiped her face. "I guess I still love the idea of him and what we could have had together," Brenda said. "But your father and I got married before you were born—yes, I went down that aisle with a big ole stomach—and went on and had a good life together for a long time."

"But it wasn't what you planned for yourself?" Paul asked.

"It wasn't; but you have to walk in your life. It is already planned for us," his mom said. "James was a good man; *is* a good man. I was joking about wanting him dead. That would devastate me. But he wasn't *the* man for me. And over time, it just got to be that I had to breathe again. I couldn't breathe being in a marriage that really didn't do anything for me.

"We had our greatest gift—you—and some really good times, times I will never forget. But you were long gone and I was left dealing with the man in front of me. And that wasn't enough—for either of us."

"Don't you feel lonely, though?" Madeline asked. "I know I do."

"Yes, you're right," Brenda admitted. "At times it's very lonely. But the peace I have within myself balances it out."

The burgers came and they ate mostly in silence—except for an occasional outburst by Paul about the football game. They enjoyed the meal and the wine and watched the Redskins defeat the Cowboys, giving mother and son some needed feel-good after Brenda's revelations.

On the way back to the car, Paul walked with Ginger and Brenda with Madeline, and the drama seemed to fade away...for a while, anyway.

CHAPTER 7
IN THE LAND
OF GRAPES

Paul settled into the car and headed toward Napa. His GPS gave him directions across the Bay Bridge, but he wanted to cross the Golden Gate Bridge.

And, surprisingly, no one argued with him.

After some wayward turns in the city, though, Ginger asked: "Can I ask someone how we get to the Golden Gate? We're wasting time."

"My instincts tell me we're close," Paul said.

"Boy, you have the sense of direction of a blind donkey," his mother said. "Ask somebody so we can stop riding around this city."

"Really," Madeline said. "I'm ready for a hot shower and..."

"And what?" Brenda asked with a smile. "Go ahead, you can say it."

"A drink, dammit. Get a drink," Madeline blurted out, and everyone laughed. Well, everyone except Ginger. She had some concern about her mother's drinking, and it increased by the month. Based on what she saw on the plane and at lunch, Ginger was now worried.

Her mother always had a healthy appetite for cocktails, but it grew exponentially after her husband died less than a year before.

"Mother, maybe we should start fresh tomorrow when we visit

the vineyards," she said. It was as delicately as she could put it.

"Excuse me?" Madeline said.

"I'm just saying that we have a lot of sipping to do and I don't want you to be sick tomorrow because you had so much today," Ginger said.

Madeline was already buzzing from the wine at lunch, and it showed. "I thought we already talked about this," she said to her daughter. "I don't need nobody monitoring how much I drink. You act like I'm gonna get sloppy drunk and embarrass you. Well, I won't.

"And if I did embarrass you it would be payback for all the times you embarrassed the hell out of me when you were a kid."

Paul found the Golden Gate Bridge, without anyone's assistance, and made sure everyone knew it. "Who told you it was close?" he said, "Me. I have the instincts of an explorer."

He said that to turn the subject; he could sense it was getting heated between mother and daughter. Didn't work.

"So that's your excuse, Mother?" Ginger said. The way she said it made Paul look at his wife. It was dark in the car, so he fumbled with the gadgets around the rearview mirror until he found the interior light switch.

He wanted to see Ginger's eyes; they told if she were intoxicated. If they were open and bright, she was OK. If they were barely open and glazed over...trouble. Some people get quiet when they get a buzz, some get loud, some get talkative, some get belligerent. Ginger was one of the belligerent ones.

"You're paying me back for what I did as a child?" she asked. "Really? Seriously? You're joking, right? I can recall some things that you did to me when I was a child that I should be mad at you about, if you want to know the truth."

"The truth is that—look—we're about to cross the Golden

Gate Bridge," Paul said, again trying to get their attention somewhere else. The women turned to look, but only briefly.

"Look," Brenda said, "you can walk across the bridge. We should do that—well not you, Paul. But I think I would do it."

"Yeah, I can do without that, Ma," he said. "Oh, wow. Look over there."

He pointed to his far right, where across the San Francisco Bay you could see the beautiful skyline of San Francisco all lit up.

"Now that's beautiful," Brenda said. "Do you ladies see this?"

Ginger and Madeline turned and admired the spectacular view. Paul drove slowly so they could take in as much of it as possible.

"The East Coast is not this pretty," Madeline said. "The mountains, the water, the skyline—this is so gorgeous."

The banter about the beauty of the area continued across the bridge and along Interstate 80. Ginger was about to address her mother again when Paul said to her: "You're up front, so you have to be my navigator. How long are we on this highway?"

It was a nice try, but Ginger was looking for a confrontation. "Here," she said to Paul, handing him her cell phone. "I programmed the hotel's address in the GPS. That will get us there."

She then turned halfway around in her seat to address her mother.

"I wasn't the one as a five-year-old kid who was left at home alone," she said. "I can recall many times when I wasn't even in the first grade and Daddy was at work and you locked me in the house and went to do God knows what."

"Child, you couldn't hardly remember that far back and that never happened anyway," Madeline said. "Look who can't handle her alcohol. You're drunk—and delusional."

"Mother, I might be drunk and at times I might be delusional," Ginger said. "This ain't one of those times. I recall clearly being hungry and scared and wondering where you were. Daddy used to kiss me goodbye; he was working the third or fourth shift at night. I was at home with you and you would leave me, make me go to bed and I'd lay there and cry and you would leave anyway."

"Ginger, that just did not happen," Madeline insisted. "I might have left you and went outside for a few minutes. But that's it. If you were crying it wasn't because of me. I was there for you."

Ginger took a deep breath. Her tone lowered, but her words were figuratively booming.

"Were you there when Uncle Ambrose came into my room that night you left me and went to the card game next door?" Ginger asked.

Whatever buzz Madeline had evaporated immediately. "What? What are you talking about, Ginger?"

"You heard me," her daughter responded.

Paul was shocked and concerned, too. He had not heard this from his wife, and when they were right, they talked about everything. At least, that's what he thought.

"Ginger, please don't tell me he did something to you," Madeline said. She was almost crying. "Please don't tell me that."

"It was a Friday night," Ginger said.

"Gin," Paul said, the concern in his voice evident.

"It's OK," she said. "I was in bed, waiting for you to come check on me, but you never did. So I finally fell asleep, but I woke up when I felt my bed move. I jumped up. I was so scared. It was Uncle Ambrose. He said, 'Hey, baby. I didn't mean to scare you. I came in here to tuck you in, make sure you're all right.'

"His voice sounded strange, like he was someone else. I was only five years old but right away I realized something was wrong. But I didn't know what to say.

"So, he slid closer to me; he was sitting at the foot of my bed at first. Then I knew something was really wrong because he pulled my covers back. I was confused. 'If he's trying to tuck me in, why is he taking the covers off me?' My little five-year-old brain could process that something was wrong.

"I could smell the alcohol on his breath; he was reeking. He put his hand on my shoulder. He said something like, 'Kiss your Uncle Ambrose good night.' Then he tapped his lips. 'Here. Kiss your Uncle Ambrose good night right here.'

"Now I was really scared. But before I could scream, Daddy came in the room. He grabbed Uncle Ambrose and threw him on the floor. He came over to me and asked me if I was OK. I couldn't talk; I nodded my head. He leaned over and hugged me and kissed me on my face and pulled the covers back over top of me.

"He said, 'Go to sleep, baby. I will be back to check on you later. Sweet dreams.' Then he pulled Uncle Ambrose up off the floor and dragged him out of the room....never saw Uncle Ambrose again."

Madeline had a look of shock on her face. For several seconds, she did not say anything. Paul and Brenda were riveted to Ginger's words and did not know what to say. Finally, Madeline broke her silence.

"It all makes sense now," she said. "I know exactly the night you are speaking of, baby. That was the night your uncle was found not far from our house, beaten almost to death. No one ever knew what happened to him.

"The last person to see him was one of our neighbors who said he swore he saw Ambrose go into our house that night. And he saw your father go into the house a little while later. But he never saw Ambrose come out. The police questioned us—everyone who was next door at the card game, the neighbors—and according to them, that was the last time he was seen in a healthy condition, walking into the front door of our house."

"What do you mean, it makes sense now, Momma?" Ginger asked.

"I'm so sorry," she said.

"For what, Momma?"

"I left you alone and my brother would have probably raped you if your father hadn't come home when he did," Madeline said. "Ambrose was sick; he wasn't playing with a full deck. There were times when everyone was afraid of him. He was liable to do anything. But your father told me—and I'll never forget his words— he said: 'Maddy, if he puts a hand on you or Ginger I swear to you I will kill him.'

"Your father had never spoken to me with such force and conviction about anything. I knew he meant it."

"What are you saying? That Daddy killed Uncle Ambrose?"

Madeline looked away, toward the mountains that sandwiched Interstate 80.

"Mother," Ginger pleaded.

"He didn't technically kill him," Madeline said, turning to her daughter. "When Ambrose was found, he was alive, but really in bad shape. He was in the hospital for several days and then one day had a heart attack and died. So, that's what was on his death certificate. The doctors couldn't tell if the beating he took played a role in his death.

"But all makes sense now. That night, when I finally saw your father, he was sweating and exhausted and acting weird, like something was bothering him. For the longest time, he seemed different. You didn't know Ambrose died because your father told me not to tell you. He said you were too young and you didn't need to know about death at such a young age.

"I went along with it because he was my husband and it wasn't an outrageous request. Richard was very solemn at the funeral, but not sad, if you know what I mean. He seemed down, but not sad that Ambrose was dead. He was carrying a heavy burden. I always felt it but now I realize that he had beaten my brother to the brink of death.

"And he was sitting there through his funeral listening to people get up there and talk about how much they loved him and how much of a good man he was. He was my brother and I did love him; we grew up in the same house. But Ambrose had some issues. He functioned OK and worked, but we used to say in the family that we wouldn't be surprised if he ended up being anything from a bank robber to a serial killer."

"Oh, my God," Ginger said. "You're saying Daddy killed a man?"

"Again, he died of a heart attack," Madeline said. "But the guy who lived next door saw Richard go in the house after Ambrose, but he didn't see either of them come out of the house. That's because Richard took him out of the back. He was found less than a mile from our house—the back of our house.

"And I was there when Richard came home—he came in through the back door. And, based on the police report, he came home long after the guy saw Richard go into the front door of the house."

"I can't even believe this," Ginger said. "I mean, I am glad my father protected me when I needed protecting. But…"

"I'm blown away, too," Madeline said. "Richard never said anything to me about him touching you or being in your room. But he didn't because he knew I would have dug up Ambrose's body and killed him again. Oh, my God."

"There goes my little high," Brenda said. "This is deep."

"Ginger, you OK?" Paul asked.

"I don't know," she said. "I mean, I'm OK. But I don't know. I know my father as one thing and now I learn he almost murdered my uncle."

"But—wait, excuse me," Brenda said. "I don't mean to be all in this but I'm right here and couldn't help but hear everything. Is it OK if I ask something?"

Madeline and Ginger both said it was OK.

"How can you not know what you feel about this?" Brenda said. "Your father protected you. He swore that he would end the person's life that laid a hand on you. This guy did and he probably led to his dying because—if what Madeline says is true—he would have been back, and maybe trying to hurt you.

"I'm not very comfortable saying this, but he got what he deserved and your daddy should be a bigger hero in your eyes than he ever was. I'm not condoning killing, but you were a five-year-old girl. What if your father hadn't come home? How many other girls had he touched and done God-knows-what to?

"I'm sorry; that's my two cents."

"It does mean a lot to me that he saved me from something that could have scarred me for life. But…"

"Ginger," Madeline said, "there are no buts. What's the word? Romanticize? I'm not trying to romanticize what Richard did. But there are millions of fathers who say they would have done the same thing. Richard, I believe, did it."

"Gin," Paul said, "if someone, anyone, put a hand on you or Helena in that way, I would kill him, too. Actually doing it is one thing. But that's what I believe. Your dad protected you. I respect him even more now than I already did."

"I wish I could call and ask him what happened," Ginger said. "I want to hear him say it to believe it."

"Well, unless you want to have a séance, that's not going to happen," Madeline said.

"I think," Paul said, "you should let it go. In the scheme of things, something that happened that long ago should not matter much now."

"I don't know about that," Ginger said. "I mean, it happened, so how can it not matter?"

Brenda said, "Everything that happens doesn't matter. And if you ignore it, it's like it didn't happen."

"You spit some knowledge, Ma," Paul said.

"'Spit some knowledge?'" Ginger asked. "Who are you?"

"Don't be mad that I am in tune with the ways of the youth," Paul said.

"*Please*. You're not in tune with the ways of the middle-aged," Ginger said, laughing.

Paul had successfully moved Ginger off her base of lamenting the possibility of her father's actions. And he was intent on keeping her away from that subject.

"OK, copilot, where do we exit?" he said, handing her back her cell phone.

Ginger gave Paul the specifics and looked out of the window at the mountainside they passed. It was quiet in the car for several minutes, with all the ladies dozing off, one-by-one.

That was a relief for Paul, who did not give the demands of traveling with three women much thought when he cooked up the idea. He was focused on reconnecting with his wife and wine. As he swerved into the valley, his mind wandered.

It was gnawing at him that he had not told Ginger of their newfound wealth. He felt a lot better about where they were going in the marriage, and that she was receptive to making it work after so much bad stuff.

Paul purchased a David Yurman diamond ring for Ginger, a gift he planned to give to her on the trip, after he was sure she was sincere about making the marriage work. He figured the last vineyard they would visit would be Sterling in Calistoga, where they would take a tram up to the top of the mountain to visit the winery.

Its website indicated and the pictures confirmed it was one of the most romantic wineries in Napa Valley, with pristine views of beauty stretching miles and miles in every direction. Out on the deck was where he envisioned presenting it to Ginger, a gift to consummate a restart of their marriage. He would tell them later, at the hotel about the money. That was his plan.

He drove past signs saying Vallejo and continued along dark stretches where he, at times, could see beautiful landscape. He let the window down for a minute to consume the breeze and the smell of fresh California air.

Paul felt more carefree than he ever had. He was on his dream trip with his dream girl and, while the trip promised some bumpy times, he anticipated the sense of family to come out of it would be worth the occasional discord.

He hoped.

CHAPTER 8
HOTEL, MOTEL, HOLIDAY INN

As if they could sense they were getting close to the hotel, the ladies all woke up within minutes of each other. Paul was glad they were close because he had to go to the bathroom for the previous twenty-five miles, but did not want to stop or disturb the sleeping women.

"How close are we now, Vino?" Brenda said. It was the first time she used her nickname for her son around Madeline.

"Vino? Who's Vino?" Madeline asked.

"I am," Paul answered. "It's my mom's pet name for me, so to speak."

"I know the next question," Brenda said. "The answer is, I was with him the night he discovered that he liked wine. It was amazing. He was like a self-taught expert, right from the start. He could taste the elements of the wine and tell you what it was. Accurately. He was amazing.

"And he was twenty-one. How many young men at that age are even *trying* wine? Well, Paul was. He was drinking it and loving it and analyzing it.

"So, one day I called him 'Wino,' and he was offended. He said, 'A wino doesn't appreciate wine. He only appreciates the next drink he can get.'

"Of course, I let that nickname go right away because he was right. So I decided on 'Vino.' Wine. If there were a word for wine lover, I would call him that. Since there isn't, I just call him 'Vino.' It fits. He's all about wine."

"All right now," Madeline said. "Vino, get us to the Marriott, please."

"You know what's crazy, Mrs. Wall?" Ginger said. "He loves wines so much and studied them. And yet, he won't do anything with this knowledge.

"I told him to go be a bartender at a wine bar. Become a sommelier."

"A what?" Ginger's mom said.

"A sommelier," Ginger answered. "A sommelier is a wine expert, someone who can pair wines with meals based on understanding wine. They know everything about wines.

"When he lost his job, there was the perfect opportunity to pursue his passion," Ginger said. "But he did nothing."

"I didn't not do anything," Paul said. "I did a lot of stuff. I just didn't do anything with wine."

"Except drink it," his mom chipped in.

It was an uncomfortable subject for Paul. Even though his life had changed with winning the lottery, losing his job scarred him. His manhood was stripped, and it affected his marriage.

"You know, life is full of surprises," he said. "Maybe I will take on something working with wines. It's never too late."

He said it so convincingly that he believed it. And then his mind started roaming. He now had the resources to do whatever he liked. He did not want to be a bartender because he did not want to serve others in that way. But he did like the idea of talking to people about wine. In just a few minutes of contemplation, he conceived of opening a wine store where he picked the wines and could host wine-tastings each month and share his knowledge.

He hadn't thought much about what to do with all that money, except save it, travel and buy wine. He told himself he would share his thoughts with the ladies before they departed.

They were all up and alert by the time he pulled up at the Napa Marriott. There were some lavish hotels in Napa that Paul wanted to experience, but they were so pricey that Ginger would have questioned why he would spend so much money.

Besides, the Marriott was nice and convenient and it served a Thanksgiving dinner, too.

Paul emptied the trunk of their luggage-on-wheels and everyone pulled their bags into the lobby, which was buzzing with people at the bar and dining in the restaurant.

When he got the room keys, a sudden fear came over him: how are the in-laws going to get along sharing a room? He made sure his and Ginger's parents were on the same floor, but down the hall from their room.

"What time is dinner?" Brenda said. "Do I have time for a nap?"

"It's at eight-thirty, but we can push it back if we need to," Paul said. "I talked to the host. The evening is open in the restaurant. And they are serving dinner until eleven."

He handed the ladies the keys and they made their way to their rooms. As Paul and Ginger headed to their room, Ginger surprised him. "What room am I in?" she asked.

"Don't even play with me, Gin," Paul said.

"I'm not playing. Who said we were going to stay in the same room?" she said.

"I did," Paul answered. He had arrived at the door to the room and slid in the card key.

"You coming in?" he said, holding the door open.

Ginger just looked at him.

"Gin, we're all the way here now and you don't want to stay in the same room with your husband?" Paul said. "Come on. That's not cool."

"It's not about cool," Ginger said. "We have problems."

"We can't work them out here in the hallway, Ginger," he said.

That bit of reasoning worked, and she entered the room, which was nothing special. But it did have two double beds, which she acknowledged.

"This is my bed," she said.

Paul ignored her, but placed his carry-on on the other bed. He zipped open his other bag and fumbled through it until he pulled out a bottle of Fairview Pinotage, a South African wine given to him as a gift by a former coworker who visited the vineyard in the summer.

"I have been waiting to crack this," Paul said. "This is the time."

Ginger's sudden discomfort could not mask her desire to share the wine. She enjoyed it—probably not as much as Paul, but she could have at least a glass almost every day.

This was a special bottle that Paul coveted, so she was moved that he brought it to share with her. But she was still damaged by his behavior over the previous several months.

Ginger realized she was sending him mixed signals, but that's what was coming out of heart and her head. They clashed.

"Be right back," Paul said. "Gonna get some wineglasses from the bar."

He made his way to the bar and was shocked by what he saw: his mother and mother-in-law sitting in the lounge together sipping wine. Paul quickly turned away and acted as if he did not see them. He did not want to interrupt their moment and he wanted to get back to Ginger.

Inhaling the Napa Valley air did something to Paul. He could smell the grapes in the air, although it was not prime grape-growing season. Still, being there and passing the vineyards on the way in improved his already-uplifted spirits and made him frisky and romantic. He wanted his wife back.

When he returned with the glasses, Ginger was in the bathroom, which gave Paul time to dig into his luggage and pull out a scented candle. He lit it and pulled open the drapes, which revealed a swimming pool.

He wiped down the glasses, but did not open the wine until Ginger came out. He wanted her to share in that moment. That's how seriously he took wine—opening a bottle was important.

"What's this?" Ginger said when she reentered the room. The candle made it cozy and romantic. She had not seen that kind of thing from Paul in at least a decade.

"It's a nice mood for us to enjoy this great wine," he said.

Ginger did not respond or resist. Her husband gave her a glass and he sat next to her on "her" bed. He cracked open the bottle. "I waited for you to be here to open it," he said.

She smiled. After pouring each a glass, Paul lifted his and proposed a toast: "To my wife. I am thankful that you are here with me in the one place I really wanted to visit. And to be here now, on Thanksgiving, really brings it all together because I am really thankful that you are my wife."

Ginger smiled. She was touched. She tapped her glass into his and they both smelled the wine, then swirled it around in their glasses, sniffed it again to see the difference from the oxidation and then took a sip.

"Oh, man," Paul said, a smile developing on his face. "What do you think?"

Ginger smiled, too. "Excellent," she said. "There is no aftertaste in this wine."

"And it is smoky with dark fruit flavors," Earl said. "Wanna hear some history on Pinotage? Remember, I studied it."

"Sure, why not? What else do I have to do?" Ginger said.

"Keep sippin' while I kick the knowledge," Paul said.

"Kick the knowledge?" Ginger said, shaking her head. "Anyway, go ahead."

"Pinotage is a unique South African grape variety that only grows well in South Africa," Paul explained. "Most wine drinkers have less experience with it than other red wines. And guess what: Some South Africans love it, but some don't like it so much because it is not European enough. It does not possess any of the flavors of French wines.

"The Pinotage grape is a combination of a Pinot Noir grape and Hermitage grape that was created in 1925 and is one of the younger red wines Thus, Pinotage. Last thing: They actually grow Pinotage in a few places in California and Virginia."

"Interesting," Ginger said. "You really should do something with all this knowledge. I mean, I've been thinking about it. With all the layoffs in the last years, many people have decided to pursue their passion, to do what they really want to do. I realize you like heating and air conditioning repair. But you love wine, Paul."

That confirmed Paul's earlier thoughts.

"I do, and I'm really surprised you said that because I actually have been thinking the same thing," he said. "Maybe, in time, we could open up a wine store and host wine-tastings. Make it really nice. Educate people."

"That sounds nice, Paul, but that costs money," Ginger said.

Paul poured more wine in her glass. "Well, you never know. Things could turn around for us. They *will* turn around for us. And when they do, that's something we can explore. I'd like you to be my partner."

"That's a long way off," Ginger said. "A long way."

"Maybe. Maybe not," Paul said, smiling. "You have to put it

out in the universe for it to become reality... But I'd rather talk about us."

"What about us?" Ginger said.

"Well, we've made some progress since we hit rock bottom—since I hit rock bottom," he said. "I think we have. We are talking. We made love. We are here in California. Two months ago, I wouldn't have expected any of this."

"Me, either, and that's why I'm trying to figure out what changed," Ginger said.

"I changed," Paul said. "I got off my ass and finally stopped feeling sorry for myself and realized nothing happens unless I make it happen."

"And that's it?" she asked.

"No," he said. Paul sipped more wine and shook his head. "No. When I took inventory, I realized that I was ruining our marriage. You're not perfect and neither am I. But you're perfect for me. I believe that."

Ginger's head was spinning. Literally. The wine took hold and Paul's words did, too. And so, when Paul slid beside her on the bed, she did not resist. He went for it.

"I love you, Gin," he said. "I will apologize every day if I have to, to get you to understand how badly I feel about the things I said. And I will kiss you right here on your neck every day, too. You like me to kiss you right there, don't you?"

Ginger did not want to answer, but her body was all his now, as if all the months of trouble and pain and concerns did not happen. Anger, disappointment, sadness...none of that mattered in that moment. When her body spoke, she listened and acquiesced to its needs.

Paul knew this, and he turned his wife's face toward his with a gentle tug. She was breathless. Between the wine and the signals her brain sent through her body—and the love she tried to suppress for Paul—she was defenseless. He kissed her on her lips, which were moist with anticipation.

His lips were thick and soft, and they met hers as two wine-glasses would meet to climax an intimate toast. Ginger closed her eyes and Paul closed his, and they delighted in a deep, passionate kiss that made Ginger woozy when their lips finally parted.

The small portion of her brain that was not covered in passion tried to resist. She stood up to catch her breath, but Paul stood up, too, to restrict her breathing by kissing her again as he wrapped his arms firmly around her.

Paul's heart beat as if he had been sprinting. It was the combination of unmitigated passion with his wife and the intensity of the kiss that heightened his desires. And so, he leaned away from Ginger and, while looking into her eyes, slowly unbuttoned the front of her shirt.

As each button came loose, Ginger breathed in, until Paul got to the end and slowly pulled off the blouse and discarded it like a piece of tissue into a wastebasket. Ginger stood there, staring at her man, feeling like she did when they first met, when they had sex as if their survival depended upon it.

That was such a joyous time in their lives, and to feel like that made Ginger finally release any inhibitions and meet Paul's desires with her own passion.

So as Paul fumbled slightly with unhitching her bra, Ginger politely took his hands and placed them over her firm breasts and she reached behind her back and released the strap in an instant. Paul knew his wife, and that maneuver meant the resistance was over. They could not dance to their rhythm.

Since winning the lottery and regaining some self-esteem, Paul dropped significant weight, making him look more like the man she married than the man she loathed. He had only had sex with his wife once in the previous two months, and she had not seen his new body in the flesh.

Paul, eager to show it off, pulled his shirt over his head and stood in front of his panting wife as if to say, "This is all yours. What you gonna do with it?"

Ginger read her husband's look and she slowly, seductively unbuckled and unzipped her pants, never taking her eyes off Paul's, who was unbuckling and unzipping his pants, too. When their underwear dropped to the floor, it was like the starter's gun to a race went off.

They attacked each other, kissing and groping in a furious fashion that somehow was in rhythm, a seductive dance that extended from one side of a queen-sized bed to the other.

Finally, the foreplay turned into lovemaking that they had not experienced in years. About two months before the trip they had a sexual encounter that was more about them having a need than having sex. This was passion. This was intense.

Ginger allowed Paul to lead the family, but she, at times, liked to be in charge of certain situations. Intimacy with him was one of them. She liked to be on top so she could control the passion: How deep Paul entered her, how rapid the thrusts, the angle of penetration.

All Paul had to do was hold on. Ginger was at her dick-riding best, squirming her saturated vagina on his hardness in swift counterclockwise rotations, which allowed for pleasure along multiple areas of her inner walls.

Paul tried to thrust upward, but Ginger's pace was fast and did not allow much for his participation. She rocked her hips and enjoyed his joystick with abashed pleasure. The wine made her feel uninhibited, and her actions spoke the truth about how she felt.

She kissed Paul deeply as she changed her sexual attack. Now she bounced up and down on his manhood. Paul stroked upward to her cadence, creating a smacking sound as they challenged each other on how deep he could get and how much she could take.

Well, she took everything he had to offer and he offered a lot. He held her by her waist and pulled her down to meet his thrusts, making it almost a violent collision of passion. Ginger moaned with each thumping, but there were moans of pleasure and pain coming together as only can happen in intense sex.

Paul grunted with each thrust, an indication of how intent he was on getting deeper and making sure his wife felt his intent. After two minutes of straight pounding each other, Paul began to sweat, and immediately he went back to their early sexual sessions that really solidified their bond.

Those experiences were few and far between over the years, but in that moment of feeling sweat develop on his forehead and slide down his face, he made a commitment to return their sex lives back to something sensual and passionate, romantic and lasting.

Losing his job diminished his sex drive, and he was embarrassed at the weak effort he gave Ginger in the first weeks after being laid off. Sex became less important because his manhood was threatened with being out of work. His erections were mild, or certainly unlike the pole-hard stiffness he banged Ginger with their first hours in Napa Valley.

Ginger noticed the difference—in how he handled her and the strength of his hardness. She might have been in control of the movements while being on top, but Paul was in control of the pleasure.

Ultimately, he won out on that battle; his forcefulness was unrelenting. He was too proud to let Ginger wear him out, and so he kept feeding her until she exploded in herky-jerky body gyrations and weird sounds that had only one interpretation: ecstasy.

Her movements were so wild that all Paul could do was hold on until she gathered herself, which took another minute or so. It was then when he flipped her onto her back and began his pleasure quest by holding up her legs and spreading them as he threw his head back and pumped deeper and deeper into her.

She took his strokes with sounds of pleasure, and Paul felt like he was having an out-of-body experience. He and Ginger had not enjoyed that kind of relentless passion in some time, so long that he could not even recall.

And when he looked down and saw the pleasure on his wife's face—a look he had not put there in months—he became so excited that he stroked her harder and harder, generating a sensation that ran through his body and exploded out of the head of his penis and into Ginger's waiting canal.

It was his turn to yell something incoherent but translated into the ultimate pleasure. He collapsed his much larger body onto Ginger's and she took him without issue, hugging him firmly as he breathed heavily over her shoulder.

"My God," Paul managed to get out after a few minutes. "I forgot how incredible we can be together."

"It has been a long time," she said.

Paul realized he was suffocating her, so he rolled over, and they both let out a sigh.

"This is how it should be all the time," Paul said. He held her hand and turned toward her. "I messed things up, but I want us to get back to where we were. And I also realize it will take time. But I hope this is the start of us getting back to where we were when we were happy."

Ginger's cautious side wanted to offer something negative, or at least something that would not indicate she was all in. And that made her mad. *Why can't I embrace what was good without second-guessing?* she wondered.

It was her nature to find the cracks and pounce on them. This time, though, her body told her to cut it out, to let go. She loved her husband and he had just put it on her in a display of passion and love that she missed—and needed.

That was the key. Ginger had girlfriends who insisted they did not need a man and could get by without sex in their lives. She did not understand that. She needed the physical aspect of lovemaking in her life and she needed the emotional connection that came with it. She wanted to believe she could have one without the other, but she could not convince herself of that.

She felt most emotionally connected to Paul when they consistently had sex. It was not the elixir to all things broken. But it was the foundation of holding things together.

So when Paul's sex drive diminished with his loss of self-esteem, their connection to each other slowly dwindled, too. Laying on her back after a vigorous round of passion with Paul made Ginger feel alive.

"I want the same thing, Paul," she said. "I do. But I'm scared. I'm scared because I don't know what brought you around and if you'll go back to that place where you were depressed and cold and sometimes just mean to me.

"It has been a very rough last year or so with you. I felt like my family was falling apart. Thank God we were able to somehow shield our troubles from Helena.

"You don't know this, but I have gone through a lot because of this. It has been a very difficult time. And I couldn't even talk to you about it because we were so fractured. Still, I believed it was a phase. I never expected to hear you say you wanted a divorce. That was very hurtful and it put me in a really bad place. I don't know. I am here, in Napa, because I want to save our marriage. And as great as it has been so far, I can't get out of my head how things have been."

"I understand," Paul said. "I do. But I was going through something that I did not know how to handle. They say you lash out at the people you are closest to when you're under duress. Well, I was under duress. I worked all my life. I provided for my family from Day One.

"To be let go after so many years and so much commitment to the job, it crushed me. And I won't even try to lie: My ego was crushed, too. We probably should have sought counseling then. Maybe it would have helped if I opened up. But I can't even say now, looking back on it, that I would have said the things necessary to heal.

"I felt sorry for myself and nothing was going to get me out of that mode until I found a job. I need to provide for my family."

"But Paul, it's not like we were going to lose our house. We saved well enough to survive for a while. And you should have known that providing for your family means more than money. You weren't the only one going through something. I needed you to be there for me, and you weren't. You were in your own world.

"Our daughter needed you to attend her events and really be more a part of her last year of high school. You were at her graduation and you were great. But leading up to that, you were not pleasant to be around."

Paul lifted his wife's hand toward his face, leaned over and kissed it.

"You haven't kissed my hand in more than a year," Ginger

said. "It might sound crazy to you, but you kissed my hand at the end of our first date. I was expecting a kiss—we had such a nice time—at least on the cheek. But at my door you told me you were glad we met, reached down and pulled up my hand and gently kissed it.

"And that was so damn erotic and sexy and gentlemanly. I was turned on. From there, every so often you would kiss my hand when I was upset or when you wanted sex or when you were just being nice. I have missed that."

Paul wanted to tell his wife at that moment about the lottery money, that their lives had changed forever, that they could do whatever they wanted without regard for finances. But he didn't. He listened to the doubts she expressed and decided to hold on to his secret a little while longer, when Ginger seemed all in and doubt-free.

Instead, he said, "I don't know about you, but I'm starting over. I'm rebuilding. I'm committed to making the effort to regain your trust and full commitment to the marriage. I understand your feelings, but I'm going to do what I need to do, what I'm supposed to do, to make things right."

"Well, that sounds good to me, Paul," Ginger said. "I guess we'll just have to see."

Paul pulled her closer to him and she rested her head on his chest. "We have about an hour, maybe ninety minutes before dinner. Let's get a quick nap and have a great Thanksgiving dinner," he said.

"I wonder how our mothers are getting along," Ginger said.

"I wonder, too," Paul said.

CHAPTER 9
MOMMA MIA

The mothers spent their time before Thanksgiving dinner enhancing their buzz with glass after glass of Cabernet Sauvignon.

"I needed this time away more than those kids of ours needed it," Madeline said. "They have their neat little lives, daughter off to college. And here we are. I'm a widow and you're divorced."

"But we can't let that keep us down," Brenda said. "I had my moments of depression, even though I was the one who wanted a divorce. But I got over it."

"How?" Madeline wanted to know. "How did you do it because it's been almost ten months since my husband died. And I feel strange even thinking about another man."

"You gotta believe you don't need another man to get on with your life," Brenda said. "I said you gotta believe that shit—but you don't have to deny yourself, either."

The women laughed and Madeline said, "I *know* that's right."

"Girl, I got on the Internet and joined a dating service and I have met two really nice men," Brenda said. "Please don't tell Paul this. He thinks he's my protector. He bought me the computer and told me to not even think about those dating sites because—how did he put it?—they attract 'the man who is not interested in nothing but having sex. They figure that you are desperate to be on a dating site, then you will be easy to get in bed. I'm not trying to hear about you being stalked—or worse—by someone you met online,' he said.

"I let him live his life, you know? He's got to let me live mine. You can believe his father is living his."

"Well, truth be told," Madeline said, "I did meet someone. He was visiting my church. Retired military. He lives in San Diego. Retired there. Said he would be in Sacramento visiting his cousin or some relative while we are here. So I might have to sneak away for a day to see him. I like him. Charming. Smart. We've had dinner and breakfast together."

"On the same date?" Brenda asked.

Madeline looked embarrassed. "What can I say?" she answered.

"Listen at you," Brenda said. "You should tell him to bring a friend and we can double date. Shoot, I ain't above no blind date."

"You know what? That's a good idea," Madeline said. "Where's my phone? I don't know how to text that well; Ginger showed me how. But that's the way the young folks do it. They send a text. I'm not trying to be that young, but I don't want to seem that old, either."

The combination of the wine impacting her coordination and the touch screen to her iPhone made it an adventure for her to complete the text. "Shoot, I guess we can have another glass of wine while you figure that whole thing out," Brenda said.

After nearly five minutes, she was done. "Damn, I'm exhausted," Madeline said. "Next time, I'm just calling. Trying to act young is too exhausting for me. And I only typed three sentences."

"I ain't that hip myself, but I know you have to abbreviate," Brenda said. "I'm glad you at least tried. You're so prim and proper."

"I might be prim and proper," Madeline said. "But I can get down and dirty when I need to. But ladies rarely go there."

"You trying to say something about me?" Brenda asked, smiling.

"Of course, not," Madeline said.

Before Brenda could reply, she looked up to see Paul and Ginger approaching. She looked at her watch. It was Thanksgiving dinnertime.

"I can't believe you are down here before us," Ginger said.

"Honey, they have been here since we got here," Paul said.

The mothers looked at Paul in a strange way.

"That's right, isn't it?" he asked. "I saw you all when I came down here to get some wineglasses. That was almost two hours ago."

"Mother, you have been drinking wine all that time?" Ginger asked.

"Not all that time," Madeline answered. "But most of it."

And she and Brenda burst out laughing, loudly. Ginger and Paul looked at each other. They were in for an interesting evening.

"I thought you wanted to shower and change clothes, Mother," Ginger said.

"I decided to sit here with Brenda and enjoy life instead," her mom said. "I'll do that later. And I know one thing: I'm hungry. Wine does three things for me: makes me hungry, makes me feel good, and makes me want to wee-wee."

"That's too much information, Maddy," Brenda said. "Yes, that's my new nickname for you. Maddy. Madeline has too many syllables."

"Oh, boy," Paul said. "They are both tipsy as hell."

"Vino, it's OK," Brenda said as she pulled herself from her seat. "We're fine. You know what, son? This was a great idea. I am so glad to be here. And you're right: Maddy isn't the bitch I thought she was."

"OK, OK," Paul said to his mother. "Maybe you should have some water."

"We're going to the bathroom; come on, Maddy," Brenda said. "Get us a table for dinner, Paul. We'll be right back."

The moms composed themselves and walked arm-in-arm to the restroom.

Ginger turned to Paul. "You called my mother a bitch?"

"What? No," Paul said. "Come on, now. I love your mother, even if she has issues with me. And why would I say something like that? My mom didn't even say that. She said she didn't believe she could get along with your mother. And I told her your mom wasn't as bad as she thought."

"That's not the same as saying you love her, Paul," Ginger said.

"It ain't calling her a bitch, either," he said. "Hold up. Are you trying to start a fight? After what we just did and what we just shared? I told you neither of us called your mom a bitch. My mom obviously is feeling the wine. So whatever comes out of her mouth is suspect."

"Or the truth," Ginger said. "You know what they say: A drunk person speaks a sober man's thoughts."

"Yeah, well, I'm focusing on the good thing and that's that they are getting along," Paul said. "I hoped for this but didn't expect it."

"Well, that's true," Ginger said. "I guess we should ride this wave as long as we can."

"That's right because even the biggest wave reaches shore and dies at some point," Paul said.

"Let's get some wine and drink to them being BFFs for now," Ginger said.

They went to the reception area and were seated near a fireplace. He held the chair for Ginger and placed her cloth napkin in her lap.

"Look who's suddenly Mr. Chivalry now," she joked. "I guess good sex brings out all kinds of stuff."

"Especially good sex after not having any for about a year," Paul said.

"Excuse me, but we had sex about two months ago and two months before that," Ginger asserted.

"That's a pretty sad timeline. But it wasn't anything like what just happened," Paul said. "We had sex then. Just now, we had *sex* and we made love at the same time. Know what I'm saying?"

Ginger blushed.

Their parents arrived at that table about that time. They had killed a bottle and a half by themselves and it was obvious. They were as giddy as schoolgirls, laughing and joking as if they were life-long pals.

Ginger and Paul were amazed.

Everyone ordered the holiday dinner of turkey, dressing, yams and greens and enjoyed it to the hilt, all the while engaging in lighthearted conversation that made it feel like a family meal.

Madeline and Brenda passed on wine with their meals, but they allowed Paul to order a bottle as a nightcap, Shiraz, and when all was poured in the glasses, he offered a toast.

"This is what family is about—enjoying each other and loving life. I've always wanted this for us, so if feels good to finally have it."

They tapped glasses and, for Paul, he felt on top of his world. He was healthy, his wife seemed to be coming around and he was a millionaire. He felt the urge to tell the ladies of his luck, but thought better of it. *Not yet*, he said to himself.

"Look at you two," Brenda said, staring at her son and Ginger. "Y'all look like you just had sex."

Paul practically choked on his wine.

"You know what? You're right," Madeline chimed in. "Look at you, Ginger. I noticed it when you first came down, but I let it go. You all been up there doing the do."

"Mother," Ginger said. "I don't believe you. Doing the do?"

"Yes, but am I wrong?" Madeline asked.

"If you were right or wrong, I wouldn't answer," Ginger said. "I can't believe you would even ask me something like that." Brenda said. "Paul's just a smiling. I recognize the look. He ain't said a word."

"'Cause he doesn't have a thing to say about that," Paul said. "This is a case when too good much wine goes wrong."

"Can we get back to the meal?" Ginger said.

"Why isn't Helena with us?" Madeline asked. "It would be perfect if she was here, too."

"I know," Brenda said. "I don't get to see my granddaughter enough as it is."

"Who's fault, is that, Ma?" Paul said. "Helena wanted to go to her roommate's home and spend the holiday there. She's loving her college experience and sometimes that's a part of it. She'll be home for Christmas.

"And this is a grown people trip. Would you be drinking as much wine as you have if she were here?"

"Yes, I would, because I'm grown and can do whatever I want to do," Brenda said. "And the reason I say she should be here is because I remember what it was like for me when I went to my roommate's hometown for a weekend in college."

"Well," Ginger said, "Miss Wall, we spoke to the young lady's parents and they are aware that they are teenagers who are young and can get wild. I'm not stupid: Helena isn't an angel, at least not around us.

"I spoke to her earlier and she said she is fine and enjoying herself. It's a parent's nature to worry. But I'm not going to drive myself crazy with it by making sure she's with us all the time. She needs her freedom to build responsibility."

"Yes, but this is family time and she should be with her family," Madeline said.

Ginger resisted the urge to snap at her mom, and instead reached for the wine. "Well, in reality, it was our decision, Mother," she said.

"I've never seen you sip so much wine," Paul quickly added, attempting to advance the conversation.

"I never *needed* to sip so much wine," Ginger said.

Paul smiled, but no one else did. He looked at his mother and the look on her face was not a good one.

"Ma, what's wrong?" he asked.

"I don't feel good," she said. "Too much wine."

"I don't feel good, either," Madeline said.

"Mother, what's wrong?" Ginger asked.

"My head. My stomach," she answered.

"What kind of wine were you drinking?" Paul said. "Both of you not feeling good? This is crazy."

"I'm feeling sick," Brenda said. She pushed away from table and placed both her hands over her stomach. Her face became flushed, her skin clammy.

"Come on, let's go to the bathroom," Paul said.

"I'm going, too," Madeline said. "I'm going to throw up."

Ginger and Paul hurried from the table and helped usher the women toward the bathroom.

"Ma, wine doesn't do this to you," Paul said. "I don't understand this."

Three feet from the bathroom door, Brenda threw up, a heaping splattering of her breakfast, lunch, dinner and drinks. Seeing that helped Madeline throw up, too.

And passersby shook their heads in disgust. Paul and Ginger went straight to caregiver roles, trying to comfort their moms.

"I got them," Ginger said, as she walked the ladies into the bathroom. She glanced down at the vomit on the floor. "Maybe you should get that up," she said to Paul.

"Hell, no," he said. "I'll get some paper towels and cover it, but that's it."

And so he did and then went back to the table to finish the wine, pay the bill and wait on the ladies. After about fifteen minutes, they came out, and he rushed from the restaurant area to meet them.

"You feeling better?" he said to his mom, as he clutched her arm.

"I feel woozy, but a little better," she said. "Seems like I've got to get whatever's left in my stomach out of it."

"I don't understand," Paul said. "For both of you to have a reaction like this over wine doesn't seem right."

No one responded to Paul, which made him uneasy, curious. They continued toward the elevator without anyone saying anything.

Finally, as they got into the elevator, the mothers looking totally worn down and intoxicated, Ginger let it out.

"They got sick because your mother ordered shots," Ginger said with anger in her voice.

"Shots?" Paul said. "Shots of what?"

"Tequila."

"Ma, you don't even like tequila," he said. "Why would you do that?"

"I don't know and I'm too sick to go into it now," she said, her voice weary.

Ginger looked at Paul with fire in her eyes. He looked at his mother with dismay as he helped her into her room. She collapsed on the queen-sized bed closest to the bathroom.

"Paul, I feel like I'm going to throw up again," Brenda said. "I need you to stay here and take care of me."

He did not know what to do, so Ginger spoke up.

"Yeah, he can stay here with you and I will take Mother to our room," she said.

Paul's head snapped in her direction. In his mind the night would be spent resuming their lovemaking of earlier in the day. Ginger knew what was on his mind.

"That's right," she said. "You stay here with your mother since she created this…situation."

She and Madeline headed out the door toward Paul's and Ginger's room.

"You're blaming this on my mother?" Paul said. "Last I looked your mother is a grown woman and I'm sure no one made her drink that tequila."

Ginger said, "My mother ordered the second shot, but your mom shouldn't have even brought tequila into the equation."

"Oh, she did?" Paul said, looking side-eyed at Ginger, who was standing in the doorway with her mother on her arm. "I guess I should be mad at your mom, huh?"

Ginger turned and slowly walked three rooms down the hallway with her mother. There, she was glad they had two beds because she and Paul had littered the other bed, closest to the window, in their passion.

Her mom said, "Let me lay down for a few," she said. "I feel so weak and so…so drunk. I need to close my eyes and get my head together and my stomach right."

Ginger took off her shoes. "I'll be right back," she said. "I'm going to get a gown from your room so you can change."

In the hallway, she encountered Paul, who was headed to his room to get his toiletry bag and something to sleep in.

"So you have attitude with me because your mother drank what she shouldn't have?" Paul said.

"Your mother had to take it to another level," Ginger said.

"My mother?" he responded. "I might have not had a good flight here, but I did notice that *your* mother had liquor in a flask on the plane. So who's zooming who?"

Ginger stormed off to the other room to get her mom's belongings. She thought Brenda was asleep, but she was not.

"Ginger, I'm so sorry," she said. "Sit down for a minute."

Ginger obliged her. "We didn't mean to ruin our Thanksgiving dinner. We took that first shot because your mother and I came to a truce and we drank to it. It was my idea."

"What was the truce?" Ginger asked.

"To make sure you and my son stay together," she answered. "We might be old—or older—but we're not blind or crazy. We knew you all have been having troubles for many months now. She blamed Paul; I blamed you.

"What we realized in spending some time together today is that sometimes it's nobody's fault. Sometimes things happen just through living. It's up to you and him to work it out. But we, as mothers-in-law, could help by being friends and not enemies.

"So, your mom asked for the second shot—for family. And that's why we got sick. Two shots. I haven't had a shot in forty years. It was too much."

"You all are something else," Ginger said. "I guess the best thing about it is that you all are now getting along after almost twenty years."

"In my heart, I only agreed to come on this trip to really learn about your mom, who she was, what she really was like. We never really spent any *real* amount of time together. Don't get me wrong: I wanted to come to Napa Valley. But that was another big part of my reason for agreeing to come."

"Wow," Ginger said, "the truth really is in the wine. And the tequila, too, I guess."

While that was going on, Madeline surprised Paul. "Don't go yet," she said as he was heading toward the door with his luggage.

"Huh?" Paul said.

"Can you sit down, for a minute?" Madeline said in a voice so low Paul had to strain to hear her. "The room is spinning but I want to apologize for that mess we caused down there tonight. I'm glad it didn't happen in the restaurant. I also wanted to say that I am glad you planned this trip.

"You probably didn't want me to come; I haven't been the best mother-in-law to you. Not because I don't like you or even love you—I do. It's just that Ginger has been my whole life. Do you know that when she was born, we both almost died? Yes, complications came up—I had some rare condition and my blood pressure dropped and it was all messed up—and they had to take her to save her. And her heart rate dropped, the cord was wrapped around her neck and she was breech.

"But she...we both made it. Doctors said we were little miracles. Your child will always be special to you, but she was even more special to me. So I am a little overboard when it comes to protecting her and wanting the best for her, no matter how old she is.

"But here's the thing: You are the best man for her—always have been."

And suddenly she was asleep. So, Paul gathered his things and headed to his mom's room. In the hallway, he and his wife's paths crossed again. The brief chat with their in-laws tempered their anger.

"Wild night, huh?" Paul said, smiling.

"Crazy," Ginger said. "I feel so bad for them. They are messed up. And we're supposed to have breakfast at nine and then start touring wineries."

"If they aren't up to it, we can drive around and see the area, eat and do wines later in the day—or the next day," Paul said. "We'll play it by ear."

"OK," Ginger said. "Let me go in here and check on this woman."

"I'll bring you a glass of wine later," Paul said. "Keep your phone near by. I'll text you."

But Paul never texted and it did not matter to Ginger; both listened to their respective mothers share news about themselves they never knew and were so shell-shocked by the information that they did not dare stop them. They listened…and listened… and listened until they fell asleep.

CHAPTER 10
HUNG-OVER & OUT

The morning brought less pain for Brenda and Madeline, but they were hardly themselves. Madeline went back to her room. She and Brenda showered and got dressed around ten o'clock and sat on the bed waiting for Ginger and Paul.

"I feel like a truck ran over me; then backed up and did it again," Brenda said.

"Same truck must have hit me, too," Madeline said. "My head doesn't hurt, but my stomach is not quite right and my body feels worn down."

"This is crazy," Brenda said, as Paul knocked on the door. "We're in the best area of the United States for wine and I don't want to even *see* a bottle of wine."

She opened it and Paul stood in the threshold, smiling, with two cups of coffee in his hands.

"OK, party animals," he said. "Here's a pick-me-up."

"Very funny," Brenda said, as she reached for a cup. "But this is exactly what I need."

"I don't even drink coffee, but if it's going to get me to feeling better, then I'll try some," Madeline said. "Where's Ginger?"

"She's gone down to get us a table for breakfast," Paul said.

He walked with the ladies to the elevator. "That was some night," he said. "I was feeling great about everything and then—"

"Do you really have to remind us, son?" Brenda asked. "It was embarrassing enough. Let's not relive it."

"I can't promise it won't come up again," Paul said.

"Did you get some pleasure out of us being so sick?" Madeline said.

"Pleasure? Seeing you all throw up in the hallway? Seeing you intoxicated?" Paul said. "Of course, not? But I did speak to both of you last night while you were in bed. Do you recall that?"

"You talked to me?" Madeline asked.

"No," Paul said, holding the elevator door open for them, "you talked to me."

"Oh my goodness," she said. "I don't remember that. What did I say?"

"That you love me and I'm the best thing that ever happened to Ginger," Paul said. "That's the abbreviated version."

And then he laughed, making Madeline uncertain if he was joking or telling the truth. The elevator doors opened and Ginger was standing right there.

"Oh, I was coming up to see where you all were," she said. "Hi, Mother. How you feeling? How are you, Ms. Wall?"

"OK," they said almost in unison.

"Well, the coffee should help," Ginger said. "And maybe some oatmeal and toast."

"That's about all I can take right now," Madeline said.

They made their way to the restaurant.

"I hope no one remembers us from last night," Madeline said. "That was so embarrassing."

"I know," Brenda said. "I almost want to change hotels."

"Well, we're not doing that, Ma," Paul said. "We don't know them and they don't know us. So it really doesn't matter."

"You weren't the one who vomited in the lobby," Brenda said.

"Touché," he responded.

They made their way to their seats for breakfast. Paul and Ginger felt refreshed. They slept about seven hours.

"On the east coast, it's about one in the afternoon," Ginger said. "I'm hungry."

"My stomach doesn't feel quite right, but I'm eating because it's time to eat," Brenda said.

And so, everyone ate. Paul sat across from his wife and between his mother and mother-in-law. He felt a distance from Ginger that he could not pinpoint. He thought they had gotten past blaming each other's mother for their intoxication the night before, but knowing her, he sensed something was amiss.

"Gin, how you doing? How's your food?" he asked.

"Fine," she said without looking up. He knew then something was bothering her.

"What's wrong?" he asked. He figured she still blamed his mother for her mom getting sick and throwing up.

"Nothing," she said.

The parents looked on, curiously.

"Come on, I know you," he said. "You can tell me. We're among family."

Ginger raised her head and looked at him. "Is there something you want to tell me?" she asked.

"Huh? No," he said. "Tell you about what?"

"About how you ended up out of work last year, which started all the drama we have had," she said.

Paul's heartbeat increased, but he remained outwardly calm—and did not say a word.

"Let's talk about it since you want to talk so much, since you want to know what's wrong with me," Ginger said.

"Maybe you should talk in private," her mother said.

"No, Paul said we're among family and I should say what's on my mind," Ginger responded. "So I'll ask again: Why did you lose your job?"

"What are you talking about?" Paul asked.

"I spoke to your mother last night," Ginger said.

"What?" Brenda said, shocked. "What are you talking about?"

"See, that's what a good buzz will do; you start telling stuff you didn't mean to tell," Ginger said. "You told me some harmless stuff and you also said, 'I know you have been having issues because of why Paul got *fired*."

"I did not say that," Brenda said with indignation.

"Ms. Wall, that's exactly what you said."

"Well, I don't remember that," Brenda added.

"Doesn't really matter if you remember," Ginger said. "It only matters if it's the truth. Paul, you told me you got downsized out of your job. But you told your mother something different. Why?"

"My mother is right," he said. "We should speak on this in private."

"No," Ginger said sternly. "Right now. What happened? You were fired? Why were you fired, Paul? I know why. I'm seeing if you're going to tell me the truth."

"It was some B.S.," he said.

"So it's true? You got fired and told me you got laid off," Ginger said. She was remarkably calm for someone so furious. "Why would you do that?"

"Because I was embarrassed," Paul said. "Embarrassed by what they did to me."

"No, if your mother is correct—," Ginger said.

"Ginger, I do not recall saying anything like this to you," Brenda said. "Where are you getting this from?"

"I got it from you, Miss Wall," Ginger said. "You said some

nice things about me and about the marriage and then you told me your son got fired from his job because of sexual harassment."

"I knew that, but I wouldn't tell you," Brenda said.

"Why wouldn't you tell Ginger?" Madeline jumped in.

"Because it wasn't my place to," Brenda said.

Voices started to rise. "Wait, can we hold it down some?" Paul said. "We already were embarrassed here last night."

Ginger ignored Paul.

"Well, you apparently felt like it was your place to go last night because you sure enough told me that," she said. "So the question is, Paul: Why didn't you tell me? You told your mother, but not your wife?"

"Gin, I didn't know what to do," Paul started.

"So it's true?" his mother-in-law asked with disdain in her voice.

"Gin, can we go somewhere for ten minutes to talk about this?" he asked.

"First of all, I'm not going anywhere," she said. "And secondly ten minutes hardly would be enough time for what I have to say to you."

Paul was trapped. There was no wiggle room, not an inch to squirm free. So he released the burden that he had been carrying around for nearly a year.

"It's true, but I didn't harass anyone," Paul said. "I'm sorry I lied to you, Gin. I really am. I didn't want you to think crazy about me because it's such a stupid reason to get fired."

"What did you do?" she asked, calmly. "It must have been really serious for them to let you go after—what?—fourteen years?"

"There was a woman on the job," he started. The eyes of the women were locked on him. The fall morning turned summer hot for Paul. "Her name was Sophia. She worked in the office. Any paperwork that I had to file after a job I had to file with her.

So, one day she asks if I would like to go to the grand opening of an art gallery. I told her I would check with you and that I didn't know.

"I asked for her number to text her my answer. When I texted her that we already had plans, she started texting me all kinds of stuff. It was crazy, like she was cultivating a relationship in her head."

"What did she look like, Paul?" Madeline wanted to know.

"Ginger, can we finish this in private?" Paul asked.

"No, keep going," Ginger answered.

Paul took a deep breath. "She's an attractive woman, Ms. Knight. But that has nothing to do with anything."

The women did not respond.

"Before she switched up on me, we would exchange text messages about harmless stuff," he went on. "After about two weeks, we became really familiar with each other. She told me she was dating and so I didn't feel like there was anything there to be concerned with.

"Well, one day, Big Al sends me a text message. It's a short video of two people doing this sex trick where a guy flips the girl over and when they stop, they are in this wild sex position. Well, I forwarded it to her, to Sophia, and she took offense."

"You did *what*?" Ginger said. "You sent a video of two people having sex to a woman? Why would you do that? That's what you wanted to do to her? You didn't send it to me, but you sent it to some woman on your job?"

"You didn't want him to send that to you anyway, baby," Madeline said.

"Mother, please," Ginger said. "Paul, why would you send something like that to a woman?"

"It was a mistake," Paul said. "A grave mistake. I thought we were friends, like one of the guys. I shouldn't have done it, of course, looking back on it."

"So what's the B.S. part, Paul?" Ginger said. "You sent a woman a very inappropriate video. Doesn't seem like B.S. to me."

"It's B.S. because she then started going back through my text messages to her and started changing the meaning, changing the context of what I was saying. So, instead of my text reading: "Wanna meet at the Ritz for a drink?" she said it read like I was asking her out on a date or to spend the night at a hotel.

"She responded: 'Aren't you married?' It wasn't intended like she was insulted or anything like that. She meant it at the time like, 'Aren't you married? You've go to go home and be a husband.' That's one of the running jokes we had.

"She would ask me about doing something and I would tell her, 'No can do; going home to the wife.' And so it became this running joke with us where she would say, 'Aren't you married?' to almost anything I said."

"Now I see where the B.S. comes in—with you," Ginger said.

"Gin, that's not true," Paul pleaded. "Listen to the rest of it. So, when she gets the video, all of a sudden our jokes became me harassing her. And because the video was pornography, they called it sexual harassment."

Ginger stared at him with so much anger. Paul did not know what to do, so he kept talking, thinking the longer she listened the clearer it would become to her. Wrong.

"It was crazy," he continued. "Here I thought she was a friend, but she turned out to be someone out to get me."

"Why was she out to get you?" Madeline asked.

"Because I would not go out with her," Paul said.

"You never met her out?" Ginger asked.

"No," Paul said. "I mean, she met all of us out a few times. It was never just her and me. She did talk about me rejecting her. She'd say, 'Married man, you need to loosen up a little. Every time I ask you something you say, 'I'm married.' So I think she simply was not used to a man being disciplined with her. And she didn't like it. I don't know what her motivation was because I never talked to her again. But she saved all our texts and interpreted them to the mediator. Meanwhile, I didn't have any text messages because I deleted them all."

"Paul, this sounds crazy to me," Ginger said. "If there was nothing going on, if you didn't have an interest in this woman, why wouldn't you tell me about her? You never mentioned her name. I always asked who was with you when you would hang out. Never, not once did you mention a woman's name.

"So, because of that, it's hard for me to believe that simple story. You lost your job because you were chasing another woman. Period."

"No, it's not as simple as that," Paul said. "I am not going to allow you to believe this nonsense."

"Nothing you can do to change it now," Ginger said. "I've been in the dark for eleven months. I came out here in good faith to mend our marriage. And yet I found out that you're a cheater and that you don't trust me enough to tell me something very personal, something that really affected our marriage, but you told your mother.

"Thanks for trusting in me."

And with that, Ginger tossed her cloth napkin onto the table and headed out of the hotel's front door. Madeline stood and stared at Paul before following her daughter.

"Ma," he said, looking at Brenda.

"Paul, I am so sorry," she said. "I promise you, I do not remember telling her you got fired. But I was so messed up that I guess I did. Maybe it was on my conscience and I didn't realize it."

"It's okay," he said. "It's my fault. I always hated not being upfront with her. Should have told her back then and faced the music."

"Well, you're going to have to talk to her—but when she cools off," Brenda said. "Saying something now is only going to make it worse. Trust me, I'm a woman."

"How can we go and have a nice day with her mad at me?"

"Easy," Brenda said. "She doesn't want to have a bad time. Plus you have your momma here. Come on, let's go. They're probably outside waiting on us."

And they were. Paul used the remote to open the doors and physically opened the front passenger door for Ginger, who stepped into the car without acknowledging her husband.

Paul revealed a printout that had various wineries listed. "So, we can go to Beringer now and hit one or two others before the day is out. And we can stop somewhere for a nice lunch," he said. "Anyone have any thoughts on that?"

Ginger looked away from him, out the window. Madeline said, "I don't feel so great, so I'm not really ready to taste wines."

"Actually, me, either," Brenda said.

Paul was devastated. He was called "Vino" by his mother because he loved wine. He traveled to California on a plane despite his immense fear of flying. He was finally in his dream location with the closest women in his life…and no one wanted to go taste wine.

But he did not reveal his frustration. Not totally. "I can't believe I cannot get to a winery now that I'm finally in Napa," he said. "But we're a group traveling together, so it's not only about me."

He started the car and sat there for a moment or so.

"I have an idea," he said. "How about us taking a drive back toward San Francisco so we can see the Golden Gate Bridge during the day? We went across it, but it was too dark to really enjoy it. There's a park right there, Golden Gate Park. We can go there and take some photos and take in the beautiful scenery.

"By the time we get back, it will be time for lunch and hopefully everyone will feel better and we can visit a winery. What do you think?"

"You know, you can walk across the Golden Gate," Madeline said. "Let's do that."

"That sounds like fun," Brenda said.

"I'm gonna leave that to you all," Paul said. "I'm sure it will be exciting, but flying here was exciting enough for me."

Ginger did not say anything. Paul hated when she was that way. He hated it because he did not know where her mind would go, but he knew it would not be a pleasant place.

"Gin, does this plan work for you?" he said.

"Fine," she said, not bothering to look in his direction.

"OK, well, I'm going to take the scenic route through downtown Napa so we can get a feel for where we are," he said.

Brenda pulled out her camera. Madeline fumbled with her phone. Paul lost himself in the moment as they rode through the charming and quaint town, laced with interesting shops and restaurants, with people milling about. The temperature was in the low sixties with the sun spraying rays over the place as if a spotlight.

"Magnificent time to be here," he said. "We could not have picked a better weekend."

"It is beautiful," Madeline said, but more to Brenda than Paul.

The foliage and yellow and red leaves in the trees and on the ground made for an image that one would see in a painting.

"I could live here," Paul said. "It's been ten minutes and I already know I could live here. It's so warm and so quaint. And it helps that there is wine all around you. I can be consumed in wine. OMG."

"It's interesting that you can love wine so much but not become a wino," Ginger's mother said.

"It's just like you liking alcohol but not becoming an alcoholic," Brenda said. She said it pleasantly, but she was defending her son, whether he wanted or needed it or not.

"I don't know if I like what you're insinuating," Madeline said.

"Don't get your Depends in a bunch," Brenda said, and everyone laughed, even Ginger.

"I'm glad to see some smiling faces in this car," Brenda added. "I'm feeling better and we should have a good time and enjoy each other."

"I agree with you, Ma," Paul said. Then he added: "OK, in honor of you ladies getting, uh, inebriated last night, why don't we share a story about an embarrassing moment that we haven't shared with anyone before."

"That's easy," Ginger said. "I married you."

"Ouch," Paul said. "That was mean. But at least you smiled. I like seeing you smile, Gin."

They were at a light before jumping on the highway headed toward the Golden Gate Bridge. They looked into each other's eyes for a few seconds before she looked away.

"Who wants to go first?" Ginger asked.

"I'm not sure what kind of story you're looking for, so Paul probably should go first," his mother said.

"OK," Paul said. "I'll go. Now, this has to be a story you never told anyone. OK? OK, about ten years ago, Helena had a school project where she had to take a coffee can, punch holes in the bottom of it and use it as a plant holder or something. I remember buying her one and then another one because something was wrong with the first one.

"So, this was a time you might remember, Gin. We were meeting in Buckhead at Phipps Plaza to go to the movies. It was the spring or fall—I can't remember which—but I had a pullover sweater on. So, anyway, I had a job in College Park and you were already in Buckhead, shopping or something. You had Helena with you. So, we were going to the movies and I rushed home, showered, changed clothes and got into the car to meet you all.

"Well, I am so anal about seeing the previews that I decided I would pass on going to the bathroom and would go when I got to the movies. So, I get on 85 North at the Connector and—bam—it's a logjam. Traffic is backed up for a few miles. So I'm anxious about getting to you all on time and I hate traffic and now I've got to go to the bathroom so bad that I'm squirming in my seat."

The ladies are laughing and hanging on to his every word. He went on: "So, we're at a standstill and I'm in the center lane with no way to take an exit. By the minute, I've got to go to the bathroom more and more. So I start looking around the car for a cup or bottle or anything because I'm about to pee on myself."

"Oh, my God," Madeline said.

"My mind is racing. Then it hits me: I bought that second coffee can and Helena left it in the trunk. So since we're at a standstill, I pop the trunk, get out of the car right there on 85 and hurry up and grab the coffee can and jump back into the car. I had no other option; I couldn't hold it much longer.

"So I'm frantically trying to open my pants, get the belt loose and the zipper down because I'm about to wet myself, which I could not let happen. I'm sweating. It's an emergency. I don't know how it is for women, but when a man has to pee badly and knows he's about to let it go, it's harder to hold it back.

"Finally, I get myself free and I position the can between my legs and—I'm sure you know the relief you feel when you've got to go really badly."

Paul started demonstrating behind the wheel his actions. He

feigned closing his eyes and throwing his head back in relief. "I had saved myself and the relief felt so good," he said.

"But then I started feeling something. My butt got warm. I looked down, and the can I was peeing in had holes in it. It was the first can I bought, not the second one. So all that pee that went in the can came right out in my seat."

The women howled, they laughed so hard. Paul was laughing hysterically, too, Then he started reenacting the moment. He pulled himself from his seat, as he did that night.

"I lifted my butt up so I wasn't sitting in a pile of pee," he said, and they burst into laughter again for several seconds. "It was a total mess. And once you start peeing, you can't stop."

Madeline and Brenda were falling all over themselves. Ginger was in tears. Paul, too. And he kept them in stitches.

"So I emptied my bladder and was sitting there on the highway in my own pee."

"Stop, Paul," his mother managed to get out between laughs. "You're crazy. I can't take any more. Please stop. Oh, my God."

But he wasn't finished. "So I was relieved in one sense, but soaking wet and pissy in another," he said, and Ginger buried her face in her hands, laughing so hard she could barely catch her breath.

"Paul, I don't believe you," she said.

"I'm serious," he said. "So now I have another problem. And we're still sitting in the same place; traffic had not moved. So I've got to do something. So I pop the trunk again to get some towels I have to wash the car out of the trunk to soak up some of all the pee on my seat."

The ladies again are doubled-over in laughter.

"I hurry up out of the car, hoping no one can see the big piss stain that covered my whole behind. I get the towels and place them on the seat and jump back into the car. I had about four towels, so they sopped up the urine pretty good."

He stopped to join the others in laughter. When he composed himself, he said, "So, I solve that crisis. I have gotten the pee off my seat. But my pants are soaking wet. Traffic starts to move a little bit and I almost swerved into someone because I was taking off my pants as I was driving."

Once again, there was laughter among the women. "You're killing me with this one," Brenda said.

"So, I use my feet to slip off my shoes and squirm my way out of my pants and drawers. I'm literally riding up 85 with my naked butt on a pile of pissy towels."

The women roll down the windows; they laughed so hard they got hot.

"So," Paul continued, "I've got about fifteen minutes max to get my underwear and pants dry."

"Oh, Lord," Ginger screamed.

"So, I turn the heat on blast and hold my drawers up to the vent."

"Ha, ha, ha, ha, ha, ha," the ladies howled.

"After about five minutes, they get mostly dry, but I'm sweating like a pig because it's burning up in there. Finally, we clear the congestion point and traffic starts to really flow. My drawers aren't quite dry, so I somehow get them to suspend on the vent so I didn't have to hold them up there. I roll down the window when I get past downtown and now I'm driving at about sixty-five miles an hour.

"So, I grab my pants and hang them out the window so they can dry as my drawers are drying."

Again, an eruption of laughter from everyone.

"I can't even imagine what that looked like: a half-naked man driving on the highway with his underwear stuck in a vent and his pants hanging out the window. The heat in the car worked good because my underwear got dry pretty quickly. They weren't fresh, but they were dry.

"I pull my pants from outside the window and position them so the wet area could take on the heat much of the way up 85 and all the way up Highway 400 to Lenox Road. By the time I get off at Lenox, the pants are not totally dry, but close to it. I put them up to my nose and was like, 'That's not good.' So, I park in the mall—you had called me twice but I couldn't pick up the phone with all that was going on.

"While sitting in the car I somehow got my stinky drawers on and pulled my stinky pants over top of them. And the only way I could think of to try to muffle the odor was to take off my sweater and wrap it around my waist."

"Oh, no," Ginger said. "I remember that night. You came in there looking crazy. And I asked you why you had your sweater around your waist. I remember."

"Well, I couldn't say, 'Because I pissed on myself and I don't want you or Helena to smell it.' I don't know what excuse I gave you and I knew I looked crazy, but I had no alternative. It was a Harry Potter movie, maybe the first one, and Helena was so excited about it. I had to be there.

"You had already purchased the tickets and I went straight to the bathroom to wash my hands. I remember Helena wondering why I didn't hug and kiss her when I first saw you all, as usual. I made sure she sat between us because she would be so into the movie she wouldn't think about any odors. When the movie was over, you suggested we go somewhere for dessert. I was like, 'You and Helena go. I'll meet you at home.'

"And that's my embarrassing story that I had never told anyone."

The women shook their heads. "I don't think anything can top that," Madeline said. "I give you credit: I might not have *ever* told anyone that story. But it was hilarious. Oh, my God."

"And the way you told it," Ginger said. "I didn't realize you had that kind of comedic timing. Just hilarious."

"It's like you've been waiting to tell that story," Brenda said. "And it didn't take a buzz from wine to get it out of you."

"You know what else I remember about that night," Ginger said. "I found it curious then, but didn't say anything."

"What was that?" Paul asked.

"When Helena and I got home, you were taking a bath," she said, and they all burst into laughter again.

"Yes, I was," Paul said. "I needed a bath that night."

They all laughed some more before catching their breath.

"I will never look at you the same, son-in-law," Madeline said. "And I mean that as a compliment. You have way more of a sense of humor than I ever thought."

"I'm a funny guy," he said. "Well, maybe not funny, but I appreciate a good laugh as much as the next guy."

"That has to be one of the funniest stories I ever heard," Brenda said.

"I'll drink to that, literally," Paul said. "Ma, look in that bag between you two."

There she found two bottles of The Prisoner wine, a delicious California Zinfandel that traveled in his luggage, and four glasses. "I thought maybe we could have a little something to sip on while we drive," Paul said. "How are you all feeling?"

"Maybe that's what I needed—a good laugh—to feel better because I sure do," Madeline said.

"I can at least sip on a little," Brenda said.

"Here, let me open it," Ginger said.

"Paul, you're driving, so..." Ginger said.

"I know. I'll get some when we get to the park," he said. "But don't think I forgot: Somebody has to tell an embarrassing story."

"If we finish these two bottles of wine, I'll be glad to tell a couple of stories," Madeline said.

"OK, I'll tell one now," Ginger said. "It won't be as long as Paul's but I never told this to anyone."

"Oh, really," Paul said. "OK, I'm ready for this."

"All right, so I get a promotion on my job to senior marketing analyst," Ginger began, "and the men in the office are livid. You know how men are—well, you might not, Paul, but I'm sure our parents do. They think women are inferior and should advance only so much.

"Well, I earned the promotion and my boss was courageous enough to give it to me knowing how the men in the office would react. So, anyway, I have a week to make this big presentation in front of my boss, his boss and the men who were angry I got the job.

"I prepared my butt off to make this presentation awesome. I needed to impress everyone. So, I go to the salon and get my hair done. I bought a beautiful new suit. I'm ready.

"I start my day as I usually do: with a light breakfast of juice and yogurt and a cup of coffee. I'm totally prepared. We get into a boardroom and I'm looking great and feeling great. I'm about to nail it, and make those guys look silly.

"So I get introduced and I get up to the head of the table where I have my stuff set up on an easel. I start great, talking about our competitor's approach to this particular project, and I can see in my boss' face how proud he is that he promoted me. But then it happened: I turned to point out something on the easel and as soon as I turned my back totally to them, I let out the loudest fart you could imagine."

Paul, Madeline and Brenda screamed in laughter. "Are you serious?" Brenda asked.

"Totally," she said.

"Wow," Madeline said. "You never told me that."

"What did you do?" Paul said.

"Well, first of all, it wasn't merely loud, but it was stinky," Ginger said, and the laughing began again.

"So I'm standing up there, afraid to even turn around to see their faces. But when I do turn around, it's like the funk rushed up my nose. And it was so strong that it jolted me; I couldn't hide on my face that it stunk to high hell."

More laughter.

"So I'm standing there, gagging on my own fart, and they are looking at me and trying to pretend they didn't hear it or smell it."

More laughter.

"So what did you do?" Paul said, finally.

"I looked at them with a straight face and said, 'That's what I think of the competition.'"

Paul, Brenda and Madeline laughed loudly, just as the men in the boardroom had.

"I can't even tell you how embarrassed I was," Ginger said. "The funny thing is that after that, I was even more loose and the guys even loosened up and somehow, my fart at the wrong time helped me and those guys have a better relationship. Don't get me wrong; I don't trust them. But from that moment on they stopped being so rude and distant with me. So it's made for a better working environment."

"Wow," Brenda said. "It takes passing gas to get men to respect you. How crazy is that?"

They settled down and the attention turned to wine.

"This is some good wine, Vino," Brenda added. "I'm feeling much better."

"Look at that," Paul said, pointing to the Golden Gate Bridge.

"Beautiful," Madeline said.

Paul drove across the bridge, slowly, and the magnificence of the view quieted the car. No one said a word. They snapped photos and admired the prodigious bridge and skyline of San Francisco off in the distance.

"Just beautiful," Ginger said.

Paul took the first exit over the bridge and worked his way back and crossed the bridge again, headed toward Napa. Dozens and dozens of people walked across the bridge.

"Look, Brenda," Madeline said. "That's gonna be us."

"But, Paul," Brenda said, "we're not walking back across, so you're going to have to come pick us up on the other side."

The traffic was heavy going back across the bridge, which was fine to the ladies; they got to take more photos and enjoy the cloudless day even more. Once they parked at Golden Gate Park, they stood outside the car and enjoyed the wine.

"I'm gonna need to walk off this wine," Brenda said. "I'm feeling it."

"Let's do it," Madeline said. "You walking with us, Ginger?"

"I think I'm going to pass," she answered. "I want to admire this view, enjoy this wine and relax. That's what a vacation is to me."

So off the seniors went, leaving Paul and Ginger in the park. She did not wait long to address her concerns. All that laughing in the car made her feel good, but it did not eliminate the angst she had about how Paul lost his job and that he did not tell her.

"I don't understand; how am I supposed to feel?" Ginger said. "You told me you got laid off, but you got fired. And you got fired because of sexual harassment. How can I believe anything you say?"

"Oh, so it's the 'Boy Who Cried Wolf' thing, huh?" Paul said. "Nothing I say is the truth? I've lied so much that you can't believe anything that comes out of my mouth? Well, if you truly believe that, then what I have to say about it won't matter. If you don't believe that—which I hope you don't—then maybe we can get past this.

"Gin, it is very simple: I sent the woman an inappropriate text message with the video. That was it. I told her repeatedly that I'm a married man. I have tried to figure out why she would turn on me like she did and I'm guessing it was because I never bit on her advances. They were subtle, but they were also obvious. And I stuck to: 'I'm going home to the wife.'"

"Do you understand that even if what you said is true," Ginger said, "the violation and the dishonoring of our marriage is in you having these private jokes and text messages; you were building a relationship with her. And if she didn't get offended by the video, you'd still have this secret relationship with her. That's the violation and the disrespect.

"If you felt compelled to never mention her to me—not even say her name—then it shows there was something to hide, or something you thought you'd want to hide in the future. And that's hard to swallow.

"I can think you asked me for a divorce because you were going to run away with whatever her name is. I could believe that you decided to try to stay in the marriage because she broke up with you. I could believe that you could still have something going with her. I could start thinking about those times you said you worked late—were you really working or working with Sophia?

"You see what I'm saying? This kind of thing triggers a whole lot of distrust and a whole lot of questions—and none of it is good."

Ginger's points were so valid that Paul pondered them for a minute or so. He looked off in the direction of the bay, with Alcatraz in the far-off distance. He did not want to react to what she said right away. To do that could mean he was more interested in reacting than actually listening, and he did not want her to think that. So he didn't say anything. And he didn't know what to say.

Finally, Ginger leaned on the car hood beside him.

"I'm sorry," he said. "I get it. The things I thought were harmless clearly they aren't harmless, even if I had no intention of doing anything with her. I'm really sorry, Gin."

"I'm not going to play holier-than-thou with you," she said. "You know, laughing in the car about your peeing on yourself was such a good thing for me. It helped me purge some of the really bad feelings I had about you. They didn't all go away. I'm not saying that.

"But what I'm saying is that even when I was laughing, I was thinking: 'He's a good man and we've had a good life together.' The last year or so has been hell. But here we are, in California. It could be worse."

Paul put his arm around his wife and looked at her. She did not look at him; she looked straight ahead.

"Gin," he said softly, "I'm sorry. Nothing like that will ever happen again. I promise. I love you."

She slowly nodded her head. With his arm still around her shoulder, he lowered it and rubbed her back. It was another of the delicate affections he used to show her early in their marriage.

And Ginger began to cry—at first tears sliding down her face and then downright weeping. Paul hugged her tightly, with both arms. He was alarmed. He knew his wife, and the way she cried was a sorrowful cry, not tears she might shed in a time of personal turmoil.

"What's wrong?" he asked.

"Nothing," she said.

"You're crying; something must be wrong," Paul said.

"We've been through a lot," Ginger said. "As soon as we take one step forward, there's one step back. I'm worn out."

"Stay here," Paul said. "We need to finish this bottle—and open the other one, too."

He went into the car and poured the last of the wine in their glasses. Ginger wiped her eyes and took a deep breath as Paul stood in front of her with the wine.

"I will do anything to get us past this," Paul said. "Let's take in the moment. Look at where we are. It's a beautiful day. Look at that bridge above us and the mountains and the city over there and the boats…and you cannot get much more picturesque than this. We have to enjoy it. We have great wine and a perfect day. No more crying, no more negative anything. Let's live."

"You said you'd do anything for us to get past this," Ginger reminded him.

"I don't like the way you said that," Paul noted. "But I *did* say it. Why?"

"I want to walk across the Golden Gate Bridge," she said.

"Gin," Paul said, "not that. We're sitting here enjoying the amazing view, sipping on wine. It's lovely."

"How we gonna let our mothers do it, but not us?" Ginger said. "That's crazy. Imagine what the view is from up there. And we can put our wine in a cup and—"

"A cup?" Paul said. "Wine is not to be consumed in a foam cup," Paul said.

"You know what you sound like? An English snob without the accent," Ginger cracked. "You can do it. You flew all the way across the country to get here… You said you'd do anything."

"Wine relaxes me," he said. "Let's finish this up and then I'll do it—only because I want to make things right with us."

CHAPTER 11
BRIDGING
THE GAP

P aul finished his wine, and another glass, before they embarked on the journey across the Golden Gate Bridge. Oh, and he carried some in a foam coffee cup, too.

He decided he'd talk as much as possible to keep his mind off of what he was doing.

"Do you know the bridge is seventy-five years old?" he said as they made their first steps across it. "I read up on it. It was built in 1937. It took almost four years to build."

Ginger sensed what Paul was doing, so she engaged him. "Tell me more," she said as she looked out at the stunning view. Paul kept talking, but she was mesmerized by the beauty and hardly heard him.

"Ok," Paul said, "the bridge is one-point seven miles long. So, it should take us about an hour and a half to walk it. We'll probably catch up with our mothers at some point.

"During construction, eleven men died falling off this bridge. They had this safety net hanging below the bridge and when men fell, it would catch them. Those who fell in it were entered into the 'Halfway-To-Hell Club.' It caught nineteen men.

"But eleven men died when a part of the scaffolding collapsed and ripped through the net. That's crazy, right?"

Ginger didn't answer.

"Here's what's even more crazy," Paul added. "More people have committed suicide jumping off this bridge than anyplace else in the country. There was a documentary I saw called 'The Bridge' that actually showed some of the twenty-four suicides off this bridge in 2004 alone. Now that's crazy."

"Yeah, it is," Ginger said. "I hope no one does that today, while we're up here... Paul, look. Look out there."

There were a plethora of sailboats elegantly drifting in the water, decorating the bay with brilliant colors. A few clouds seemingly strategically placed gave the image the feel of a painting.

Paul looked, and the view was so breathtaking that he stopped talking.

"My God," he said. He sipped his wine. "Unbelievable. I imagined it would be beautiful, from what I saw while driving across the bridge. But this? This is crazy beautiful."

Ginger looked up at him. "I know," she said. "You cannot tell me there is not a God. Man built this bridge. But all that out there...the water, the island, the mountains, the sky...that's God's work."

They walked the next five minutes without saying a word. Ginger could hardly take her eyes off the view. Paul watched the people. He could tell the locals; they walked briskly and hardly glanced to admire the stunning scenery. The first-timers or visitors took it in slowly, walking at a deliberate pace while stopping often to take and pose for photos.

"Since I'm up here," Paul said, "we might as well get a picture."

"You're gonna need to get up against the rail," Ginger said.

"OK," Paul said with confidence that he did not have. But he decided to do it instead of thinking about it.

So, he stopped at an angle where Ginger could capture the magnificent San Francisco skyline behind him. But people walked by, between them, so she had to wait a few minutes before it was clear to take the photo.

In the interim, Paul sipped his wine and then made the mistake of looking straight down at the water. The combination of the waves, the height at which he stood and his fear of heights, set off a minor scare. It was like the blood in his body was draining.

But he was determined to not let it mess up his experience. So he closed his eyes for a few seconds and told himself, "Hold it together." When he opened them, he was a different person. He felt relaxed, like wine can induce, but also alert and excited.

He posed showing the "peace" sign and smiled the biggest smile he had in some time. He felt on top of the world, literally and emotionally.

Paul again looked down over the railing at the waves, to test himself. Bad move. He got dizzy and disoriented. Ginger could see it coming on and immediately came to his aid.

"Here," she said, putting his cup of wine to his mouth. "Concentrate on this."

It worked. Paul pulled himself together rather quickly and they continued their walk—hand-in-hand.

Ginger looked down when Paul clutched her hand to make sure what she felt was real.

"You have not held my hand in at least ten years, Paul," she said. "These changes in the last month or so have been dramatic. Maybe I should get you drunk so you'll finally tell me what's really going on because it has to be something."

Paul smiled. He looked up at the expansion of the bridge and the view beyond it to take in the beauty of it all. And it almost came out right then. He wanted badly to tell Ginger that they were millionaires and their lives, as they knew it, had changed.

Telling her right there, on the Golden Gate Bridge, would be symbolic of how he felt about their future—they were above the world. But his mom was not around, and in his mind, he wanted to tell all three of the women at the same time at the top of the mountain at the Sterling Vineyard. That was the new plan he came up with. So, he held back, hard as it was.

About a half-mile in front of them were Brenda and Madeline, who were becoming faster friends. They walked at a much less brisk pace than their children. And they talked the entire time, learning that they had been compatible all along.

"Finally," Madeline said, looking down at her cell phone.

"What?" Brenda wanted to know.

"Mitch finally texted me back," she said.

"OK, what did he say?"

"He said he has a friend for you and that they will be here either tonight or tomorrow night. We can decide."

"I'd like them to come now, but it's probably better that they come tomorrow," Brenda said. "This is our first night. We probably shouldn't separate from the kids tonight."

"That's true, but if I know my daughter, she will try to escort us tomorrow," Madeline said. "It amazes me that she tries to be the mother sometimes. I agree tomorrow is the better day to do it, but..."

"But Paul will be all in it, too," Brenda said. "I guess it's better than them just saying, 'Do whatever.' We should talk to them about it tonight so they'll be clear about it tomorrow."

"Should I ask about his friend?" Madeline said. "We should know something about him before he gets here."

"Yes, you should call him," Brenda said.

And Madeline did. "I'm glad you called because it took me ten minutes to type that text message," Mitch said. "Texting for me is only in case of emergency, if I'm tied up in a truck and being kidnapped or something."

Madeline laughed. "You're funny."

They chatted and laughed and Brenda got a little jealous. She could see how much Madeline enjoyed Mitch and looked forward to seeing him, and Brenda did not have that in her life. She was not "hating" on her new friend, but she *was* envious.

"So what's up with his friend?" she asked.

Madeline said, "His name is Lionel and he's retired military, too. He says Lionel is a fun man, a good man."

"Yeah, but that doesn't mean his interesting," Brenda said. "But, at this point, how can I complain? Let's see what happens."

Madeline set it up for the men to drive to Napa from Sacramento and meet them for dinner the next night. "My son-in-law did a lot of research," she told Mitch." So I'm sure he will have some place to recommend for us."

"You know what?" Brenda asked. "This walk has been great for my energy and my stomach. I feel a lot better."

"Me, too," Madeline said. "Almost like new. By the time we get back to Napa Valley, I'll be ready to really eat."

Brenda's phone rang before she could respond. It was Paul.

"We're almost on the other side," Brenda said. "How's the park?"

"I don't know because we left the park," Paul said.

"What? Well, where are you?" she asked.

"Right behind you," he answered.

Brenda turned around to see her son and daughter-in-law about twenty yards behind them.

"Look," she said to Madeline.

"Oh, my goodness," Madeline said. "I thought you were going to stay at the park and pick us up on this side of the bridge."

"We couldn't let you all outdo us," Paul said.

Madeline looked down at their clutched hands and smiled. She had viewed Paul as a slouch—or at least someone who was a good man but not a great achiever, which is what she wanted for her daughter. So, while she never protested Ginger's choice for a husband, she never gave him a ringing endorsement or fully embraced him.

Watching Paul with Ginger on the trip gave her an appreciation for her son-in-law that she did not have. She listened to him speak, *really* listened, and determined that he was much smarter than she realized and much more cultured and definitely far more humorous. She, indeed, took him to be a humorless person, someone who could not enjoy a good joke and could not tell one.

His self-deprecating story on their way to the Golden Gate Bridge shed a new light on Paul, the man. Seeing him hold her daughter's hand gave Madeline a much more favorable feeling about him.

At the same time, Brenda assessed Ginger—and told her so.

"Can I steal your wife from you for a few minutes?" Brenda said, grabbing Ginger's free hand.

Paul didn't answer. He released her hand and they walked in front of Paul and Madeline.

"I want to tell you," Brenda began, "that already I have seen more of who you are since yesterday than I have in almost twenty years. And you know why that is? Because I probably wasn't looking before now. Why that was the case, I cannot really explain except to say that as a parent, you can sometimes see your child as so special that no one is really good enough for him.

"I have seen the kind of mother you are and I have seen how nice a house you keep and how hard you work. But I couldn't pull myself to believe you were right for Paul. And I'm sorry for that."

"But what has happened for you to feel differently, Ms. Wall?"

"My son is perfect to me but he's not perfect," Brenda said. "He has his little—what do they call them?—idiosyncrasies. And I see where you manage them very well. You got him to get on an airplane. Let's start with that. And even though you didn't sit with him—and even though I was drinking with your mother—I saw how you checked on him and reassured him, helped him get through it. I saw that you really cared—even though things haven't been that great with the marriage. I know what's going on—some of what's been going on. I commend you for that."

"Thanks, but I've always cared about Paul and always tried to be a good wife," Ginger said. "We've had our problems, but no more than anyone else. I would like to ask you something, though."

"Go ahead," Brenda said.

"In the last month or so, Paul has been different," Ginger said. "He's been happy and positive and it has thrown me off."

"I noticed the same thing," Brenda said. "I actually was gonna ask you if you knew what was going on with him."

"What are y'all talking about?" Paul said from behind them.

"You," they said in unison, and laughed.

"Forget it," Paul said. "I don't even wanna know."

"Well, I know this," Madeline said. "I'm not walking back across that bridge."

"I'll go back and get the car," Paul said. "I'll call you when I cross the bridge and turn around."

"Paul," Ginger said, "you sure you don't want me to go with you? I don't feel so good, but I'll go with you if you want me to."

He smiled. "You do care about me," he said. "If you're tired, you should stay with them. I'll be fine. I can walk a little faster so I can get back here as quickly as possible."

Paul went on his way, and the ladies crossed the bridge and found a place where they could rest and talk.

"Might as well tell you this now, Ginger," Madeline said. "We have a dinner date tomorrow night."

"Excuse me?" Ginger said. "A dinner date? With who?"

Madeline explained and Ginger was not happy.

"I don't think that's the point of us coming out here," she said. "You don't really know these men. And you think I'm going to let you run off with them? I don't think so."

"I wasn't asking your permission, child," Madeline said. "I am your mother, not the other way around. I was giving you the courtesy of letting you know what we were going to do. I know this man and it's not like we're in jeopardy—or that we won't be in a public place."

Ginger turned to Brenda. "Have you told Paul this?" she asked.

"Not yet," she answered. "And I'm sure he will have the same feelings as you, that we shouldn't go. But we're not some young kids who don't know what we're doing. We invented dating."

She and Madeline laughed. Ginger did not. And the look on her face told of her over-the-top concern. She had read about the Craigslist killer and the guy who met a woman on Christian Singles.com and killed her. Ginger could not see any good in them going out with men they hardly knew.

"Why is it that you young folks think we don't know what we're doing?" Brenda asked.

"Exactly," Madeline chimed in. "We raised you. I taught you how to deal with young boys and then men. So you know I know what I'm talking about because you've told me as much. So, it really comes down to this: You think I have lost it as I have gotten older? You think all the stuff I shared with you has somehow departed my mind and I'm some lost little girl going out into the dating world?"

"I'm not saying that, Mother," Ginger said. "I'm saying that things are different now. People are more crazy than ever and you have to be careful about who you sit across from at dinner."

The back-and-forth went on for several minutes, with neither side budging. Finally, Paul called to say he had crossed the bridge in the rental car and had turned around and was headed their way. He met them near the tollbooth and they jumped in the car and headed back toward Napa.

"By the time we get back, it'll be time for lunch," Paul said. "You all feeling better? Think you'll be ready to eat? I found this cool place online where we could stop and eat outside if it's warm enough when we get there."

No one said anything. "Hello?" Paul said. "OK, what happened?"

"These senior citizens are talking about they're going on a blind date tomorrow night," Ginger blurted out.

"Oh, now we're senior citizens?" Brenda said.

"You're not too old for me to whip your butt," Madeline said.

"Wait a minute," Paul said. "What do you mean?"

"What she means is that my friend, Mitch, is visiting his cousin in Sacramento and he and his friend, Lionel, are going to come up and take me and Brenda to dinner tomorrow night," Madeline said.

"You have a problem with that?" Brenda asked, almost daring her son to challenge her.

"Ah, yes, I do, as a matter of fact," Paul said. "Who are these people? And I thought this was a family trip."

"It is a family trip, and us having dinner with someone else will not take away from it, Paul," Brenda said. "And you and your wife can have a nice dinner together without us around. It works out for everyone."

"Why can't we all have dinner together?" Paul asked. "The six of us."

"Because we don't need you and Ginger trying to chaperone us," Brenda said. "What are we? Teenagers?"

"I can't believe we're still talking about this," Madeline said.

"We appreciate your concern. But we're not going skydiving or mountain climbing. We're having dinner. So relax."

"And I don't want to talk about it anymore," Brenda said.

Paul drove on and glanced over at Ginger, who shook her head.

"Wait, what, exactly, is the problem?" Madeline said. "Could you please tell me? If it's something more than you thinking we shouldn't go with them because they are men and we don't know them that well, you can keep quiet. But if there is more to it, then please share with me."

Again, Paul's and Ginger's eyes met.

"Well," Ginger began, "it's basically like this: I've never seen you with another man or even heard of you with another man or even conceived of you with another man. It was always you and Daddy; that's all I know.

"So to tell me you're planning to go out with someone, well, that doesn't sit well with me. And I realize it might sound crazy; I do. I'm a fully grown woman but you're still my mother."

"I appreciate that, baby," Madeline said. "But your dad—God rest his soul; he was a good man who was good to me—but he's gone. It took me a while to accept it, to deal with it. I'm *still* dealing with it. But it has been almost a year and I have got to live my life, whatever time I have left. And it's not like I'm trying to marry this man. I met him at church and I have seen him a few times.

"He lives in San Diego, but he happens to be visiting his family near here. Why wouldn't we see each other? What's the harm? And above all, why wouldn't you trust me enough to enjoy the company of a man without dishonoring your father? And I knew him better than anyone in the world. Your dad would not want me mourning him for the rest of my life."

Ginger appreciated her mom's points.

"If he's her friend," Paul asked his mother, "how did you get involved in this, Ma?"

"Because I asked Maddy to ask if he had a friend," she answered. "Why not? I'm single. I like adult male attention, too. And don't bring up your father. I'm sure he's living his life, which is what he should do. I have to live mine."

Neither Paul nor Ginger had any retort of consequence, so they rode on in silence, admiring the wonderful landscape.

When they got into Napa, they took Route 29 all the way in to St. Helena, a quaint little mountainside town in the heart of the Valley. And they really liked it because of its name, Helena, same as their daughter. They admired the wineries they passed along the way: Beringer, Sutter Homes, Peju, Milat, and the endless row of restaurants and shops that begged for a visit.

"You feel like eating?" Brenda said to Madeline.

"I finally feel like myself, for the most part," she answered. "Well, at least I can eat. My body isn't quite right, but that walk did me good. Shoot, I'll be ready for some wine with lunch."

"I have a cool place for us to eat," Paul said. "It's up ahead, I think. Looked it up on the Internet. It's called Gott's Roadside."

"There it is," Brenda said, pointing to the left. And so it was. It had an American flag hanging in front, high above the street, and a huge patio filled with umbrellas, people everywhere and smoke rising from its chimney.

"It must be good because it's packed," Madeline said.

"Very cute," Brenda added.

Paul parked the car and they made their way in and ordered. They were lucky; they were able to secure a table under an umbrella up against the white picket fence that surrounded the patio.

Madeline had the Chinese Chicken Salad, Brenda the Shrimp Tacos, Ginger a bowl of chili and a Classic Tuna Melt and Paul the Classic Tossed Cobb Salad and garlic fries. He also ordered a bottle of LaFollette 10 Pinot Noir for thirty-three-dollars.

"Can't have good food without good wine," Paul said. And no one argued with him.

Madeline said grace and they ate. "Hey," Paul said, looking at his and Ginger's moms, "you all think you're slick. You were supposed to tell us an embarrassing story that you haven't told anyone."

"That's right," Ginger said. "Who's going first?"

"I'm not sure I can tell mine now; we're eating," Madeline said.

"That's a cop out," Brenda said.

"OK, fine," Madeline said. "You have to get closer because I don't want to say this too loudly."

Everyone leaned in. "It's not a long story," she began. "I was about twenty-two and dating this guy that I really liked. He was strong and smart and funny and he liked me for me."

"Sounds like Daddy," Ginger said.

"Ha, ha. It *was* your Daddy," Madeline said. "So, we're dating like three months and we'd never been intimate. We spent a lot of time together because we enjoyed each other so much. I was holding out—not because I wasn't attracted to him or even really liked him. I was in love with him and I had to make sure he respected me.

"You know how men can put you in a category if you're too forward. They start thinking you're that way all the time and never once consider that you could only be that way with them because of something they did with you that freed you up."

"Right," Brenda jumped in. "Don't get me started with the double standard of how women are viewed by men."

"That's a whole different talk show," Madeline said. "But anyway, I had to make sure that he knew I wasn't easy. So, I was having a hard time sleeping and took some sleeping pills one night right before he came over to my place. My mother was sick, I was thinking about graduate school; there was a lot on my mind and when it was time for bed, I would lie there on my back, looking at the ceiling.

"Well, I also had been sick—stomach problems—and when I was growing up there was no such thing as hot mint ginger tea. My mom gave us a laxative. So that's what I took to feel better."

"Uh-oh," Brenda said. "I see where this is going."

No one else did. "So, he's over my apartment," Madeline went on. "We're talking and having a good time and it's about two or three in the morning and we're both asleep on the couch. When I woke up, I couldn't ask him to go home.

"So I tell him to come on, 'Let's go to bed.' He perks right up and I guess thinks we're gonna do something. Anyway, I change into a gown and he's in bed in his boxers. And we're hugging and kissing and I'm so tired that as soon as we stop, I fall asleep. The sleeping pills took over.

"I guess after a while your dad fell asleep, too. Around six in the morning, I wake up. The pills were so strong that I'm a little bit disoriented. I see him resting there peacefully. The sun is peeping through the blinds. Just a perfect little morning.

"Then I start to smell something. I start sniffing him, seeing if it's coming from him. I sit up in the bed and I'm looking around the room, and the scent is getting stronger and stronger. Now it's plain old stinky. So I move the sheets back and the funk bursts into my face. Again, I thought he had passed gas. But the reality was crazy."

Madeline leaned in even closer so that she could lower her voice and they could still hear her. "It turned out that it wasn't him," she said. "I looked between my legs and there was a small pile of shit in the bed, all runny and wet. I had shit on myself in my sleep."

The group burst into laughter so loud that almost everyone on the patio turned to see what was happening. Paul got up from his seat and leaned over the white picket fence, laughing uncontrollably.

It took them a few minutes to get themselves together.

"Mother," Ginger said when it calmed down. "Are you serious?"

"The moral of this story?" Madeline asked. "Don't take a sleeping pill and a laxative at the same time."

And the laughter started again. It took them a few minutes to calm down.

"I tell you what," Brenda said. "If he married you anyway, he really loved you."

"Wait," Paul said, "how did you explain to him what happened?"

"Oh, well, that was funny, too," Madeline said. "So, I was, as you might guess, panicked when I realized what happened. So I tried to cover up the pile with the sheets to mute the funk and then ease out of the bed without waking him. But all the movement woke him up. So, I tried to hurry to the bathroom, but it was on his side of the bed, so I had to walk right past him.

"Remember that nightgown I said I put on? Well, it was white and the back of it looked like I sat in a giant pile of dark chocolate. It was crazy. I tried to hide it but there was too much mess."

Laughing, Ginger asked, "What did Daddy say?"

He said, "You OK?"

"I hope you said, 'No,'" Brenda said.

"I did. I told him to not move; I didn't want him to—God forbid—roll over onto that mess or pull the cover off of it. So, he just lay there. I cleaned myself up and told him to get out of the bed as I pulled the sheets off.

"He never said a word. He just looked at me. And I never said anything about it. It was so stinky and nasty. But that's the kind of man he was: He didn't want me to be any more embarrassed than I already was."

"No offense, but he still married you?" Paul said. "Now that's love."

"So if that were me, you wouldn't have asked me to marry you?" Ginger said.

"Gin, you can do-do right here and I'd clean it up and keep it moving," Paul said. Everyone laughed, and the tension of the parents' double date the next day was gone.

"I have never told anyone that story; I actually tried to forget it," Madeline said.

"When you really think of it, it's romantic," Ginger said. "You showed yourself at a vulnerable position and Daddy still wanted you. It didn't matter to him. He did not care. He loved you."

Paul poured everyone more wine. "See, this is what I'm talking about," he said. "A beautiful day, good food, good wine, lots of laughs and family."

"How you feeling, Mother?" Ginger said. "Your stomach."

"I feel like I'm back to normal," Madeline said. "Bring on the wine tasting."

"I feel a little sluggish, but I'm ready to go, too," Brenda said.

"Speaking of going, it's your time to go," Paul said. "What's your embarrassing story?"

"I haven't had enough wine yet to tell it," she said. "Let's keep drinking and go to a tasting and then let me tell my story."

No one argued with Brenda. They had laughed so hard at Madeline that they needed a break anyway. So they enjoyed the mid-sixties November temperatures and absorbed being in Napa Valley.

"I said it already, but I could live out here," Paul said. "There's a feel of peace and calm out here that I never had before."

"Yes, but I'm sure it's the idea that there is wine all around you that makes it even more appealing," his mother said. "Look out there. Vineyards everywhere."

Ginger wanted to talk about something else. "I probably didn't handle it well on the bridge, but can I ask you something, Mother—and you, too, Miss Wall?" she asked.

The ladies nodded their heads.

"It hasn't even been a year ago since Daddy died and I haven't gotten over it," she began. "I still dream about him being here and I wake up so devastated and even angry when I realize that it was a dream. I can admit—I was a daddy's girl and I haven't moved on. I want my father here. So, how do you do it? How do you move on?"

Madeline took the defensive at first. She didn't want her daughter to think she loved her father any more than she loved him as her husband. But she surprised herself by her ability to eschew her personal feelings and, instead, seek to give Ginger some clarity.

Madeline sipped her wine and motioned for Paul to pour her more. He did and she took a sip of it and reached across the table and held her daughter's hand.

"I guess we're one big happy family here, so I can share this right here, right now," Madeline started. "I miss your father more than anyone could possibly know. You don't love him or miss him any more than me, I can promise you that. I can hardly remember my life before him. His love is infused in my body, in my heart. No one could ever replace who he was to me, who he remains to me, even in death. I learned how to love through your father. Everything good in me came from my parents and your dad.

"I am so glad to hear how much you love and miss him. It's

only right because you were the crown jewel of his life. He loved me, sure. He coveted you, Ginger. You know what he said one time? He said, 'Maddy, I can die a proud man knowing I helped bring my daughter into the world.' That's how much you meant to him—everything.

"So I guess you thinking I must be crazy to not still be totally devastated by his death. But you're wrong, honey. Do you have any idea how upside down my life has been since he died? Do you have any inkling what it is like to have one of your arms cut off? That's what it is like for me.

"So, my answer is, I don't know how to tell you to move on. I'm living my life, but I haven't moved on. This man lives in me every day and always will. I knew him better than anyone on the planet. He shared so much with me, and me with him. And because I know him, I know he hardly wants me sitting around playing the victim and not living my life. That's the man he was.

"I never dishonored my husband in life and I damn sure won't in death. And he would want me to live my life. I have to, Ginger. If I don't, what happens to me? I don't have my husband anymore and you can rest assured I'm not OK about that. I have the same dreams you have about him being here, only to wake up in tears. We got sick last night and while I was in bed, I thought about how he would have reacted to me throwing up in the hallway of a hotel. And you know what? He would have made sure I was all right, cleaned up the mess and once I started feeling better, laughed his ass off at me. He would have made me laugh at myself.

"Think about it: He never ran stuff into the ground. He was always about moving on to the next thing. He was positive, Ginger. And so I'm not going to be the widow so devastated that she sits in the house with the shades drawn. And you know why? That's not what my husband would want me to do. And so I am honoring him by living my life. And that's what you have to tell yourself and believe it. Your father wants you to live your life."

With that, Madeline wiped the tears that streamed down her face. Ginger did, too. And so did Brenda. Paul practically popped an eye muscle he worked so hard to prevent crying.

In a very real way, one he never articulated, this was the kind of thing Paul wanted to happen on their trip. The more he thought of their parents going with him and Ginger, the more he thought it was an ideal way to bring the families together for more than holidays, graduations or funerals.

There was a divide between the families stemming from unfounded perspectives. Brenda perceived Madeline's self-assuredness as arrogance and snobbishness and Madeline interpreted Brenda's unfiltered tongue to a lack of sophistication. Their discord was as transparent as glass, and so the families hardly spent time truly getting to know each other because Brenda and Madeline spread misleading rumors and sometimes all-out lies about their child spouse's family.

It was pathetic, yes, but it was their way. Paul saw this cross-country venture as an opportunity to end the madness, to bring together the families and form a bond. It was a truly noble idea, especially with women in their sixties who were stuck in their ways, however warped.

But it was working. Something about being away from home opened them up, batted down their guards and they allowed the other to see her for who she really was. Madeline's explanation to Ginger silenced the table, except for the tears.

Paul looked at his mother and he knew she had a new respect, a new appreciation for Madeline.

"Let's have a toast to your husband," Paul said, as the women wiped away tears.

Ginger rose from the table and came over to the other side and hugged her mother. "I'm sorry, Mother. I'm sorry," she said softly.

Madeline, crying again, nodded her head. Brenda reached across the table and handed her a napkin. Paul and Ginger's eyes met, and she resumed crying.

It was a heart-tugging moment, a moment that was awkward on the patio of a crowded restaurant. Most people went about their business. A few people noticed the outpouring of emotion.

"OK," Paul said. "Let's have this toast before people start thinking we're weird or something."

Ginger let her mom go and went back to her seat. But Brenda came over and hugged her. "It's OK to love your daddy and to be emotional about him," Brenda said into her ear. "Trust me, he feels good about it."

"Here we go," Paul said, raising his glass. He was not being disrespectful; he was trying to move beyond it because Madeline got more and more emotional. He recalled attending his grandmother's funeral and the pastor inciting emotions instead of offering comfort. His posturing seemed contrived. Brenda and Ginger were sincere.

"To Richard Price," Paul said, "a man who remains loved by many and never forgotten."

They tapped glasses and took a sip of the wine. To loosen things, Paul offered an evaluation.

"Next time, I want you to taste it with all your senses," he said. "I want you to put your nose in there good and smell it. Then I want you to twirl it around in your glass to let it oxidize or breathe. Red wine needs to breathe so all its flavors and aromas can come out. Then I want you to lean your glass over and let the wine reach the rim of the glass and then turn it back upright and watch the 'legs,' which is how the residue of the wine goes back to the bottom of the glass. If it's really fast, then the wine is pretty young. But if it flows back slowly, then it's older.

"Then, before you sip it, smell it again—you will notice a difference. It'll be more flagrant. That's what twirling it around does—it brings out the aromas... Now sip it."

The ladies followed his instructions.

"Wow, it does taste better," Madeline said. "It's like all that stuff woke it up."

"That's actually a good way to put it," Paul said.

"It tastes sort of peppery but fruity," Ginger said.

"I can taste the spiciness, too," Brenda said. "Very interesting. I've never paid this much attention to tasting wine before. I sucked it down. If it wasn't bitter, it was OK with me."

"I don't know how or why I was never that way," Paul said. "I, somehow, always appreciated wine."

"I can see a few days with you and Ginger and I'm gonna be a wine snob," Brenda said.

"Well, that's not a bad thing," Paul offered.

They laughed and conversed about the wine, the weather, life and family. Paul excused himself and went to the bathroom. When he returned, he stopped about twenty feet from the table and admired the women—*his* women—laughing and getting along over a glass of wine. And he felt at peace.

CHAPTER 12
THE FAMILY BUSINESS

Peace can be fleeting, especially among a group of strong-minded people who have strong opinions and are strong debaters whose senses have been heightened by an overconsumption of wine.

And so it was with Paul, Brenda, Madeline and Ginger. They took their lunch love fest to Beringer Winery, where they were impressed with the mere mass of the facility and the quality of the wines. Paul had looked down on Beringer because it was a "common folk" wine, available in grocery stores.

He was delighted to learn it had excellent, high-quality wines far out of grocery store price points. They sipped on the 2009 Modern Heritage Chardonnay Carneros, the 2010 Modern Heritage Riesling and 2010 Modern Heritage 3 Acre Red Knights Valley.

They then went on to three more wines from the Beringer Private Reserve Cabernet Sauvignons 1996, 2003 and 2006. After tasting a half-dozen wines, the ladies were good and tipsy. Paul felt the effects, too, but he was more himself than the others.

"How we going to another tasting?" Brenda said. "I don't think I can drink anything else right now."

"As much as I'd like to have some more, maybe we should sit down for a while," Madeline said. "After last night, I definitely don't want to push it."

Paul was a little disappointed; he was ready to move on to the next spot, St. Supery Winery. He had a glass of its 2009 Chardonnay at The Lamb's Club during a bus trip to New York the previous summer and loved it so much he tracked it down on winenthusiast. com and located it at Savi market in Atlanta.

He told the ladies they could remain in the tasting room as he went to the Beringer store to order a case to have shipped home. Ginger said, "I want to go." She approached Paul, who whispered to her: "They're buzzing right now. We might not want to leave them alone."

Ginger agreed and went back to sit with the parents. Paul made his way and ordered a case of a combination of the Beringer Reserve wines that totaled more than twelve hundred dollars. That's why he did not want Ginger with him in the wine store— she would have serious questions and demanded answers about him ordering wine that expensive.

He shopped around the expansive store, looking at wine accessories and finally decided he would rejoin the ladies and take them into downtown Napa to shop and see the landscape. But as he approached, he saw expressions on their faces that were not pleasant.

Paul picked up his pace. "How's it going?" he said in a cheerful way when he arrived at the table. But no one else was cheery. "What's going on?"

"We're fine," Ginger said, but they weren't.

"What's going on?" Paul asked again.

"Helena," Ginger said.

"What? What about her?" Paul asked with concern in his voice.

"Your daughter is fine," Brenda said. "But we were arguing— no, discussing—whether you should tell her that she is adopted."

Paul sat down. That was a major point of contention between

him and Ginger. He did not want to tell her. Ginger did. Their child was eighteen and totally unaware that her parents were not her biological parents.

"How did you all get on this subject?" Paul said.

"She texted me a photo of her and her friend and I showed them the photo," Ginger said.

"Yeah, she texted me the same photo," Paul said. "And…"

"And I said it's remarkable that she looks like Ginger even though she's not her mother," Brenda said.

"Ma, what do you mean?" Paul said, his nose flaring open.

"That's what I'm talking about," Ginger said.

"I didn't mean it that way," Brenda said.

"Ginger is the only mother Helena will ever know, so for you to say that is so insulting," Madeline said.

Their happy family had deteriorated in the time it took Paul to purchase a case of wine.

"Ginger, I am sorry; I really didn't mean it that way," Brenda said. "You're that child's mother and you've been a great mother, too. That's why she's such a fine young lady, because of you and Paul. I'm sorry. I was not trying to disrespect you. Why would I?"

"Well, thank you for saying that, Miss Wall. I am very sensitive around this subject. That girl feels like she came out of my stomach," Ginger said.

"And that's why we don't have to tell her about her biological parents," Paul said. "She's as much a part of you as if she came out of you."

"But that's not right," Madeline said. "She should know where she comes from. She should understand her history."

"That's right, Mother," Ginger contributed.

"But even if that history is not going to make her feel good?" Brenda said.

"It's not a pretty history," Paul said, "and I don't want my baby thinking anything less of herself because of the sperm donors' horrible lives."

The divide and animosity was palpable: mother and son felt one way; daughter and mother felt another. And as sweet and wonderful as it felt at the restaurant, it was that sour and antagonistic at the winery.

They sat at the table in the tasting room, which had all but emptied, and had a knockdown drag-out. Paul and Brenda's position was based on the knowledge that the natural parents of Helena were criminals who would not see freedom for another five years. The mother, in fact, gave birth with one arm handcuffed to a hospital bed.

A week from delivering a child, she and her co-criminal boyfriend robbed a gas station convenience store and were caught after an extended high-speed chase. They shot the worker, although he gave up the money without hesitation. The pregnant mother was the driver of the getaway car police followed for miles through Atlanta traffic before finally being cornered, ironically enough, on Freedom Parkway.

There was a shootout for several minutes or until they ran out of bullets. It was then that they surrendered. Had the television cameras not been present, they likely would have gotten shot, despite giving up.

Two days later, Helena was born—in the Atlanta Federal Penitentiary hospital. The mother got a day to recover and was back in her cell where she faced multiple counts of armed robbery, attempted murder of a police officer (because of a shootout with authorities) and possession of an unregistered gun and stolen goods, among other charges.

The father was in prison on the same charges when the baby

was born. They were a criminal team that worked in tandem wreaking havoc for years, robbing people, assaulting people and generally being a menace to society.

They both expressed no interest in even seeing the baby. And because their families' lives were just as troubled, there was no one to turn the baby over to if they wanted; no one who could do the child good, that is. Even in their psychosis of committing crimes, they understood the best option for the child was to put her up for adoption.

"Take it out of me and give it a chance to do some good," the woman said before going into labor. "I don't deserve nobody to call me 'Momma.' What can I do for a baby? If I wasn't going to jail, what can I teach a child? How to be a criminal? That's what happened to me. I might have messed up my life, but I ain't trying to create another me. I know enough to recognize that's wrong."

"And you want me to tell my daughter that's where she comes from?" Paul said. "That's not fair to her. It would be one thing if they said, 'Let me at least see the baby. Let me hold her.' They said the opposite. So if they don't want to know the baby at all, why should we put her in that crazy world that they come from? It could make her look at herself in some kind of crazy way. I think she's fragile enough to be affected by it."

Ginger saw it differently. "That's so wrong, Paul," she said. "We all should know where we come from. And although we raised her from her first days on this earth, she has natural parents that she should know about. And knowing about them shouldn't break her or make her look at herself in some strange way; we raised her to be strong and independent.

"It would be very selfish to prevent her from knowing this truth, Paul. That's not how it should be."

"And," Madeline contributed, "I was a nurse for thirty years.

The fact that you all do not know her family's health history is not good. So many health issues and conditions are handed down through bloodlines. Heart disease. Diabetes. You just don't know. And even mental health issues. If her parents were both doing criminal things, there could be a gene that triggers such behavior. All this is very important."

"Haven't you all been on top of her visiting the doctor and taking all sorts of tests?" Brenda asked. "You've done your part. You think you're going to get the information you need from that family about family history? It's as dysfunctional as it gets. I don't have to tell you this. You did the research. You knew from the beginning that they would be in prison and they wouldn't be the kind of people you'd want Helena associated with. So why now, when she's in college and her life is great? All it's going to do is upset her. No good will come out of it."

They had asked for a bottle of Cab while Paul was in the bathroom, and it arrived just before Ginger was to add to her argument. The server wanted to pour the wine, but Paul told her, "I got it. Thanks," so she went on and they went on.

"Nothing bad will come out of it, either," Ginger said. "I…"

She went silent. "I don't feel so good; a little queasy," she said.

"No more wine for you for a while," Paul said, handing her a glass of water.

"You OK, Ginger?" her mom asked.

After a few sips of water, she sat back in her seat.

"This argument is making me sick," she said. "Paul, Miss Wall, what if Helena finds out about her parents from some other source? What if they are rehabilitated while in prison and in a few years—they are eligible to be released in five years—and they decide they want to at least meet the child they created? And they find us and approach Helena. You've seen the movies and how that turns out; it's ugly.

"I have never seen or even heard of a case where a kid is not upset when he finds out that his parents did not tell him about his birth parents. There is a natural interest to know where you come from, whether it's good or bad."

"I don't know about that," Paul said. "I wouldn't want to know that my parents were criminals. That wouldn't make me feel good."

"But would it make you feel good," Madeline interjected, "to learn that your parents who raised you made a decision to be dishonest with you about something really important?"

"Well, who says she has to know?" Brenda jumped in. "Who's going to tell her?"

"Brenda, that's not the right approach," Madeline said. "We can't have something like this hanging over her, over the families."

"It's been like this for eighteen years and I don't feel bothered by it," Paul said. "And Helena is living her life, having a great time. It's not hanging over her, either."

Paul sipped his wine and it began to settle in. He felt a little lightheaded, which intensified his emotions.

Ginger stared at her husband from across the table. It was not an angry or a comforting look. It was as if she could see what was in his heart.

"You're scared," she said to Paul, who swirled his wine as if he did not hear Ginger. "Look at me, Paul. You're scared."

"Scared?" Paul said, looking confused. "Scared of what?"

"Scared that your baby will look at you differently," Ginger said.

Paul just looked at her.

"Paul, honey, don't you know nothing could change who you are to her?" Ginger said. "You are the apple of her eye, and vice-versa. She's a daddy's girl. You're a girl's daddy. No one comes before you."

Paul's eyes began to water. Alcohol increased his emotions.

"You took her to her doctor's appointments when she was a baby," Ginger went on. "You taught her how to ride a bike and how to drive a car and everything in between: basketball, golf and cards and even how to get what she wanted out of me.

"When I dropped her off at college, we both cried in the room. I said, 'Why are you crying?' She said, "Cause I miss Daddy already.' You and I have had our issues, yes. But that is your daughter. She loves you more than anyone in the world. You've got to know that."

Tears rolled down Paul's face, and he did not even bother to wipe them.

Brenda put her arm around her son. "Is that it, Vino?" she said in a comforting voice. "Is that what you think? Oh, no, son. You can't lose that girl. You're everything to her."

She treated him as if he were a three-year-old, wiping his face clear of tears. He just shook his head.

"It's OK," Brenda said.

"I just... We just put so much of ourselves into her," Paul said. "I don't want anything to take away from that."

"But nothing can, Paul," Brenda said. "Because we've put so much into her we must be honest with her on this. Remember when she was a tiny baby and we sat in the living room, on the couch, and you held her in your arms and you looked at me and said, 'She deserves us and we deserve this little angel.'"

"I do remember that," Paul said. "I'm shocked you remember it. That was eighteen years ago."

"I remember it because it was important," Ginger said. "You said she deserves us because you knew we would never let her down and teach her and mold her and protect her and be there for her. She deserved that. Well, she also deserves to know about her parents. To not tell her would not be protecting her. It would be letting her down."

And those were the words that turned Paul—and his mother. The idea of letting down Helena did not compute with him. It was not an option. He lavished her with love and attention—and all the latest technological gadgets, too—but mostly with love. The fact that he considered breaking up his family spoke to how jumbled his mind and self-esteem were at the time.

"You're right," Paul said. "It would be letting her down—and not believing in the bond we have—to keep it from her. So, how do we tell her something so delicate? When do we do it?"

"Should have already been done," Madeline said. "I thought four years ago, when she went to high school was the time. But…"

"Well, we can't go back in time," Brenda said.

"She's coming home for Christmas," Paul said. "That gives us about a month to figure out how to tell her."

"Drink plenty of wine," Brenda said. "It will help the truth come out."

They laughed, finally, and lifted their glasses.

"To Helena," Paul said. "My daughter. *Our* daughter." And they tapped glasses and drank of the wine.

CHAPTER 13
AND THE PLOTS THICKEN

Because Madeline and Brenda were afraid to drink more, considering how the previous night ended, and with Ginger complaining of a queasy stomach and lightheadedness, the group decided to go back to the hotel after the discussion.

"How about I order some appetizers and we sit by the pool and relax?" Paul suggested. "There is still some sunlight left in the day."

Ginger pulled Paul aside. "So you just insist on spending all your money?" she said.

"No, that's not it," Paul answered. "I want to maximize this trip, this place. It's beautiful out here."

"Don't you think maybe we should talk some more about Helena?"

"OK," Paul said. "I thought we were done. Can we do it out here? It's a nice day to sit outside and talk."

"Fine," Ginger said.

Madeline and Brenda told their children they would connect with them for dinner. "This was a really nice day, Paul," Madeline said. "I enjoyed all of it."

"Me, too," Brenda interjected. "Looking forward to a nice dinner—after I get a nap. Between last night and the wine tasting, I need to rejuvenate."

And off they went. Paul grabbed Ginger's hand and led her to the pool area, where he ordered a glass of Viognier. Ginger passed.

"The truth of the matter is I have something that needs to be said," she started. "I don't know if it's the wine or if it's my conscience. It's probably more the wine because I haven't felt the need to say this when I'm totally sober."

She looked around to see if anyone was near; they were the only guests by the rectangular-shaped pool. The sun was brilliant, so much so that Ginger dug through her purse to pull out a pair of sunglasses. She had Paul's in there, too, and handed him his.

"What's wrong, Gin?" Paul wanted to know. "It's OK. I agree with you and your mother. Let's tell Heather about her natural parents. I'm OK with it."

"I'm glad you are," she said. "But that's not it. Well, that's not totally it. Talking about it today, telling you that she deserved to know it and that we owed her the truth, made me realized I owe you the truth, too."

Paul's thoughts were all over the place. Was she speaking of his firing because of the sexual harassment complaint? Had that woman contacted her? He met a woman at Whole Foods one day, got her phone number but never called when the woman indicated she worked at the same building as Ginger. Could she have said something to his wife? Did she know about him winning the lottery? *How could she*, he thought. He only told Big Al, and he knew Big Al was as trustworthy as could be.

He pondered all those possibilities as quickly as he could to come up with an answer that might minimize the presumed trouble he was in. But Ginger wanted to speak of something else.

"I must preface this by saying that there was a period several months ago where we were over in my mind," she began. "And if the wine didn't have me buzzing, I probably wouldn't even say anything now. Anyway, you told me you wanted a divorce and that you didn't want me anymore. And—"

"I've apologized about this time and time again," Paul said. "And I will continue to apologize about it. I wasn't in my right mind. You've known me for more than twenty years. That was like someone other than me was speaking. I was in a bad place. But that's part of why we're here, to get beyond that."

"I know," Ginger said. "But this is something else. Please, let me get it out. I think it's the reason why I was so upset that day I told you I was all panicked in the garage. It was more than having to live with you without Helena there as a buffer. It was living with myself, what I did, that was also bothering me."

Paul's mind immediately switched to infidelity. What else could it be that she would have trouble living with herself? And in an instant he was mad, furious, embarrassed, humiliated, jealous. It is with that speed a man can get to all those emotions when he believes his woman has betrayed him.

"What did you do, Ginger?" he said. He needed to hear the words. Not that they would be soothing. "What did you do?"

The server arrived with his glass of wine and Paul did not bother to even acknowledge her. "Ginger," he repeated, "what did you do?"

She looked into his eyes, eyes that were far from comforting. "Paul, after you told me you wanted a divorce, I was lost and hurt and didn't know what to do with my life," she began. "In that moment, I realized that my life was hinged on our marriage. I sunk everything into you and Helena and now it was falling apart. I didn't know what to do."

Paul sat with his arms folded, waiting for the real news.

"The day before you told me you wanted a divorce, I learned I was pregnant," Ginger added. Paul unfolded his arms and sat up in his chair.

"What?" he said, amazement all over his face. "I thought, I mean…the doctors said…you know…"

"I know; they said I couldn't get pregnant," Ginger stepped in. "We tried for years but nothing happened. Well, that one time when we basically just needed to be physical with each other—we were in the middle of all our drama—produced a pregnancy."

Paul was relieved, shocked and delighted.

"Are you telling me we have a baby coming?" he said, smiling while looking down at her stomach.

His response made the news Ginger had to share even more devastating.

"No, Paul, we don't," she answered softly.

"But you said you were…" His voice drifted off as the realization of what happened hit him.

"I had an abortion, Paul," she managed to get out.

Paul literally shook his head, as if the words would be jumbled and came out to mean something else. But there was no mistaking what she said.

"You had an abortion? What are you talking about?" Paul said, sounding confused.

"You told me you wanted a divorce," Ginger said. "You said you didn't want me anymore. What was I to do? Bring a child into a world where we were going to split up? It seemed crazy to me at the time. I don't hate anyone, but I truly detested you. You were mean and cold and totally dismissive of me, as if I was some rag doll."

"Still, Ginger, you don't get rid of a baby without talking to your husband," Paul said. He noticed his voice rose and looked around to see if anyone was there to hear. There was not.

"We weren't talking at all, Paul," she said, tears forming in her eyes. "What was I supposed to do? You didn't want me. That's what you told me. How could I think you'd want a baby?"

Paul shook his head. He never expressed to Ginger how much he always wanted a child born of his genes. Instead, at the time, he comforted Ginger when the doctors told her she could not conceive. He loved Helena as if she were of his body. But if they could have had a child between them, it would have meant everything to him.

"An abortion?" Paul said. "I know we weren't talking. I know what I said. But, still. That's a pretty big deal, Ginger. You... Didn't you know how much I wanted a child with you?"

"No," she said. "The next day after the pregnancy test came back positive—you didn't even notice that I was sick and sluggish—you came home and told me you didn't want me anymore. That's what I remember. And I knew then what I had to do.

"It was the hardest decision of my life. I wanted a baby so badly, too. But I wanted a family more. And if I couldn't have a family with you, it didn't make sense to have a baby...I was devastated when I couldn't have a child and I was shocked when I was pregnant. It told me the doctors do not have power over God. I was so happy.

"Why do you think I cooked that nice meal that night? We hadn't been talking or anything. But I had a nice meal and sat there with you at the table. That was the night I was going to tell you, hoping that the news would bring you around, make you see we had something to bring us back together. And before I can say anything, you tell me you want a divorce. I was livid and hurt and, to be honest, devastated. But mostly, I was confused. There was nothing to say after you so coldly told me what you wanted."

"Oh, my God," Paul said. "You might not understand it, but that was an unselfish act I was trying to make that night. I was basically saying you deserve better than me. I wasn't being the man I needed to be for you. I was at a low point and I didn't see any way to come out of it. The way I lost my job, which you didn't even know about. The terrible job market. Doing the odd jobs to keep food on the table. I felt like I was dissolving into nothing. You deserved more."

His voice drifted off. Ginger wiped her face and reached over to hold Paul's hand. He pulled it away.

"But you took the one thing away from me that could have changed my life," he said, the anger in his voice distinctive. "You knew how much a child would have meant to me. We talked about it for years. Helena brought us the best joy we could have received. But she also was a blessing because we loved her so much we stopped talking about not being able to have a child. And now, you somehow get pregnant—a miracle—and you kill the baby? How could you do that?"

"Paul, that's a very mean thing to say, way to put it," she said. "I didn't know what to do. I was confused. I—".

"That's when you talk to your husband, dammit," Paul said. "You don't go off and get rid of a baby without talking to your husband. I don't care what I said to you that night. What you did was bigger than what I said."

Ginger's emotions ran high, but she remained poised. "You've got to know that was not an easy decision for me," she said. "But I had to do what I thought was right. I have beaten myself up about it every day since then. But I'm not going to let you beat me up, too. If you had been more of a man and faced your challenges instead of giving in to them, we wouldn't even be here. That's the hard truth and I'm sorry I am saying it to you like this. But it's the truth. So, you can blame me all you want—and I understand why you would—but you know the truth."

"Oh, so it's my fault that you went out and did what you did?" Paul said.

"It's my body and my life," Ginger said, getting angry. "I'm not going to let you make me feel more upset about it than I have already been. But until the last several weeks, I didn't feel that badly. I felt like I did the right thing. You weren't fit to be a father to a baby. You were acting like a baby yourself."

"Kiss my ass, Ginger," Paul said, rising from the table. He turned to walk away, but turned back to pick up his glass of wine off the table and stormed off, leaving his wife there with her thoughts.

She was so angry she could not even cry. He made her question her decision, but she believed she did the right thing at the time. Still, his words could not be ignored. Maybe her decision was hasty. Maybe she should have thought about how the news of her pregnancy would positively influence Paul. Maybe she should have taken her friend Serena's advice, which was to consult with Paul. But she did not want him to want the marriage for a baby; she wanted him to want *her*. But her struggle with the decision from that moment on was an indicator of knowing she was not happy with her decision.

Ginger decided she would find Paul and let him know how she felt. But when she got to the room, he was not there. She called him on his cell phone, but it rang in their room; he left it there. She was frustrated, and went to the parking lot to see if the rental car was still there. It wasn't.

Paul had taken his drink and his anger and his pain to the car. He started driving with no destination in mind. He needed to get away, to clear his head, to figure out his feelings. The disappointment in Ginger did not diminish his feelings for her. But it did upset him in a way he could not articulate or even identify. His mind took him to several dark places—Ginger going under the knife to have the abortion; what the child would have looked like; and even his role in her decision. Paul was a mental wreck.

He ended up on in the northern block of Napa's downtown district at 1313 Main, a swanky wine bar that had a warm and inviting feel. That was exactly what he needed.

Paul was lucky to get a small corner table on the lovely patio that was fenced in by lush greenery. After nearly fifteen minutes of contemplation, he ordered a bottle of Caymus 2008 Cabernet Sauvignon. It cost $163. He did not care. He wanted to lose himself in the wine.

He did not bother to ask his server about the wine. He wanted to test his senses. He looked around at the mass of people smiling and enjoying each other and it saddened him. He learned something about his wife that he thought it was best he did not know: That she had the capacity to deceive him.

Never mind that he kept the truth from her about why he lost his job. That did not come into his mind. He could only see what was in front of him, and that was that he had a chance to father a child and Ginger took it from him.

When the wine came, he had to shake himself of his thoughts. The Caymus was a lush wine, rich in color and flavor. He inhaled it deeply to let the aroma rise through his nostrils. He closed his eyes to appreciate it.

He then set it on the table and placed the stem of the glass between his index and third fingers and began slowly swirling it around, to help the wine breathe and to release all of its flavors. After a minute or so of that action, he smelled it again, and this time the aromas seemed to burst into the air, causing a small smile to crease his face.

He was having the best time—and he hadn't even tasted the wine yet.

He swirled it some more and finally, deliberately moved the glass toward his mouth. It was a delicate and careful maneuver, as if he were placing one of Ginger's breasts in his mouth. When he finally creased his lips to place the rim of the glass between them, he took in another deep smell of the wine, and he was almost mesmerized by it.

The wine funneled into his mouth and he let it wade there so his tongue could consume it all. He detected a complex mix of dark fruit, blackberry and plum with a hint of licorice and spices. It was a full-bodied wine, one that had a strong finish but no aftertaste.

Paul was in love.

It was the best wine he had ever consumed, and he treated it as such, pampering it and seducing it as he ingested it. It was so good and fulfilling that for a time, he did not even think about Ginger and the mess he considered his life to be.

By the fourth glass, he was officially on buzz—and the reality of his life came back to him. He wished Ginger had kept that secret to herself. Knowing it confused him. Part of him despised that she made such a major decision without his input; another part of him admired her honesty. Those conflicting emotions and the wine clashed to make his head spin.

One moment he thought of calling her to talk it out, but it was then that he realized he left his cell phone in the room. The next moment he actually pondered getting a hotel room and staying away for the night as a way of clearing his head. The truth was that it would be a way of punishing her, and, as mad and disappointed as he was, he couldn't bring himself to torture his wife.

As he finished the last glass, he wondered what Ginger was doing, how she was feeling about him not being accessible. He was always in reach of her. To be as disconnected as he was at this time with the issue hanging over them had to be driving her crazy, he thought. And he did gain a little pleasure out of that, but not so much that he would allow it to linger much longer.

He enjoyed the last sip, paid for the bottle with his debit card and headed to the car to go back to the hotel and face the issue that was impossible to ignore and likely would take quite a while to overcome. Before leaving, his server asked if he would like a glass of water; he could sense Paul's equilibrium was off.

"I can't put water on top of a wine like that," Paul said. "Thank you, though."

And he made his way to the rental car and started back to the hotel, well enough, considering his thoughts were all over the place and that he was drunk. He did not know if he could ever forgive Ginger for aborting his child, and that scared him because he loved her. He was anxious to talk it out with her to see if he could arrive at a different emotion.

However, when he reached the second light on Main Street, he stopped in the middle of the intersection. He was not sure why. He thought the light turned red and that he actually stopped at the proper place. He also thought he heard sirens, so he stopped in adherence of the emergency vehicle.

But he was certain there were police lights behind his car a few seconds after he stopped. He looked into his rearview mirror and said, "Damn."

"Pull your vehicle out of the intersection," the officer said through his loudspeaker.

Paul did as instructed, but he knew a bottle of wine—not to mention what he consumed at the hotel—probably took him over the legal limit for alcohol consumption while driving. He did not want a DUI. Worse, he did not want to go to jail.

So, before the officer reached the car, Paul closed his eyes to gather his balance. "You can do this," he said.

The officer approached and tapped on the driver's side window.

"Sir, are you all right?" the officer said, looking as much into the car as he was at Paul.

It was dark out now, around eight o'clock and the cop shined his flashlight into Paul's face.

"I'll be doing better if you didn't have that light in my face," he said.

"Why did you stop in the center of the intersection?" the officer said, the light still in Paul's face.

"I got confused, officer," Paul said. He got the words out, but did not enunciate as clearly as normal. "I'm visiting here for a few days and I was looking around at the town and looked up and it seemed like the light turned red and I lost where I was. I thought for that second I was behind the crosswalk."

"I see," he said. "Can I see your rental car contract and license?"

Paul looked in the car's glove compartment, but the contract was not there. He feared Ginger took it with her, as she was holding it some of the ride to Napa from the airport. Then he checked the center console, found it and handed it over to the officer.

"Sir, have you been drinking?" the police officer asked.

"Yes, I just left the wine lounge, 1313, a few blocks away," Paul said. He figured lying was not going to work, so he surmised that giving him something would be the better strategy. "I had the best glass of wine in my life. A 2008 Caymer: amazing wine, especially considering it was so young."

"Where are you staying?" the policeman said.

"Not too far away, at the Marriott," Paul said.

"Can you turn off the engine and step out of the car?" he told Paul.

"Is this really necessary? I got confused about the light and where the crosswalk was," Paul said.

"Yes, it's necessary," the officer said, his tone much more

aggressive. "The fact that you couldn't determine where to stop is a problem. You admitted you were drinking and you smell like more than one glass of expensive wine. And your eyes are glassy."

"I'm just sleepy," Paul said as he exited the car. "I've traveled all the way from Atlanta. Still trying to adjust my body to the three-hour time change. If I were at home, it'd be going on eleven-thirty and I would already be in bed."

The officer was not having it. He directed Paul to the side of the street away from traffic. People walking around and driving by in the quaint town could not help but notice Paul going through a field sobriety test.

He was not happy. He was embarrassed. And he felt the pressure of proving that he was not inebriated. But he didn't. He couldn't. Too much drinking impaired his center, so he could hardly walk a straight line in the awkward fashion cops demand: one foot literally in front—heel-to-toe—then turn around and do it again. Stand on one leg with arms stretched out, extend right hand away from body but touch the tip of the nose. Then do it with the left hand.

"This test is not a fair test," Paul told the policeman. "How can you test me on something I have never done before?"

"Sir, that is the law and nothing I can do about it," he answered. "Furthermore, turn around please and place your hands behind your back."

The officer placed the handcuffs on Paul and walked him to the police car when he did what people see on television all the time when someone gets arrested: He put his hand over Paul's head and held it down as he folded into the back seat. He even said, "Watch your head."

Paul sat in the scrunched-up seat totally uncomfortable and completely humiliated. His high was gone. He was going to jail, and that fact ripped away all the feel-good of the wine he experienced a few minutes before.

Worse, he started to feel nauseous and lightheaded. It was warm in the car and he began to sweat. The officer stood outside the car speaking on a wireless device about having the rental car towed. Paul began breathing out of his mouth to get more air, trying to prevent a panic attack. For someone who had a fear of flying, being confined in cuffs in a cramped space was tantamount to torture.

He felt caged, trapped…like a prisoner. The officer finally came back to the car.

"I don't feel good; it's hot," Paul said. "Can I get some air, please?"

The cop turned around and looked at Paul and saw the distress on his face, the sweat on his brow. He nodded his head and blasted the air.

"We have to wait here another ten minutes or so for the tow service to get here," he said. "Meanwhile, I'm going to do some paperwork to make this whole process quicker."

"Can I get a phone call? I'm not trying to spend the night in jail," he said.

"Well, you're likely going to do that," he said. "By the time you get a bail bondsman and he gets it over to the jail, it'll be several hours. Unfortunately, it's not a quick process."

"What's the charge?" Paul said.

"Suspicion of driving under the influence of alcohol," he said.

"Ah, man, come on now because of that sobriety field test?" Paul said. "That's pretty unfair."

The officer did not respond at first. Finally, after an extended pause, he said: "You'll be able to make a phone call when I get you to the station. You have someone here who can post bail for you?"

He said, "Yes," but it was not a call he wanted to make. He was fortunate that he even remembered Ginger's number. Hers, his mom's and Helena's were the only phone numbers he committed to memory.

His instinct was to call Ginger, but the pettiness in him moved him to call his mother. This would be a slap in Ginger's face. Not on the same level as her getting an abortion without consulting him, but a slap in the face nonetheless.

But that would have to wait. It was another fifteen minutes before the tow truck arrived. The officer filled out paperwork in silence and Paul listened to the calls from the dispatcher come in on the radio.

There was an arrest at Lincoln and California of a man who ran a red light—on his bicycle. The bigger problem for the guy was that he was in possession of a meth pipe with meth in it. He was headed to the Napa County Department of Corrections/County Jail.

Then there were officers and medical personnel called to the 700 block of Lincoln Avenue. A two-year-old male was suspected of taking medicine a two-year-old child was not supposed to take. He was transported to Queen of the Valley Medical Center for evaluation.

And then there was a fifty-nine-year-old man who was caught walking out of the local Target on Soscol with a jacket and sweater he did not purchase. An employee made a citizen's arrest, holding him until police arrived.

Focusing on those crimes helped Paul to calm down and take his mind off the discomfort he felt. Finally, the officer began the short drive to the jail on First Street. Paul looked at the people on the streets going about their lives without the specter of being placed in a prison cell. It made him feel worse.

They arrived and immediately Paul was struck by how the correction officers had either disdain for him or looked at him as if he were invisible, not even a person. He was lumped into the lot of criminals because he drank too much and got behind the wheel. He felt less than whom he was.

The cuffs were finally taken off and he rubbed his wrists that were pained by them. He wiped the remaining sweat from his face and poised himself. The police turned him over to the correctional officers, who would "process" him.

The place did not look horrible—it wasn't Alcatraz. But there was an air of oppression about it, a feeling of troubled souls resonating the place.

Shit got real for Paul when he was told to stand on the blue line and look at the camera, turn to his left and to his right—his mug shot. That didn't feel good at all. Then he was taken to the finger-print area where a woman did the honors, one by one placing his fingers on a machine that resembled a copier that captured his prints.

He was amazed at how routine the processing in process was. It sobered him up. He was as coherent and observant as he could be. He understood completely that he was an inmate.

"Excuse me," he said as an officer led him to a cell that was narrow and smelly, with aluminum benches on either side. Best of all, it was empty. The last thing he wanted was to have to deal with others. "Can I make a phone call?"

The correctional officer led him to a phone that sat on the desk at the command center. On a pillar next to the phone was a list of local bail bondsmen. Under it was a sign that read: "5 Minute Limit on Phone Calls… No Exceptions."

Paul dialed his mother's number. He was worried that she would not answer; she did not take calls from numbers she did not know.

But Brenda was concerned about Paul after Ginger told her that he left in a huff and without his cell phone. She was hoping it was her son.

"Vino?" she said into the phone with a sense of desperation, bypassing the traditional, "Hello."

"Ma. Hey," Paul said. "I'm in—"

"I know," she interrupted. "Don't even say it."

"Jail, Ma," Paul said.

"DUI?" she asked.

"He said 'suspicion of DUI,' which makes it, to me, hard to prove," Paul answered. "I didn't take the breathalyzer. So he's going by what he believed."

"It's his judgment as an officer to determine if you're a threat behind the wheel," she said. "Why the hell did you leave us here at the hotel anyway? Ginger wouldn't say."

"We can talk about it when I get out of here," Paul said, "which is the reason I'm calling."

He gave her three options of bail bondsmen from the list by the phone. He could hear Ginger's voice in the background, and she was not singing.

"Here's your wife," Brenda said.

"Paul, you're in jail?" she said.

"Yeah."

"So why didn't you call me? You called your mother?" she asked.

"Doesn't feel good, does it," Paul responded, "when something important happens and you turn to someone other than your spouse?"

"This is why I had an abortion; you can be so mean," she said.

Paul heard Brenda's response in the background. "Abortion? You had an abortion? Madeline, you knew about this?"

Then he heard all three of the women's angry voices talking all over each other. It was audio confusion.

"Hey, hey, hey," Paul said so loudly into the phone that a correctional officer came over and warned him about his volume. Ginger finally got them to stop bickering. "Can y'all do that later— *after* you get me out of here?"

"Well, I'll let your mother handle that since that's who you called," Ginger said with attitude.

She passed the phone back to Brenda. "You OK, Vino?" she said as if she were talking to a kid.

"Ma, I'm fine," he said. "I'm at the Napa Correction Center/ County Jail. It's not that far from the hotel. They just told me my fine is five thousand dollars, but I can bond out for five hundred. Can you work on this now so I can get out of here? Please?"

"OK, I will," Brenda said. "But we've got a lot to talk about— you driving and drinking and your wife having an abortion? Really?"

"OK, I gotta go, Ma. I won't be able to call you again, so please get me out of here now."

And with that, he hung up and was led back to the cell, which, in those few minutes had welcomed three guests: a twenty-something young man who reeked of alcohol and the streets; an elderly man who seemed to be either drunk or mentally challenged; and a man close to fifty who laid on his back on one of the benches.

It was close to ten o'clock at night the day after Thanksgiving and Paul Wall was in the Napa jail, a place he never even considered when he planned the trip to his dream destination.

CHAPTER 14
YOU HAVE THE RIGHT TO REMAIN SILENT

"Y ou can forget about getting out of here tonight," the elderly man said. He was disheveled, with long, dirty-blond hair and thick facial hair, a sort of a filthy Santa Claus. Paul studied his face and determined there was a younger man than he first thought beneath all that hair and behind those wrinkles.

Paul was not interested in having conversation with his fellow inmates, but had to respond to the man.

"How do you know?" he said.

"How do I know?" the man responded. "You ever seen *The Andy Griffith Show*?"

"Andy Griffith? Yes," Paul said.

"Well, I'm Otis from *The Andy Griffith Show*," he said.

"Who's Andy Griffith?" the younger man asked. He had tattoos of snakes and a skull and bones and other random images on his arms and shoulders and around his neck.

The man looked at Paul, who explained: "He's an old-school actor who had a TV show before you were born. He was the sheriff in a small town called Mayberry. Otis was…he was…"

"He was the town drunk," the older man said, "who spent a lot of his weekends in jail, so he knew how the system worked."

"So you saying that about yourself?" the young man asked, smiling. "You're the Napa town drunk?"

"Pretty much," he said. "But you can call me Otis. Funny thing is, that's actually my name."

"You," he went on, looking at Paul, "you don't live here."

"How you know that?"

"Because you have a Southeastern accent, probably from Georgia," he said. "The way you almost sing certain words. Your accent is not as bad as could be. You're educated. Went to college, but probably in the Northeast, didn't you? In Virginia or Washington, D.C., or Philadelphia. That region."

Paul looked on in astonishment. The man was right about everything.

"How could you know that?" Paul said. "I haven't even said ten words. Haven't been sitting here but three minutes."

"Wait," the young man said, "he's right? All the stuff he said is right?"

"He's right," Paul answered.

"How could you know that, old man?" the kid said. "You just said you're the town drunk. But you're psychic, too?"

"Not psychic," the man said. "To be psychic is to be outside human knowledge. What I do is not that."

"How do you know these things?" Paul inquired. "I'm amazed."

"I wasn't always the town drunk," he said. "I once, not that long ago, worked for a government agency that shall remain nameless. I was a profiler. My job was to study human behavior.

"For instance, I can tell by how you are sitting that you've never been in jail before, that you're…put off by this whole experience."

"I wouldn't call this an experience," Paul said.

"Are you kidding me? Everything is an experience," Otis said.

"So what happened to you?" the kid said. "I mean, you're obviously smart and had a good job. What happened? How you end up being the town drunk—no disrespect."

"Neither of you would be here long enough for me to explain it in full," he said. "Let's just say that some things happened in my personal life that I didn't—and still haven't—handled so well."

For Paul, that meant death. What else could eat at a man so much that he let his life disappear into dust. Having experienced losing his job and the depression it brought him, Paul could imagine how something more serious—death—could overtake a man's psyche.

Before the conversation could continue, the man lying on the bench sprung up. "Damn, ya'll ain't got no respect for a man trying to get his beauty sleep," he said. He was smiling. "I'm fucking with you. I had to get a power nap to get my head right. Been a long night and it's still early."

The young man laughed. "I was thinking the same thing," he said. "What you in here for?"

The man stretched and yawned and said, "Quota. These cops gotta get their quota of arrests," he said. "It's the end of the month. More people end up in here the last eight, ten days of the month than any time in the month. I'm telling you some good shit."

"That may be true," Otis said, "but they arrested you for something."

"Oh, yeah, they got me on some bullshit," he said. "Said I had an open alcohol container in my car. It was a beer can from earlier in the day that I had drank."

"But why did they stop you?" the young guy said.

"Oh, 'cause I was doing sixty-seven in a forty-five," he answered and then laughed.

"What you want from me?" he added. "I had a lot of things working against me: I was late to this girl's house for a little, you know; I had to piss like nobody's business; and I don't like driving the speed limit."

Then he turned to Otis. "I heard you say you can tell about people based on their body language. What's my body saying about me? I want to hear this."

"You're a liar," the old man said immediately. "You lie to distract you from the truth that pains you. You lie to hide the pain."

"What are you talking about, old man?" he said to Otis. "You don't know what the hell you're talking about."

"You asked me to tell me what I noticed about you," he said.

"What have I lied about?" the guy responded.

"You lied about why you're in here," Otis said. "I watched you. Not one word about your arrest was true."

"Did you lie?" the young guy asked.

The man did not respond at first. Finally, he said, "How can you know this shit?"

"I just do," Otis said. "It's instinctive but it's also a learned skill."

"But, if you don't mind me asking, what happened to you?" Paul asked.

Otis ran his hand through his thick beard and briefly looked away. He was not sure if he should share his story because he was not sure they would get something out of it. But then he looked at Paul again, and he knew he could take away something that might influence his life. He thought of asking Paul what bothered him. Instead, he told his story.

"When I was young and dumb, I didn't even give the idea of marriage a thought," he began. "I didn't trust women, didn't need them for more than sex and felt like most young men do: the goal in life is to get as much sex as possible."

"That's right. What's wrong with that?" the young man interjected.

No one bothered to answer him. Otis went on: "Then I met Darlene Wilkinson on a blind date. My friend introduced me to her. He gave me the buzzwords that meant she was just OK: 'nice,' 'sweet,' 'smart.' A young man wants to hear 'sexy,' 'hot,' 'cute.' He didn't give me any of that because he knew, while it mattered, in the end I was gonna need substance and heart and a good mind.

"Well, I was mesmerized by Darlene and less than two years later we were married. I had never envisioned what true love could feel like. But we had it. There probably is no such thing as a perfect person or a perfect relationship. But she was perfect for me and our relationship was perfect for us.

"Two years ago, she got pregnant. When she told me, I cried. I was overwhelmed with knowing she and I would produce something so great together: a child."

Otis' voice got lower and the words did not come out of his mouth so freely.

"She carried our child, a daughter, for almost nine months. I was away for work and she experienced pain and then hemorrhaging. Our neighbor rushed her to the hospital. Doctors could not figure out what was wrong for a while. I will spare you the technical details, but she had a rare condition that flared up.

"I cut my trip short to get back and be there with her. But by the time I arrived, my daughter had died."

None of the men knew what to say, so they didn't say anything. A pall fell over the cell.

"It was beyond devastating. My wife, who was a strong woman, could not get out of bed for a month. She literally stayed in bed all day. She didn't eat. She hardly slept. She just cried and cried.

"You see, we had tried for years to get pregnant, but couldn't. Doctors told us she just would not. Well, maybe eight months after they told us that—after we had considered artificial insemination and adoption—she was pregnant. It was the happiest time of our lives.

"She was a beautiful pregnant woman. And happy. No aches. No morning sickness. It was a beautiful experience for her and for me. But to lose our baby killed her spirit. She died when the baby died, except hers was a slow decline in health to where she passed from a broken heart. One night, as I held her and wiped away her tears, she fell asleep and never woke up. She died in my arms.

"So, in six months, I lost the person I was closest to in the world and the baby we talked about bringing us even closer together. So, what happened to me, you ask? A big part of me has died, too. The person I was, the life I had and thought I was going to have…it's all gone.

"There's no other way to put it. Others have experienced similar tragedies and they moved on, eventually. I think their 'eventually' just came sooner than mine. Mine will come. One day. Maybe. Hopefully. But until it does, I have to function the best way for me to function—through drinking to escape this hell that's living in my heart."

Otis amazed Paul again, but in a different way this time. How could he share such an emotional story in a jail cell to three strangers? And how ironic that his story had to do with his pregnant wife?

"Damn," the youngest man said.

"Otis, man, I am really sorry to hear this," Paul said. "I cannot even imagine."

No one else said anything for several minutes. Paul thought about how he would react to losing Ginger and Helena and it saddened him. It scared him. Maybe he would be just as floored as Otis.

It made him realize that having Ginger and Helena was the world to him. Another child from his bloodline would have been great. But he had his wife and daughter. That was a lot to embrace, far more than Otis.

He absolutely was angry and disappointed about Ginger having an abortion. But hearing of Otis' losses made him appreciate his family more than he ever had.

It came down to the whole "life is short" thing. Whenever there is a tragedy, people are reminded to appreciate life, that it has an expiration date, that not living it to the fullest is wasting time, that it could be worse than it is, that someone is worse off than you. Paul felt all that, and he was so moved that he wanted to hug Ginger and not strangle her.

Once he let go of his feelings of anger and disregard, he was able to feel for Ginger. Otis' wife also was told she could not conceive, but defied the medical expectation and got pregnant. Losing her child killed her. Paul thought about how Ginger lost their baby through abortion, and how, as a mother, that had to be a gut-wrenching decision.

And this was important: The fact that she did and Paul not even sense something was wrong spoke to how disconnected he was to her. And he started to feel bad and ashamed. He understood better how hopeless Ginger felt and how, if he were not wallowing in self-pity, he might have been able to sense something with her and thereby spark a conversation that led to a different outcome.

Back at the hotel in Ginger's room, she, Brenda and Madeline were in the throes of drama.

"I can't believe what I just heard," Brenda said to Ginger. "You had an abortion?"

"Now just wait a minute, Brenda," Madeline jumped in. "You're not going to attack my daughter, especially when it was your son who basically pushed her to this."

"How in the hell did Paul push her to do something like that?" Brenda asked.

"By the way he treated her—or didn't treat her," Madeline said.

They stood practically nose-to-nose, close enough for any loose spit to hit the other's face. "He said he wanted a divorce. Why would she want to have a child with a man who wants out?"

"Why would a woman who was told she couldn't get pregnant, actually get pregnant and then get rid of it?" Brenda said. "That was a blessing from God. He told those doctors who's in charge and performed what the doctors considered a miracle, I'm sure. So to just get rid of it…that, I do *not* understand."

"You don't have to understand," Madeline said. "This isn't about you."

"And it's not about you, either, Mother," Ginger said from across the room. She sat in the single chair by the window with her feet up on the ottoman. There was a calm about her that was surprising.

"You all are talking about me and my life as if I'm not here. Well, I am here and I have heard enough. I love you both. I do. And I am glad and appreciate that you all care so much about Paul and me. But this is our business, our life and we have to work it out—or not work it out. Not you.

"So, you two can talk about me all you want after I'm gone. I am going to bail my husband out of jail. And I want to do this by myself. I will catch a cab and will call you later to let you know what's going on."

With that she rose from the chair and walked past the ladies and out of the room.

Brenda and Madeline sat on the double beds across from each other and didn't say a word. They shook their heads and sat there for a minute. Then Madeline said, "I'll be honest: I didn't agree with Ginger's decision, either. If she had told me what she was thinking before she went to the clinic, I would have talked her out of it. And I would have called Paul. I understand why she did it. I just don't understand how she could do it."

"I don't, either," Brenda said. "Kids today are so emotional. I wasn't really ready for a baby when I got pregnant with Paul. But I didn't think about an abortion, either. I guess it's a different time."

"You know what?" Madeline said. "I guess we should go to the bar and have some wine until they come back."

"Good idea," Brenda said.

CHAPTER 15
SAY WHAT?

Before stepping out of the room, Ginger politely took the sheet of paper from Brenda listing the bail bondsmen in the area. She did not bother to look back at her mother and mother-in-law. She just kept it moving.

When she got out in the hallway, though, she breathed a sigh of relief that was so big that she got lightheaded. She gathered herself and went to the front desk, where the manager called a taxi for her.

While en route, she called Awesome Bail and gave the information about Paul's situation. She figured that would expedite the process. But hardly is anything easy in times of trouble.

The company wanted all kinds of documents that she did not have—pay stubs, social security card, passport.

"We live in Atlanta; we're here on vacation," she said. "He left his wallet in the room; I have that. There are all kinds of documentation about where we live, credit cards, whatever. We're not criminals. We are not trying to jump bail. I'm just trying to get him out."

"Miss, there is a mandatory forty-eight hours of jail time with your first DUI charge in California," he said. "So, even if he were to post bail, he would still have to serve two days."

"What?" Ginger said.

"The only thing that could change that is if the judge rules the time could be converted into work service," the man added. "But because you all live in Georgia, I don't know if that's a possibility."

"Do they hold court on Saturday here?" she asked.

"You're lucky; not all of California does, but here we do," he said. "So, he will see a judge in the morning and will determine what happens."

Ginger had the cab driver drop her off at the jail. There, she found a worker who gave her the deal: Paul would have to spend the night. He would have an eight o'clock appearance in front of Judge Davis. His bail was set but the judge would determine in the morning if he would have to serve another night behind bars and his court date.

Ginger was upset. She wanted to get Paul out; she felt somewhat responsible for him being there. Having to stay another day would totally ruin their trip; they were scheduled to leave on the red-eye Sunday night.

She did not have much cash on her, so she sought to piece together the money. She was not sure how much Paul had in his account, but she had a duplicate card to his account and she knew the PIN number. He'd had her use it in the past and the PIN was the address to their first apartment: 2406.

So, she walked to the nearest ATM and was astonished when the balance read: $48,106. She wondered if the bank got it wrong. There was a time, years back, when her account balance read five hundred dollars more than she actually had in the bank. When she tried to get out more than she knew she had, she was refused. That had to be case here, she surmised.

If that was the case, it did not allow her an accurate balance, so she was not sure if there really was eighteen hundred available.

That made her nervous because the last thing she wanted to do was have to go to her mother for the money to help bail out her husband.

Before she could contemplate that much more, Ginger got woozy. She had been feeling strange off and on, but this time she felt really disoriented—and scared. It was not like what she considered a panic attack in the garage several months before. It was more of a lightheaded, dizzy feeling and an uneasiness in her stomach.

Her family had a history of bleeding ulcers, and she was always fearful she would get one, too. This time, she was more fearful than ever. Ulcers can be brought on by worry, and she certainly had been worrying and was worrying quite a bit about Paul—and her marriage.

Instead of trying to dismiss it, Ginger found a bench on the street, took a seat and used her phone to call a taxi—and locate the nearest hospital.

Before she could do either, however, Madeline called her.

"Ginger, what's going on? Is Paul out?" she inquired.

Ginger explained the dynamics to her and told her she would be back at the hotel later and that she was working on the bail money—anything to get her off the phone.

She succeeded in that and contacted Black Tie Taxi to pick her up near the detention center. She waited on a bench with her mind racing to many places: a potential ulcer, Paul, the abortion, Helena, her mother, her marriage. None of the thoughts gave her comfort.

"Queen of the Valley Medical Center on Trancas Street," she said when she hopped into the back seat of the cab.

It was a short ride from where she was, maybe ten minutes. During that time she texted Helena, although it was around two in the morning on the East Coast. She missed her and always found a base of comfort in communicating with her child.

Unlike many mothers and daughters that go through antagonistic crises during the child's teenage years, Helena and Ginger had no such issues. They got along more like sisters who actually liked each other.

"We are having an adventure here in Napa. Lots to share when we get back. Hope you're having fun. Sure you're at a party. Be safe," was her text message to her daughter.

A return message came back in less than a minute. "Surprised to hear from you. Is everything OK?"

Ginger sent her back a smiley face because she did not want to lie. Then Paul's phone chimed. She took it with her from the room. It was a text message from Helena.

"Daddy, is all OK? Mommy just texted me. I am at a party, but I wanted to check on you all b/c Mommy texted me when you all should be having fun."

Ginger texted her back from Paul's phone. "Hi, sweetheart. All is good. We just miss you. We love you."

At least she had that to feel good about as she exited the cab and walked into the hospital's emergency room. She actually felt better than she had, but decided to go anyway. An ulcer gets progressively worse, and so she was intent on dealing with it at that moment.

The receptionist greeted her with a smile, had her fill out paperwork and she took a seat in the waiting area. She looked at the others waiting for service and wondered what their ailments were. It was a calm waiting room, much unlike when they had to rush Helena to Piedmont Hospital in Atlanta when she tripped on a street curb and cut her hand, requiring seven stitches. There was blood in that waiting area, and it was not all Helena's.

One teenager had a bruised shoulder and neck from apparently falling off a skateboard. *Probably was riding on the railing of some steps*, Ginger thought. *If that's the case, then he probably deserves this. Maybe he'll cut out that nonsense.*

The other few people looked to be not sick at all or battling something internal, like she was.

Within minutes, she was called to the back to see a nurse, which shocked her. *That would never happen at home*, she thought. She explained her symptoms to the doctor, who examined her family history, took some blood and a urine sample and gave her some ginger ale to help settle her stomach.

All her vital signs were fine. "Is this your first time in California?" Dr. Margolis asked.

"It is," Ginger said. "Beautiful place. The feeling I'm having is getting in the way a little bit. It's nothing dramatic, but the dizzy spells concern me."

"And they should," the doctor said. "Dizziness should never be taken lightly. It could be some kind of brain issue. I'm not saying that at all. There's no reason to think that at all. I'm just saying that in general, the brain is so complicated and sometimes it gives us clues that something isn't quite right. So it's important when we get those clues that we explore them."

"I have so much going on in my head right now, I wouldn't be surprised if my brain exploded," Ginger said.

"Well, let's not have that happen," the doctor said, and they laughed.

He told Ginger she could rest on the examination table until he returned with the blood work results that might give him some clue as to why she felt as she had.

She lay there thinking about her cousin, Rita, who was sick for months and went to many doctors who could not figure out her health concerns. The not knowing drove Rita batty. Ginger fretted the doctor coming back and telling her there was nothing they could find out of order.

Finally, she dozed off on the table and dreamed the doctor came back to tell her she had an ulcer, appendicitis and a stomach virus. When she looked at him with concern, the doctor said, "Well, at least you know. That's what you wanted, right? To know?"

Before she could get too scared, the door opening awakened her. It was Dr. Margolis.

"Doctor," she said as she got her bearings. "Did you find anything?"

"Let me ask you something," he said. "Have you been drinking a lot of our wonderful wine we harvest up here?"

"Yes."

"Well, that's it," he said.

"What do you mean?" Ginger asked.

He said: "As good as our wine is, it does not go down so well when you're pregnant."

Dr. Margolis walked toward the door, turned and added, "Congratulations."

Ginger did not respond. She sat on the table, dumbfounded.

CHAPTER 16
A NIGHT TO
NOT REMEMBER

If Ginger's head was spinning before Dr. Margolis' discovery, it was *really* going with the news that she was pregnant. Again.

"Doctor, how can this be?" she asked. "I mean, I was told in no uncertain terms that I could not get pregnant. Now you're telling me I am?"

"I'm going to tell you a secret that I don't want you to repeat," Dr. Margolis said. "This is covered under doctor-patient confidentiality, OK?"

Ginger nodded her head. She anticipated the knowledge he was about to share.

"Sometimes," Dr. Margolis said, "doctors are wrong."

And then he laughed. And she did, too. "That's the only real, honest answer there is," he said. "This is not an exact science, as you know. Sometimes, no matter all the research and knowledge, we don't get it right. I'm kind of glad the doctors missed on this one. And I bet you are, too."

"I am, doctor," she said. "You have no idea."

Dr. Margolis left the room and Ginger looked down at her stomach as she placed both hands over it. Then she looked toward the ceiling, and with tears flowing down her face, said, "Thank you, God. Thank you."

She spent a few minutes in the room, rejoicing at the blessing bestowed upon her, the miracle she never even considered. *And they say lightning doesn't strike twice in the same spot?* Ginger thought.

When she left the hospital, with pamphlets on healthy eating as a pregnant woman, breast-feeding and exercise, she didn't even bother to call a taxi. She began walking.

Her cell phone rang and she expected it to be her mother, who was looking for her to return to the hotel by then. She was not ready to speak to her. But when she looked at the phone, she saw an unfamiliar number. Immediately, she thought it was Paul, so she answered.

"What's going on?" Paul said. "My mom said you were working on the bail."

"I did," she said, "but there's nothing that can happen tonight. I was told you'll have to see the judge in the morning and he'll determine if you have to stay another day."

"What? Another day? Are you serious?" he asked. "Where did you get that from?"

"Paul, we have a lot to talk about," Ginger said. "Are you OK?"

"I'll be OK when I get out of here," he said. "They let me use the phone again, so I only have a few minutes. Who told you about staying here two days?"

"That's the law out here," she said. "Only the judge can make an exception. I'll be back at court in the morning at eight. I can use a debit or credit card, so I'll have the bail money—it's hard to get a bond because we don't live here—and let's hope the judge lets you go."

"This is so messed up," Paul said. "This guy didn't even give me the breath test. He went on his instincts. How can I get a DUI based on his beliefs?"

"That's what you should tell the judge," Ginger said. "I hope he lets you go."

"Yeah, me too," he said. "Well, I gotta go."

"I'm sorry this has happened, Paul. I really am."

"Thanks. Me, too. But it'll be all right. See you in the morning."

Paul got off the phone and was confused when a correctional officer directed him and the others to another area of the building. It was then that his little arrest experience turned totally humiliating and dehumanizing.

They were ordered to strip, and Paul watched in amazement as the men got naked, turned their backs to the officer and bent over so he could determine if they had stuffed "contraband" up the cracks of their anuses. When it was his turn to do so, Paul felt numb, like he was in a horrific dream.

He felt like cattle, like he was less than the man he was before entering that building. The officer ordered him to place his clothes in a paper bag and to grab a towel, a set of jail-issued clothes, plastic flip-flops and to take a shower in the stall that reeked of filth.

Paul did so in a daze. He could not believe all this was happening to him. But it was. He was no longer someone arrested on a DUI charge. He was an inmate and treated as such.

Once clothed, they were directed to a pod where there were two levels of cells and an open sort of recreation area. It was after midnight, so the televisions were off and the other inmates were already in bed.

Please put me in an empty cell, Paul prayed to himself.

It did not work out that way. He was walked to a cell on the upper level, in the center. He walked in and when the officer shut that heavy metal door behind him, Paul's heart dropped. He truly was in jail.

Adding to his misery was someone on the lower bunk that Paul thought was sleeping. *What if this guy is crazy and I have to fight him?* he thought.

He placed the toothbrush kit he was given on a small table and climbed on the top bunk, banging his knee in the process.

He had never seen and even heard of a mattress as thin as the one he stretched out on. It was about four inches thick. Paul was totally uncomfortable, but not because of the bed. He was an inmate.

He didn't like breathing the air, and the idea of actually going to sleep was far-fetched. He tossed to try to find a manageable position to rest, which apparently irritated his cellmate.

"Hey, if you gonna flip and flop all night," he said, "we gonna have a problem."

Paul was not sure how to respond. He didn't want to punk out, although he hardly was some roughneck. But he had his share of fights in his day and had gotten himself in shape in recent months. He thought he'd better let dude know he was not to be played with.

"Man, go to sleep," Paul said. He was not sure where that came from, but he blurted it out. "Don't worry about me."

He held his breath, hoping the man would not respond or would not take it as a declaration of war. Paul's response seemed to disarm the man. "That's what I'm trying to do," he said.

Paul did not respond. He felt lucky he got away with those reckless comments. He didn't want to push it. So he found a relatively comfortable position on his back and looked up at the cold ceiling. Paul counted the minutes, and they went by molasses-slow.

"Hey, why you in here?" the guy in the lower bunker asked.

"I thought you were trying to sleep," Paul answered.

"*Trying* to, but can't," he said. "First time in jail. I ain't too comfortable, you know?"

Paul was relieved. Maybe he didn't have a serial killer as a cellmate.

"Same here," he said. "I came out here from Atlanta to enjoy the wine. I guess I had a little too much last night."

"Wow, same here," the man below said. "I live in L.A. Having some drama on the job and at home and said, 'Let me get away.' This is my refuge. Been coming up here for years. Love it up here. Right now, though, not loving it so much."

"Tell me about it," Paul said. "I got my wife, mother and mother-in-law here with me. So imagine what I'm gonna face when I get out of here."

"Damn. I'll pray for you," the man said, and they both laughed.

"So you're into wines?" the guy asked Paul.

"Love wines," he answered. "Trying to get more into them. So this is an important trip for me. Had some great wines already, though. Had the best wine I ever had tonight."

"The crazy thing about this place is that if you went out every night out here, you could probably say that every night," the cellmate said. "That's why I come up here. I watch the movie *Sideways* and I get on the road."

"Ah, man—what's your name?" Paul asked.

"Roger."

"I'm Paul, Roger. I can't believe you mentioned *Sideways*. I watched it before I left, too. There are so many scenes I like. But there's this scene where Virginia Madsen's character tells Paul Giamatti's character why she loves wine… What she says and how she says it, it makes you want to drink wine."

"Paul—Paul, right?"

"Yeah."

"I know the scene you're talking about," Roger said. "I know it by heart."

"Come on, man. No way," Paul said.

"OK, check it out. She says, 'The more I drink, the more I liked what it made me think about…like to think about the life of wine. How it's a living thing…like to think about what was going on the year the grapes were growing, how the sun was shining, if it rained? I like to think about all the people who tended and picked the grapes, and if it's an old wine how many of them must be dead by now. I like how wine continues to evolve. Like, if I opened a bottle of wine today it would taste different from if I opened it any other day, because a bottle of wine is actually alive and it's constantly evolving and gaining complexity. That is, until it peaks…and then it begins its steady, inevitable decline… And it tastes so fucking good.'"

"Oh, shit," Paul said. "That's amazing. How could you—wait. You said you live in L.A… You're an actor."

"Yes," he said. "Typical struggling L.A. actor. But I loved what she said and I used that as one of my monologues for auditions. It's easy to do because I agree with what she says, so it's almost an emotional thing, like it's really coming from me."

"That's crazy you would recall *that* particular scene," Paul said.

"I know," Roger said. "I wish I could write like that. Just thoughtful writing."

"And the person had to be a wine-lover," Paul said. "How else could he be so emotional about wine?"

Paul's experience took a turn for the better. He was paired in a jail cell with a wine lover and actor who loved to talk about wine. In Atlanta, Paul had a few friends that appreciated wine, but none of them could really discuss wine the way they would sports or the stock market—with passion and knowledge.

"I'm like you—someone who likes wine and wants to get better at understanding them," Roger said. "I was up here one time and happened to meet someone who took me to a sommelier event where there were about thirty of the best wine experts in the world in one room.

"So there is this contest—whatever sommelier that can identify this one red wine would win ten thousand dollars. I was standing there, saying to myself, 'This is going to be fun.'

"Well, it wasn't fun, really."

"What?" Paul said.

"It was amazing," Roger said.

"These guys…let me tell you what happened. So, the wine is in this decanter. They pour each sommelier some of it. They're sitting around this huge table. So, you realize there are millions of wines in the world. Millions. But they have to identify the year, the region of the world and the actual name of the wine.

"I'm thinking, 'How can this be? No one can do that.'

"So, they get the wine and everyone looks at it on the table for about, I don't know, seven, eight minutes. They just stare at it. Then they pick it up and hold it above their heads and look at it again, trying to determine the age. The next thing was to smell it. So they stick their noses damn near in the wine. It was crazy. They got a clear, deep smell of the wine.

"They do that a couple of times and then they begin swirling it in its glass—two fingers between the stem and circulate it while it's sitting on the table. They're helping it to breathe. This goes on for about five minutes. And I'm like, 'I don't care what you do. No way someone gonna be able to figure out one out of a million wines. No way.'"

Paul listened as a child would a bedtime story. He was totally engrossed.

"So, it's literally about forty-five minutes later," Roger continued, "and no one has said a word. They are all studying this wine, swirling, it, smelling it, staring at it. Finally, after all the foreplay, they finally start tasting the wine. Still, no one has said a word because the one thing they can't afford to be is wrong. It would be horrible for their reputation.

"So finally, almost an hour into this thing, one guy raises his hand. He says it's a 1976 Chateau so-and-so from Southern Italy or some place. I can't remember exactly what it was. But he was *right*. Can you believe that? This guy figured out this wine forty-something year-old wine from Italy from just studying it and tasting it. The other guys clapped politely for him. I wanted to give my man a hug and a high-five. It was amazing."

"Damn," Paul said. "That's what you call being an expert in your field."

Both men were quiet for a moment as they took in the story. For those few minutes, they were not in jail. They were in that room with some of the best wine experts in the world.

"What was the wine that made you fall in love with wine?" Roger asked.

"It was a Fairview Pinotage 2002, I believe," Paul answered.

"A South African wine?" Roger said.

"Yes. My boy, D.J.'s wife, Wanda, went there for a visit and brought me back a bottle," Paul explained. "I had never had a Pinotage before. It's grown only in a few places in the world but especially in South Africa. Something about the soil. Well, I loved it. It made me feel like wine could be a meal. It was hearty and fruity and robust. It was different from any wine I had ever had. It was the wine that brought me all the way in."

"I understand how you feel," Roger said. "What did it for me was a 2008 Tobin James Fatboy Zinfandel. I always liked wine, but this one goes down smooth, like an expensive cognac. All the dark berries are evident. And it's 16.2 alcohol content, so it gets you there. I heard a guy call it 'sex in a bottle.' And you know what? You drink a bottle of that with your woman and you'll get lucky for sure."

They talked of wine—viogniers, pinots, chardonnays, merlots— until the sun came up, starting a day they hoped would not end like the day before. They talked because they couldn't sleep and because discussing wine kept them from thinking about where they were.

So into the discussion was Paul that he hardly thought about Ginger and the abortion. And he was glad about that because he still had not figured out how to process it. But Ginger said they needed to talk and he hoped something would come out of it to make him feel better. But that would be later.

Paul and Roger were corralled along with about twenty other inmates and shepherded to the courtroom in the detention center. Paul felt the weight of his trip as he stood for before Judge Jenson, who looked fresh and alert. He had an upbeat spirit.

Paul looked around the courtroom and spotted Ginger, who offered a reassuring smile. He was glad to see her; he smiled back. Paul watched how the judge interacted with the inmates before him. He was expeditious, thorough and seemingly fair, giving Paul a sense of hope. When it was Paul's turn, Judge Jenson said, "OK, you look like an upstanding citizen. What's your deal?"

It was a rhetorical question and Paul realized it, so he did not say anything as the judge examined the paperwork. "OK, Mr. Wall, I don't see any results of a breathalyzer. Did you take one?"

"No, your honor."

"I see," he said. "Looks like you took the field sobriety test. Didn't do so well, huh? What were you drinking?"

"Sir, I had the best wine of my life at 1313 Main — a bottle of Caymus 2008 Cabernet Sauvignon."

"That place is great," the judge said. "I go there on occasion… OK, let's see here. So you stopped in the middle of the intersection, didn't fail the sobriety test but didn't pass it, either. The officer used his judgment, which he is entitled to. But he did not administer a breathalyzer. Can you pay the bail?"

Paul turned to Ginger, who nodded her head.

"Yes, I can, sir," he said.

"OK, Mr. Wall. They don't have much of a case against you without the breathalyzer, but because it is a DUI case, I'm going to set a court date. See the clerk on your way out and then pay the bond, which is ten per cent of five thousand dollars. And, if I were you, I'd hire a lawyer to negotiate this thing so you don't have to come back out here just for this."

"Thank you, judge."

And just like that, Paul was again a free man. He looked at Roger, who was a few feet away. "Good luck, man. Call me," he said, and Roger nodded his head.

Paul saw the clerk, got some paperwork and went through a side door to claim and change his clothes. Ginger, after paying the bail, waited in the lobby for her husband, unsure of how he would receive her. It was her news that she aborted their child that led him to leaving her at the hotel and the ensuing drinking binge. *Would he blame me?* she worried.

At the same time, she remained flummoxed by learning she again was pregnant. *How could I go from not being able to get pregnant to pregnant twice in about five months? When do I tell Paul? My mother? Helena? Are we ready to have a child?*

She was overwrought with concerns and not confident on what to do. She was sure she would tell Paul, though. *This pregnancy was a blessing from God, a chance for me to redeem myself to Him and regain whatever I lost from my husband.*

Then she thought: *What if he's so angry with me that he wants out? What if he believes he can't trust me?*

She was going to play more games with her mind, but Paul emerged from the locked doors. Their eyes met...and there was no animosity between them. There was relief.

Otis' story about losing his daughter and wife resonated with Paul. He wasn't sure if he would not deteriorate as Otis had without his girls. And now that he had financial means, it was the time for them to come together, not pull apart. He faced the fact that while Ginger's decision on abortion was extreme, she never would have taken that path if he hadn't lost all confidence in who he was and said he wanted a divorce.

Ginger was remorseful that she acted out of spite and anger instead of calm and responsibility. Despite Paul's claims, she came to the belief that it was her responsibility to share her pregnancy news with her husband and let them decide together what route to take. She told him what she did as a way of overcoming her guilt, but it only heightened animosity in the relationship.

So now they were face-to-face after so many personal revelations, and they were unabashed in their remorse and shared responsibility for their plight.

"Thank you for being here," Paul said, hugging Ginger. "I'm sorry about all this."

"I'm sorry, too, Paul," she said, holding her man tightly. "I am so sorry."

They hugged for an extended period. When they finally let go, Ginger used the back of her hand to wipe away tears.

"It's OK," Paul said. "I'm OK, and we're OK. Let's get back to our vacation. We have one more day in California. I have some plans for us."

Ginger pulled out her vibrating phone. It was Brenda, Paul's mother.

"He's right here," Ginger said, handing over the phone.

"I'm good, Ma. No problem. Everything's fine. We're headed back to the hotel. Ah, huh. Yes… It was bad, but… Ma, we'll be there in twenty minutes. No, maybe longer. We've got to go get the car. They impounded it. So we'll get the car and be there in the next hour… OK. Ma, I'm fine. OK. Love you, too."

He ended the call and looked at Ginger. "It's not like I was in Sing Sing or Alcatraz," he said.

"A parent will be a parent until the end," she said.

He nodded his head, grabbed her hand and they headed out to retrieve the rental car.

When they got back to the hotel, Madeline and Brenda were in the lobby, waiting.

"Let me look at you," Madeline said to Ginger.

"Why are you worried about her? I was the one in jail," Paul said.

"You don't know?" Brenda said.

"Know what?" Paul asked

"I wasn't feeling well last night," Ginger said, "so after I left the jail I went to the emergency room."

"You OK? What did they say?" Paul asked.

"I'm fine," she said. "Better than ever. Just had some stomach issues."

"What did they say, though?" Paul asked.

"That I'm fine," Ginger answered. She did not want to tell him standing right there in the lobby. She was not sure the best scenario to tell him, but she knew that was not it. "I had some ginger ale and I felt better."

She was convincing enough that no one questioned her.

"Well, what's the plan for the day?" Paul said. "I've got to get a nap. I did not sleep at all last night."

"I bet you didn't; I wouldn't," Brenda said. "How bad was it?"

"Terrible. Humiliating," he said. "But I met some interesting people. But I can't talk about it now. I need a good, long shower and at least a two-hour nap. Let's have lunch by the pool around twelve-thirty."

They agreed to do so, and Ginger walked with Paul back to their room. The in-laws went for coffee and fruit.

In the room, Paul hardly delayed in getting into the shower. "I have to wash away that experience," he said. Under the hot water, he felt himself come back to life, the smell and grime and aura of the jail flowed down the drain. He spent an extra ten minutes in the shower, letting the flow douse his hair, the water serving as therapy.

"This has been a crazy trip," Ginger said when Paul exited the shower. "You feel better?"

"I feel like I washed the Napa Valley Correction Center/County Jail off me," he said. "I don't get why a jail has to be so disgusting."

"I'm just glad you're out," Ginger said. "But it's not made to be a resort, you know?"

Paul, with his silk robe wrapped around him, nodded his head knowingly, and rested on the bed. He let out a sigh of relief. Not too long before then he was on a super-thin "mattress," staring at the ceiling and wondering how his life degenerated to that situation. Being in the confines of his hotel room was so welcomed.

Ginger had the television on ESPN, but the sound was down, and Paul rested on his back as if he were in a coffin: hands clasped together across his chest.

She went to the bathroom and returned after several minutes. "Paul, we really need to talk. There's something important I need to tell you," she said. Ginger had gathered the courage and the words to give Paul the news that would turn his mindset.

Paul's response? He snored.

"That was fast," Ginger said. She sat on the adjacent bed and stared at Paul as he slept. She looked down at her stomach and put her hand over it. And she started to cry—tears of joy and regret. Then she figured out why she cried so much. Her hormones were screwy.

Life is growing inside of me, she thought to herself. And when she thought of the abortion, she cried more. *God, please forgive me.*

To have a second chance when much of her life she was told she had no chance to get pregnant, well, it made the miracle of child bearing that much more miraculous. She was anxious for Paul to wake up. She wanted to apologize to him again and to share news with him that she was sure he would embrace.

But he slept and slept—and Ginger alternated between staring at him and reading the literature on how to eat for two. She knew right away she would be obsessed with making sure she gave her child the best chance to be born healthy.

She also thought about how to tell Paul; what to say, where to say it, how to say it. Her mom and Brenda were not going to join them for dinner later that night, so Ginger thought it would be better to tell Paul first, over dinner, before sharing it with anyone.

Make it a special announcement in a special place, she thought. Paul had identified French Blue in St. Helena as their dinner destination. There was something special about that place because it was in a town named after their daughter.

Yes, that's the place to tell him, Ginger thought.

CHAPTER 17
DAWN OF A
NEW DAY

For the first time in their lives together, Paul's snoring did not bother Ginger. There were times when she slept in the guest bedroom or demanded he sleep elsewhere because the noise was so distracting. But on this day, with the news she had to share and all that they had been through, she wanted to be close to her husband.

She was in a remarkable place in her life. All the pain and hurt and disappointment of a few months before were gone. Ginger lay cuddled up with her snoring husband feeling as alive and womanly as ever.

As much as she felt like a mother in raising Helena, she was shocked that knowing she would birth a child changed how she felt about herself. She was so broken and disenchanted when she was pregnant several months before that she never gave herself the opportunity to embrace the magnitude of the responsibility.

This time, she did, and even though she was in the very early stages of the pregnancy, she intuitively placed a hand on her belly often, as if she was protecting the fetus from impending danger.

Mostly, she felt extra womanly. She knew it was a silly notion; she was a full-fledged woman all along, a mother, a wife. But having life growing inside her injected Ginger with a sense of pride and self-esteem that she had not felt. Ever.

I have a life growing inside of me, she said to herself while resting in the bed. *Oh, my God.*

Before she fell asleep, she thought about names for the baby and how the child would look and how her mom would spoil it and how she wished her dad were alive to see the baby, to see her pregnant. She also thought about Helena. She was such a delightful young lady, a teenager without the teenage attitude or sense of entitlement. She prayed her child would have the same temperament.

But mostly she prayed that Helena would forgive her and Paul for not telling her that she was adopted. Theirs was parents-raising-a-child, genuine love that was strong and everlasting. But Ginger could not help but wonder how Helena would feel about not being told the truth about her parents all these years.

For a second, she thought that maybe Paul was right. *What good would it do to tell her? We're her parents*. But that thought passed swiftly. *As her parents we are obligated to tell her*, Ginger told herself.

Still, the effects it would have on her concerned Ginger. Would Helena accept hearing the truth and not judge her parents? Would she want to meet her birth parents? And with Ginger pregnant, how would Helena receive that news? Would she resent the forthcoming child?

All those scenarios scared Ginger. Helena was her world, and she could not fathom their relationship not being the same as it always had been. Telling an eighteen-year-old she was adopted at virtually the same time as revealing her mother was pregnant would be a lot to take in at once.

It was a lot for Ginger to take in, and so she finally closed her eyes and drifted off to sleep. She rested peacefully, with dreams of Helena posing for photos with the new baby, proud that she was a big sister.

Paul, meanwhile, dreamed of being in jail and having to fight his way out of closed-in places to prevent being raped. There were two guys, one bigger than him, one smaller. They approached with caution and bad intentions. "Been waiting for this since you got here," the little one said. "You gonna be mines."

"And mines," the bigger guy added.

Paul grabbed a bottle of wine, a 2011 Alouette Pinot Noir and blasted the smaller man across the head with it, knocking him out and breaking the bottle at the same time. In his hand was the neck of the broken bottle with its sharp edges. Confidently, he approached the big guy and stabbed him in the gut with it, and he fell to the floor.

Paul let out a primal scream, and raised his hands in victory. He had conquered them. But in his salutations, he realized he had become one of them, and it scared him so much that he shook himself out of his dream and woke up.

His movements in his sleep startled Ginger, who moved away so she wouldn't get struck by a flailing arm.

"Paul, you OK?" she said. "You must have had a bad dream."

"Oh, man. I did," Paul said. "I dreamed I killed two men—or at least hurt them badly while I was in jail. Hit and stabbed them with a wine bottle."

Ginger laughed. "A wine bottle? You had a wine bottle in jail?"

"I did," Paul said, wiping his face. "And a good bottle of wine, too."

They laughed. Paul turned his body and embraced Ginger. It was just before 1 p.m. "I tell you, Gin," he said, "I hate we have gone through some of this drama. But I really believe it can—it will—make us stronger and closer.

"Jail was not a good experience, but I'm almost glad I went through it. I ain't that religious, but I can say with confidence that I believe God puts us in positions that are uncomfortable so we can learn from them. I felt like I was sub-human part of my time last night. It's humiliating to be in handcuffs and to be locked into a space. But I met people with *real* problems. It makes you understand that as bad as something may seem to you, it's not even as bad as it could be.

"You would think we would know that. But we take it all for granted. I mean, I met this man who looked so haggard—he was in the holding cell with me when I first got there. But I could see that he really wasn't as old as he looked. He was just unkempt. Anyway, the man could look at you and tell you about certain things about you because of your body language.

"He worked for probably the CIA or FBI—he wouldn't say. But he lost everything when his newborn baby died as his wife was delivering. And then his wife eventually died because she never got over losing the child. And those two deaths broke him down. He lost his job and is basically a bum. Said his name was Otis, like Otis from *The Andy Griffith Show*, the town drunk, frequently locked up. It was really sad.

"But it was also an eye-opener for me. I thank God that I didn't totally lose my mind with losing my job. But I did let it change me."

He rubbed Ginger's arm. "And I am so sorry for that," he said. "When you look back on things, you see things better. At the time, I felt less than a man; I couldn't provide for my family. But I should have been thinking how great it was that I had a family. That's the positive over negative thing. If I had done that, I probably would have handled that situation a lot differently and you'd be pregnant with our baby…I'm sorry, Gin."

It was then that she was going to tell Paul. Over dinner would have been more romantic or dramatic, but him saying that at that time let her know how much he wanted a child with her.

Before she could utter a word, however, Paul kissed her deeply; so deeply that she got dizzy. She was not sure if it was the kiss or more effects of being pregnant, but she lost her equilibrium for a moment.

She looked at her husband and she saw the kind of love in his eyes that she saw at the height of their marriage. She kissed him, and they caressed each other like lovers do.

As Paul lay on his back, Ginger tugged the belt on his robe and pulled it open, and his rocket-hard penis sprung up like a telescope. She immediately stroked it gently, causing him to moan.

At the same time, Paul meticulously handled her ample breasts, squeezing them at first before centering his attention on her thimble-sized nipples. They were Ginger's sensitive spots, her hot spots, and in response she stroked his manhood with more fervor. He leaned over and began licking and then sucking her nipples, and the pleasure rifled through her body.

She held his head as he sucked her titties, and she breathed heavily and spread her legs. He knew his wife, even if their love life had become far less frequent. And so he placed his hand between her legs, and he could feel the heat rising from her like steam.

She shifted her weight to her upper back and raised her hips off the bed, and Paul pulled down the drawstring pajama pants she wore. One side first, then the other...until they were at her ankles.

Ginger kicked them off using her feet, and bent her legs again so Paul could insert his middle finger into her. And he did, with great care and attention to her desires. The moisture from her insides doused his finger and she slid her body up and down on it to manage how deep she wanted it to go.

Her eyes were closed but her heart was open. She needed passion in her life, and the closeness that came with it. She missed the physical pleasure it brought her. After several minutes, Paul slowly dislodged his finger, and Ginger rolled on her side, her back to her husband.

Paul did not hesitate to angle himself so he could enter her from behind, and the initial insertion made Ginger flinch. Inside her, he adjusted his body so he could grab and smack her ass as he stroked her slowly and deeply. She moaned and he kissed her on her back, and the feeling that only intense passion can bring covered them.

"I love you, Gin," he said, still inside her, still pushing himself deeper.

She tried to answer, but the force of his movements stifled her breath. She could hardly get a word out that made any sense. She grunted and moaned as Paul pounded harder and faster and penetrated her until he could go no deeper.

Ginger needed a good fucking like that. They both did. So many pent up emotions, so many frustrations, so many desires. It all came out in this lovemaking session that traveled from one bed to the next, from one position to another.

"Damn, baby. You're getting it," Ginger said to Paul, her legs on his shoulders.

He extended her legs out and held her by her ankles as he pounded in rapid-fire succession, like a jackhammer. "Yes, baby," he managed to get out. The rest of what he said was profanity: "Shit." "Damn." "Goddamn." "Fuck." No sentences. Just single words that, in this context, meant pleasure.

"Get it, Paul. Get it," Ginger implored, and those words charged Paul to stroke harder and deeper and come in from different angles to touch all her walls. She was in pain and pleasure at the same time. Only during sex could this happen.

Someone's cell phone rang, but neither of them entertained

answering it. They were in the throes not only of making love, but truly reconnecting after a period of discomfort, distrust and uncertainty.

Paul finally felt the sensation of an orgasm rise at once from his feet and descend from his brain to converge and explode at his penis, swelling it up even bigger as it unleashed a load of semen into Ginger, who felt the tingly feeling of being suspended that climaxing brought.

"Oh, God," she yelled. "Oh, God."

She held him tightly as they reached an orgasm in unison, an event that was rare but significant because it epitomized their connection. Paul thrust on until his almost limp body collapsed on top of hers. They breathed heavily into each other's ear.

"Damn, Paul," Ginger said. "Damn. That was so good that I think I'm pregnant."

Paul laughed and Ginger kissed him on his chest. They lay together in silence, exhausted and fulfilled, and before long he dozed back off to sleep.

Ginger cried.

CHAPTER 18
ANTICIPATION

Madeline was giddy. She received a phone call from Mitch, who seduced her with his words. There were not Don Juan type of sentiments, but they seemed sincere and honest, and that's what she needed.

Getting over the death of her husband was a daily chore. First of all, she did not know how to move on. More importantly, she did not know *when* to move on. What was the perceived "proper" time to pick herself off the floor and date again.

She aged gracefully and, when she wanted to, had a younger woman's spirit about her. Mitch was not the first man who expressed interest in the widow. But he was the first to be chivalrous and humorous and who did not pressure her. The words that sold her on him were these, uttered about six months after her husband's sudden death:

"The last thing I want to do is come into your life as some whirlwind. At the same time, I do not reject when I have a chance to add good people into my life. I could be wrong—I was once—but I see you as a good person. So, just know I am here to build on what we started when you are ready."

It was an approach that made so much sense, which explains why so many men didn't get it. Madeline had a few men her age approach her as if she was some horny, lonely woman, dying to have someone warm her bed. "Everybody needs a little loving, you know?" one man said to her on their second phone conversation. That was their last talk.

Other men figured she must have had some life insurance money, so she was financially secure and could take care of them. One man told her: "So, I think we'll get along. You seem like a woman of today. You understand the value of being the bread-winner. I'll do my part—keep you feeling good and take out the trash."

She told him: "Leave. When you do that, you'll be taking out the trash."

Mitch was strong on his own merits, but clowns like those magnified his stature in Madeline's mind. She figured she would always, in some way, grieve for her deceased husband. But she knew the only way to have a fulfilling rest of her life was to live it. That did not mean with another man. It meant being open to another man who was worthy.

"So," she said to Brenda in the lobby as Paul and Ginger made love, "Mitch said they will be here at seven-thirty to pick us up. He said he had an Italian restaurant in mind."

"Girl, it could be Waffle House at this point," Brenda said. "I just look forward to having fun, good conversation with good men. If we get that, then I will be fine."

"I can't speak for Mitch's friend, but Mitch always has a lot to say about a lot of things. So, we'll be fine."

They noticed it was time for their kids to be downstairs and they were not. So Brenda called. No answer.

"The car is right there, so they have to be in the room," Madeline said. "They might be sleep. Paul had a long night. Come on, let's go knock on their door and wake them up."

So they took the walk to the room, chatting the whole way. But just before Brenda could knock on the door, she heard something and pressed her ear against the door.

"Madeline. Listen," she said.

And they blushed as they took in the lovemaking sounds of their children.

"Come on, Brenda," Madeline whisper. "This isn't right."

"OK," Brenda said, and they tiptoed off.

When they got to the elevator, Brenda said, "That was weird."

"Kinda creepy," Madeline said. "I remember Ginger walking in on me and her father one time. She was young, around five, and she heard all this noise and I guess she was concerned. Girl, it was embarrassing. I was bent over, holding on to the rear of the bed and her father was behind me doing his business."

Brenda laughed loudly. "Oh, no. How did you get out of that?"

"Shoot, we didn't," Madeline said. "I just said, 'Ginger, go back to bed' and she turned around and left. And we kept doing what we were doing. Thinking about it now, she might have just stood there and listened to us.

"When I saw her in the morning, there was this awkward feeling I had."

"It probably was just you feeling that way," Brenda said. "Kids have a way of moving on."

"I hope so," Madeline said. "I'd hate for her to have that image of me burned in her memory."

"I know what you mean," Brenda said. "Paul never caught us doing it. But we caught *him*. One night my husband went in his room to get a basketball—he was still playing at the time—and I went to check on Vino. Well, he was so into masturbating that he didn't even realize we were standing in the doorway. When he did, he just stopped and pulled the covers over his head."

"Wow," Madeline said. "Did you ever address it?"

"I didn't; his father did," Brenda said. "I don't know what he said, but he told me he had a talk with him—man-to-man—and we never talked about it again. But Paul did seem a little strange or embarrassed when I saw him the next day. He was about twelve."

"I think we're going to be waiting down here for a while," Madeline said. "So, let's have some wine."

"How about a white? Paul loves reds, but I like some whites, too," Brenda said. "A chardonnay?"

"You pick it, I'll drink it," Madeline said.

"So how do we handle this date thing?" Brenda said. "I'm a little out of practice. Haven't really dated in a few decades."

"I know what you mean," Madeline said. "You know why it's sad? Because even though we were married, we still should have been dating our husbands. That's where marriages go wrong. We get stuck in the rut and let it slip away.

"Having a so-called 'date night' wasn't enough. You do that once a month or so. What about the other twenty-nine days?"

"I know," Brenda said. "It's amazing how people don't get it with relationships. Older people who have been through stuff should be the relationship experts. What do these youngsters know?"

They kept sipping the wine and before long, they were feeling especially good.

"I'll tell you what the real problem is with relationships," Brenda said. She was on her third glass. "Not enough of what our kids are doing right now is going on."

They gave each other a high-five and fell all over each other laughing.

"Seriously, though, the problem," Brenda continued, "is that we make wrong decisions when we choose life partners. Sounds like you got it right—your husband was your soul mate. But most of us choose a husband or a wife for all the wrong reasons or not enough of the right reasons."

"As an example…," Madeline said.

"As an example, I'll use myself," Brenda said. "James was a good man, overall. But he did not have that energy and real zest for life that I wanted in a man. Still, I ignored it, even though it bothered me. I felt like I could change him or that he would grow into the man I wanted him to be.

"Having fun and laughing and being joyous are important to me. We had fun, to a degree, but he was more conservative and laid back than I needed. I needed a take-charge man. He wasn't that. And I knew it and yet I went along with it anyway because I figured he was a good man who was going to be good to me.

"As it turned out, that wasn't enough. I knew it wasn't enough a long time ago—*years* ago—but I literally suffered in silence. And when your kid moves on, that's when it really hits, you know? Then it's just you and him and it all comes out in a rush. Even at that I took it, stayed until I couldn't take it anymore."

"One thing you said," Madeline chipped in. "You said you thought you could change him. That's one of the big mistakes people make in relationships. You can't change anyone. Now, you can *inspire* someone to change by how you act. Maybe. But people's natural defenses come up when you are clearly trying to change them.

"They're like, 'What's wrong with me? Why do I need to change?' And instead of getting what you want, you get more of what you don't want. But I agree with you on decision-making. You know how many friends and family members I know who married someone that I knew wasn't right for them? A *lot*. If I knew it, they *had* to know it, too. But some people just want to say, 'This is my husband' or 'I'm married.' And that's the mistake."

"Yes," Brenda chimed in. "They say the divorce rate is fifty percent. I say of those who stay married, more than half of them wish they weren't married. They stay because they feel trapped or that it's cheaper to keep her or easier to stay—even though they are unhappy.

"I tell you, it took everything in me not to cheat on James. I was bored to death. Nice man. But he wasn't for me. And at the end, when I realized I had to leave, is when simply looking at him irritated me. I was in a bad place."

"Well, I give you credit for doing what was the strong thing to do," Madeline said. "My sister right now has been married eleven years and unhappy with nine of them. Just not happy about how she's living, where she's living and who she's living with. But she won't do anything. She said she's stuck. It's sad."

"I tell you, I was concerned about Paul and Ginger," Brenda admitted. "I never saw my son as he was. He never said it was Ginger, but what was I to think? Finally, he told me he lost his job and how that really knocked him off his feet."

"And it knocked Ginger off hers, too," Madeline said. "There was a time when she was miserable, very upset. There was no communication, that's what I gathered."

"Well, they are communicating now—in the language of love," Brenda said, and they laughed again. And when they looked up, there were Ginger and Paul, smiling.

"So," Paul said, "how many drinks are we behind?"

"A bottle and a half," Madeline said, "and you're not gonna catch up because we ain't stopping."

"Oh, boy," Ginger said. "That doesn't sound good."

"What have y'all been doing?" Brenda asked. "We've been waiting on y'all."

They were not about to say what they *really* were doing. But

Paul didn't want to lie, either. So he told the vague truth. "We were in the bed," he said.

"Yeah, I bet you were in bed," Madeline said.

"Mother? What does that mean?" Ginger asked.

"Nothing, child. Let's go eat. You've got to be hungry," Madeline said.

"We're going to a place in Yountville called Bistro Jeanty. Supposed to be good," Paul said. "Then we have a four o'clock at Sterling Winery."

"Oh, I read about Sterling," Ginger said. "Up on a mountain with a great view of the valley." And then she thought: *That's the best place to tell Paul he will be a father again.*

Which would have been great if it wasn't where Paul had planned to tell Ginger he hit the lottery for $8 million.

CHAPTER 19
MOUNTAIN HIGH

They drove to Yountville for lunch, which was on the way to Calistoga, where the Sterling Winery was. The sun was brilliant; it was another day that highlighted the magnificent of God.

The conversation was light, but everyone wanted to hear details about Paul's night in jail. He wasn't so keen on talking about it. Not because he did not want to share, but because he was not sure if they would get why it was an experience he was glad he endured.

"I can sum it up this way," he said. "It was embarrassing, dehumanizing, funny, enlightening and interesting. Overall, I'm glad I went through it. It's a crazy system, the prison system. Even in a little town like this people are troubled by guns and drugs and violence.

"I told Ginger about the man in the first cell I was in as they processed me. He had a great career in the government but his daughter and his wife died within months of each other and he was just broken down. He lost it and now he's an alcoholic who can't let go of his grief.

"Thank God I didn't lose my family, but I understood how important family is to me because I put myself in his place. It made the things that bothered me seem inconsequential.

"And then there was a guy there who said he was arrested for speeding. But the other guy, Otis, told him he was lying. He could tell you about yourself through your body language. Like, he said I was from the southeast, that I was educated up north. This wasn't like some fortuneteller. This was a man who studied my speech patterns and body language and could tell me about myself. I was blown away.

"So this other guy has all this mouth. He's saying how he was in for speeding. Otis told him he was lying. Told him he could see in his eyes and how he shifted his body. The guy got mad and eventually admitted that he had shot someone, someone he thought had been seeing his girlfriend. Turned out it wasn't the even the right guy."

"I have a question," Brenda said. "When someone catches his or her mate cheating, why is it they want to beat up or shoot the other person? You shouldn't go after anyone; you should walk away. But if you just *had* to shoot someone, shoot your mate. That's the person who really did you wrong."

"Or just shoot yourself," Madeline said.

"I liked it better when you said don't shoot anyone," Ginger said.

"Anyway," Paul concluded, "it was an interesting experience. Met a guy in my cell who was in for the same reason I was—and he loved wine. An actor from L.A. I got lucky: We talked about wine all night. It helped us forget where we were."

They drove along mostly in silence for the next several minutes, taking in the sights and admiring the beauty and quaintness of the place. Then Ginger spotted an ideal picture-taking spot: A roadside sign in Yountville with glorious mountains in the background, that read: "Welcome To This Famous Wine Growing Region: Napa Valley...and the wine is bottled poetry."

So Paul pulled over and they took turns taking photos of each other in front of the sign and in different groups. And they got another tourist to take a few group photos of all of them.

Brenda and Madeline were a little tipsy, so their excitement was magnified. They wanted several photos of themselves—alone and together. And they kept checking the photos after they were taken and not approving before finally Paul took control of the moment.

"The car is leaving in thirty seconds. I'd like you all to be in it when I pull off," he said. "But if not, I know where to find you after I eat."

"I guess it's time we get in the car then," Brenda said.

Everyone piled in, and Ginger turned and looked at her mother-in-law. "You think you're slick, don't you?" she said. "You never told your embarrassing story."

And everyone reiterated Ginger's point. "OK, OK," Brenda said. "I wasn't trying to get out of telling it. I just forgot."

"Well, remember now," Madeline cracked.

"OK, so, as cute as I am now, I was even more cute when I was younger," Brenda began. "I was in my early twenties and my hair was pretty long. But it wasn't long enough for me, so I got this long, flowing wig that went almost down to my butt, girl."

Madeline laughed.

"And there was this guy I really liked. His name was Peter Richardson. All the girls liked him but I heard he liked me, too. We were going to meet at this club, this beautiful place with really high ceilings, candles burning on candelabras, velvet drapes, dancers in cages, the works. We were in New York.

"I have on this chiffon dress that's falling off my shoulders—really sexy and cute but not too revealing. And so Peter is there, looking handsome and in charge. And my friends tell his friends

I'm there looking good and his friends tell my friends we should meet up near the bar area.

"So we do, and it's like a movie, like he's moving in slow motion toward me and I'm moving in slow motion toward him. The crowd parts and it looks like everyone in the club, hundreds of people, has their eyes on us and excited about us finally coming together.

"Now, I'm a little nervous but not that nervous because I had a few drinks—top-shelf Long Island Iced Teas. Yeah, I was drinking big girl drinks back then. So, anyway, I get closer to Peter, about five feet away, and all of a sudden, he has this strange look on his face. Then he starts backing up and pointing at me and the whole place gets loud and I'm looking around like, 'What the hell is going on?'

"Then I started to smell something; smelled like something was burning. I looked around and didn't see anything, but my friends were pointing at me and screaming. Finally, I felt this heat—my wig was on fire."

Ginger spit out the ginger ale she was drinking and Paul and Madeline were in stitches.

"And I'm not talking about a little flicker; my wig was an inferno. I pulled it off and threw it and it landed on one of the drapes and set the drape on fire."

"Get outta here," Madeline screamed.

"Someone threw something on the drapes before the whole building burned down. But I was standing there with the stocking cap on my head looking crazy. Peter tried not to laugh, but he couldn't hold it back.

"One of my friends came over and grabbed me and rushed me to the bathroom…I was never so humiliated. But I was lucky that fire didn't catch my chiffon dress. I could been a crispy critter."

They all laughed a good long time. "That was a good one, Ma," Paul said. "And it didn't involve someone's bodily function, either."

"I'll be sure to look out for candles tonight," Madeline said.

"Huh?" Ginger said.

"We have dates tonight, remember?"

"I'm not sure about this," Paul said.

"You don't have to be sure about it," Brenda responded. "We're more grown than you are. We're not some rookies trying to find our way. How do you all say it? We got this."

"Well, we need to know where you're going—and I want to meet them before you go."

"I want you both to meet Mitch and Lionel—that's his friend," Madeline said. "He's a nice man."

"Yeah, well, we'll see," Paul said.

They arrived at Bistro Jeanty and were attracted by its charm outside with beautiful flowerbeds on either side of the entrance, under red and white striped awning. Inside, it had the feel of a French bistro, cozy with wicker-backed chairs, food specials written on a blackboard, French art and waiters clad in long white aprons.

The menu was expansive and pricey, but no one fretted over it, especially after indulging in the delicious treats and wine. Ginger had water with lemon, green bean salad with warm goat cheese over roasted tomatoes and honey vinaigrette.

Brenda had the short rib, roasted carrots, pearl onions and buttered egg noodles. Madeline had the chicken, mushrooms, black and red wine sauce and Paul had the grilled rib eye with fries and a side of Brussels sprouts.

There was not a lot of talking during lunch. Every so often someone would throw out a random comment, which usually was about how outstanding the food was.

"Ginger, I can't believe you're passing on the great wine," Paul said. "It wasn't as great as the Caymus I had last night—that was the best wine I ever had—but this Syrah, Novy Family, it's good."

"My stomach still isn't right," she offered. "The doctor said I probably should lay off the wine for a few days."

"Damn, baby, that's too bad," he said. "We're in Napa, for Christ's sake."

"You haven't called me 'baby' in so long I can't remember," Ginger said.

"Well, it's a new me and we have a new marriage, as far as I'm concerned...baby."

"I read on Facebook on a post that said what your man should do," Ginger said. "I can't remember everything, but it said a few things like: 'A man should make a woman laugh and he should call his woman 'baby.' I do remember that."

The bill came and the women started digging in their purses for their wallets.

"Let me get this, baby," Paul said, smiling. "We're celebrating my freedom, our last full day in Napa and family love."

They agreed with Paul. But when Madeline and Brenda went to the bathroom, Ginger said to her husband: "You know, when I went to the ATM with your card to get some bail money, the balance said forty-something thousand dollars."

"What?" Paul said, trying to act surprised. "Is that all?"

"I'm serious," she said. "It was crazy."

"That's happened to me before," Paul said. "Not that much of a difference in the balance, but a few hundred dollars. I even tried to take out the money I knew wasn't really there. It didn't work."

"Same thing happened to me once," she said. "Anyway, you should check it when you get a chance."

"I will," Paul said. He felt he quickly needed to change the subject, so he said, "I'm kinda glad our moms are going to dinner. We can have one night out by ourselves at a nice restaurant. It will be nice."

Almost immediately they both thought the same thing: To share their big news over dinner instead of at the winery. It would be more private, more personal.

And then we can tell our parents the great news together, Ginger thought.

And then we can share the news with our parents together, Paul thought.

"I can't wait," Ginger said.

"Me, either," Paul said.

"When was the last time we looked forward to spending time together?" she asked.

"That's part of the proverbial marriage trap," Paul said. "You're married long enough, you start taking some things for granted. Some things, not people. It's not intentional. It just happens."

"Well, I don't want that to happen with us anymore," Ginger said. "I want something different."

"And that's what you will get because that's what I want, too, baby," Paul said. "I mean that."

Ginger smiled at him.

"Now let's go taste some wine," Paul said.

And so, they did. They cruised to Sterling Vineyard, where the line to get tickets for the tour was long. But Paul had paid for theirs online in advance, so he went to the Will Call window where their passes awaited them. He chose Sterling as one of their stops because of its reputation of having the best view in Napa Valley.

Problem was, getting to the top of the mountain required a two-minute ride in a small tram that swung back and forth in the wind. For someone who was afraid to fly, it was not comforting to step into that little carriage-like contraption suspended in the air by a cable.

It only sat four, so they went in as a group. Each of the three women paid Paul special attention. "It's going to be fine; it's a short ride up. Enjoy the view," Brenda said. "Right, Vino?"

Paul took a deep breath. He said, "I'm all right," but he didn't feel all right. He felt uneasy, like he was confined.

"Should we really be on this thing?" Madeline said. "I mean, there are a hundred wineries here. Why are we at the one that he has to go up in the air to get to it?"

"It was my choice, Miss Price," Paul said. "I'm OK. It'll be all right. It's not like we're flying."

"Look at that little boy," Brenda said, pointing to a kid around eight years old who was in the tram behind them. "Look at him. He's perfectly fine. So why aren't you?"

Mother knew best. She knew how competitive Paul was, so to be compared to a kid, well, that ate at his pride.

"Trust me, I am good," he said. "Let's go."

And up they went, ascending above the earth at a methodical pace. The view got more and more beautiful the higher they rose. "Oh, my, look at that," Madeline said, pointing down at the fountain that spouted out water into a pond.

"And look over there," Ginger said, pointing. The sun illuminated the full, green trees, the vineyard below and the prodigious mountains that virtually surrounded them. "Just beautiful."

Paul looked out briefly, but quickly turned back to the kid, who was posing for photos and having a good time.

"Where's the camera?" he asked. "Let's capture all this beauty."

And so, Ginger, who had the camera around her wrist, began firing away, documenting the beautiful nature all around them.

Paul relaxed some and while he was not as carefree as everyone else, he did not have any overblown anxieties, either.

"That wasn't bad," he said as he stepped out of the tram. "But do we have to take it back down, too?"

He was joking, but figured he'd worry about that an hour or so later, when they would be ready to leave. It was on to the tasting.

Sterling Winery was ideal for the gorgeous, sixty-five degree, clear afternoon on the expansive deck that overlooked the valley. They made they way there after tasting three different wines that they all seemed to enjoy but were not particularly excited. The chardonnay poured on the deck, though, was light and fresh and went with the day's weather.

And although they were only tastings, the sum total of the wines provided a nice buzz—not that Madeline and Brenda didn't already have one since before lunch.

They walked back into the building to read some of the history of the winery and to get another look at the huge barrels where the wine was fermented.

Paul and Ginger stayed outside. They found a corner over-looking the valley and beautiful landscape, an image a painter would put on canvas. "Maybe we should take you back to the doctor. You love wine, and yet you're feeling so bad that you can't even taste some?" Paul said. "That's not a good thing, especially where we are. This is the purpose for coming here."

"I thought the purpose was for us to find our marriage, Paul," she said.

"That's the main reason we came here," Paul said. "But we could have gone anywhere to try to reconnect. We picked Napa because we love wine so much."

Ginger, with her right hand over her stomach, nodded her head. "Gin, what's wrong?" Paul asked.

She could not wait any longer. Holding it in another few hours would have been torture. She looked around at the wonderful setting and looked up at the man she loved—the man she crushed when he learned she had aborted his child. It was time to share her wonderful news.

"God is so good," she said, shaking her head. "God is so good."

Paul just looked at her, concerned. Confused.

"Honey," she said, "when I went to the doctor last night, he told me the news. I was in shock."

Paul was clueless. It was not registering for him. "What?"

"I'm pregnant."

It was as if Paul was frozen stiff by a genie. He didn't move. He stared at her, as if he was waiting for her to say something else. But she had said enough.

"What do you mean?" Paul asked.

"What do I mean? I'm pregnant," she said, smiling.

He looked down at her stomach. "But you said you had an abortion."

"Paul, that was four months ago," she said.

"You mean, you're pregnant *again*?" he asked, still not quite getting it.

Ginger smiled and nodded her head.

"Are you serious?"

"*Yes*, Paul."

"Oh, my God," he said as he hugged her. Then he pushed away from her. "Oh, I'm sorry. I don't want to hurt the baby."

"It's OK. It's not a baby yet," she said. "I'm in the first trimester."

"I can't believe this," he said. And then he did something Ginger had never seen: He cried.

"Baby, this is crazy…crazy in a good way," Paul said. "I can't believe it. I mean, I believe it, but…I guess I'm shocked. Oh, my

God. God knew we wanted a baby. He knew we *needed* a baby."

Ginger started crying again, profusely.

"Through all this, you're carrying our baby. This is God's will. This is God's will."

They hugged and cried and would not let go of each other. In the distance, Madeline and Brenda, returning to the deck, could see them embracing.

"Oh, Lord, what's going on with them now?" Brenda said.

"Come on, let's go find out. But let me get another shot of this wine here before we do," Madeline said. "I might need more of a buzz."

"Yeah, good idea," Brenda said, and she had some chardonnay, too. Then they walked over to the elated couple.

"Hey, what's going on?" Madeline asked.

They separated and turned to their curious parents. Brenda saw the tears of her son and got nervous. "Paul," she said with anxiety in her voice.

"We have something to tell you," he said. He looked over at Ginger.

"You're going to be a grandmother again," she said. "I'm pregnant."

And all three of the ladies started screaming, drawing the attention of everyone on the massive deck.

"My wife is pregnant," Paul announced to the onlookers.

People clapped and came over and congratulated them. One couple stopped and told them: "You picked a good place to tell him this," the man said. "This is where I proposed to my wife— right over there, in that corner. That was twenty-nine years ago and a day a lot like today. Just a beautiful day."

"Beautiful because I said yes," his wife said. "It was overcast that day. It had rained."

"No, it hadn't," the man said. "It was sunny and seventy degrees."

"Listen, you were so happy that I said yes it seemed the sun came out," the wife said. "But it was a cloudy day. I remember it like it was yesterday."

"You can't even remember where we parked the car twenty minutes ago."

Paul and Ginger laughed at the hilarious, lovable couple.

"You all go ahead and enjoy your day. Congratulations," the man said. Then he turned to his wife. "Now see if you can remember to walk away when you should. Come on."

Everyone laughed as they left and playfully bickered as they did. Madeline, Ginger, Paul and Brenda found a table and sat down.

"How can this be?" Madeline asked.

"Paul and I already talked about it," Ginger said. "This is God's work."

"Amen," Brenda said. "That's what I was going to say. To get pregnant twice in the last whatever the timeframe is? This is a gift from the Man above."

Paul threw his head back so that he was looking skyward and closed his eyes. "Thank you, God," he said. "Thank you, God."

CHAPTER 20
GOOD NEWS,
AWKWARD NEWS

The rest of the Sterling Winery tasting was wonderful but overshadowed by the news that Ginger was pregnant. She had not seen Paul so buoyant since they brought home Helena eighteen years earlier.

"Look at him," Brenda said. "He's beaming."

"I know," Ginger said. "I was trying to wait until the right time to tell him."

Paul returned from a bathroom run. He had purchased them the Gold Experience, meaning they had a private tasting of three more Sterling wines: a 2008 Reserve Chardonnay; a 2010 Malvasia Blanca; and a 2011 Viognier. The staff wine steward serving them enjoyed their celebratory spirit so much that she also poured them a 2007 Sangiovese and a 2007 Reserve Cabernet Sauvignon.

Ginger had water.

"Baby, I am so sorry you cannot taste these wines," Paul said. "They are so good. Then again, I'm not sorry."

"Me, either," Ginger said. "I was telling your mom that I was waiting for the right moment to tell you. I was in shock myself for much of last night. I hardly slept. I almost told you in the room before we left. But we were talking about a romantic dinner and I thought that was the best time.

"But being out there in the sun, looking at all that God created, it felt like the right time and place."

"It was perfect," Paul said. "Perfect."

"We've got to tell Helena," Ginger said. "And we also have that other news to tell her. Thinking about that last night gave me a headache. What do you all think? How should we handle this? I don't want to burden Helena with the news that she was adopted and pile on that there's a new baby coming."

"Sometimes kids have problems with a new child because the focus won't be on them anymore," Madeline said.

"But Helena is eighteen; she should be beyond that stage," Brenda said.

"She should be but she's been spoiled all her life and gotten all the attention," Madeline said. "When she comes home next year for a visit from college, will she be OK with seeing everyone give so much attention to the baby?"

"Well, she's gonna have to be OK with it. And she will be," Paul said. "When a new kid comes the older kid has to adjust. That's how it is. We have to make sure Helena doesn't feel left out. Plus, she's so sweet. She'll be a great big sister."

"But I'm worried about the dynamic of her learning she's adopted and learning about a new baby coming all at the same time," Ginger said. "Should we tell her both things now? Should we wait on telling her about the adoption?"

"You've got to tell her everything," Madeline said. "Now. That's my opinion. She's a good young lady, mature. She'll handle it all. It might be a lot in the beginning, but she won't go off in hiding or anything. She's pretty expressive."

"Ginger, I get your concern," Paul said. "She learns that we are not her birth parents in one breath and then learns that we have a baby on the way in the next breath. Does she feel like she means less to us because of the baby?"

"She knows how much she means to you both," Brenda said. "I do. I was against telling her at all that she was adopted. But I have changed on that. She deserves to know. But the reason I changed is because I thought about the person Helena is. She's a great kid. She calls me every week—from college. And I am sure she calls you, too, Madeline. What teenager calls her grandparents consistently while they are away in college?

"So I'm sure she's calling you both all the time. My point is, family is important to her. You all mean the world to her. She's going to be strong about it. She's not going to feel you all will love her any less."

The discussion went back and forth for several minutes, all the way in the tram down the mountain to the car. It was so involved that Paul didn't even bother to be bothered with his fear of heights and enclosed places. He simply rode with it.

They headed back to the hotel feeling great physically from the wine and great mentally from the news. But they could not come to a consensus on Helena. "So, if we tell her both at the same time, which do we tell her first?" Paul asked.

The car fell silent. "Well, if we tell her the baby is coming first," Ginger said, "she'll be happy. She'll be excited. Maybe with that joy in her she will not be so impacted by learning she's adopted."

"See," Madeline said, "I think differently. If you tell her the hard news first—that she's adopted—then telling her the good news lifts her spirits. It's like, 'What do you want to hear first? The good news or the bad news?' Most people say, 'Gimme the bad news first, so the good news can make them feel better.'"

"Not necessarily," Brenda said. "I would want the good news first so it could cushion the bad news. And then there's the chance that she could receive the adoption news so strongly that it cancels out the good news."

"It has to be in how we position it," Paul said. "We can't position it as bad news or as something that's so disconcerting. We have to present it to her as news that she's old enough and mature enough to accept. We should say we probably waited too long to share this with her—put the burden on us, where it should be. Tell her that we will find her parents for her and take her to visit her parents if she'd like.

"I have a friend who learned she was adopted when she was twenty. She learned it because her natural parents' family found her. She wasn't upset with her parents; she knew they loved her and that they were trying to protect her; that they were not trying to deny the child anything, despite how it looked. I will tell her that story."

"And you also tell her that you and her mother and her grandparents love her more than life itself, which is true," Brenda said. "And tell her that her little brother or sister will need her to help raise him, to teach him, to guide him, to set the example for him. Give her some responsibility in her sibling's life."

"Yes," Ginger said. "You're both right. We have to let her know that she's even more important to us now. Let her know we want her to be a strong influence on the baby's life, which we really do."

"That's true," Paul said. "I kinda hope it's a boy because I don't think I can take another girl having me wrapped around her finger. I need a boy to wrap his mom around his finger."

"Oh, I cannot wait," Brenda said. "We haven't had a baby to play with in eighteen years. That's too long. I have missed being a grandmother to a little one, watching her grow up, learning to walk and talk and get into things."

"Yeah, that Helena was a mess," Madeline recalled. "She'd come to my house and right away run to her grandpa. She loved her granddaddy. I never saw him so proud as when she sat on his lap and would fall asleep there."

"I thought about that, too, Mother, last night," Ginger said. "I wish Daddy would be here to see the new baby. He'd be so happy."

Her voice trailed off and she got a little teary-eyed. Much of the focus after her father's death was on her mother and how she would handle losing her mate of more than forty years. But even as he was dealing with his loss of job around that same time, Paul monitored his wife. She was a daddy's girl who took his death hard.

Most people did not see her pain. Paul pulled her through, although she would never get past not having her daddy.

"Losing your father probably has something to do with why you're so emotional about this, Gin," Paul said.

She nodded her head. "I still miss my daddy," she said. "There's no other way to put it. The pain I feel won't go away. I can put it off from time-to-time. But it's there. And that's what kind of scares me about this thing with Helena: What if she feels she's losing you, losing us?"

"We have to make her understand she'll never lose us," Paul said. "I believe she already knows that, but we'll make sure she does."

They arrived at the hotel after stopping at a grocery store and picking up some sparkling cider. They wanted to toast with Ginger.

Paul stopped at the hotel restaurant and picked up four champagne glasses. In their parents' room, he made a toast.

"To my wife, who I love so much; to our unborn child, who we will love with all of our hearts; to Helena, our daughter and granddaughter that I could not love anymore than we do; and to God, thank you for blessing us with this incredible gift of growing our family."

They tapped glasses and drank up.

"I cannot wait to see you with your little baby bump in a few months," Madeline said.

"I'm gonna keep it sexy," Ginger said. "I refuse to be some

oversized human blimp in frumpy clothes with swollen feet, sliding across the room."

"Yes, we can't have that," Paul said.

"Look who's talking now," Brenda said. "He's gotten himself together and lost a bunch of weight and now he can talk?"

"That's right," he said. "I earned it."

"Well, I can tell you right now that I'm breastfeeding—they say you lose weight quicker that way," Ginger said.

"How do you know this?" Madeline asked.

"I got some information from the hospital last night, some pamphlets," she said. "I couldn't sleep. Between thinking about Paul in jail and Helena and being pregnant, it was too much for me to sleep. So…"

"I would have done the same thing," Madeline said. "I'm so happy you are pregnant. Isn't it something to realize you have life growing in your stomach? How big of a miracle is that?"

"That's why I keep touching it. There's nothing to feel yet," Ginger said, "but it's in there growing, little by little. An embryo, to a fetus to a baby to a real live person. It's amazing."

"It is amazing, but we're going to have to set up very regular doctor appointments," Paul said. "You're not a spring chicken anymore—although you still look young; don't look at me like that. I don't want anything to go wrong."

"He's thinking about this man he was in jail with last night," Ginger said.

"Hold on—that sounds too casual, like I'm always in jail or something," Paul said, laughing.

"Never know," Brenda said. "This could be the start of something."

"Not here," Paul said.

"Anyway, before the pregnant woman was so rudely interrupted,

I was going to say that we have to be positive. Nothing negative; not even thoughts. I'm going to eat right, drink right, rest, exercise, take vitamins. These nine months are going to be the most disciplined of my life. And it's going to be easy. As much as I love wine, I didn't look at you all drink it and feel like I had any urge for it. I am so into this."

"That's the right attitude," Brenda said.

They chatted for another ten minutes or so, but never came to an agreement on how to share the important news with Helena.

"We don't have to figure it out today," Paul said.

He and Ginger headed to their room to relax before going to dinner at French Blue. They planned to meet their mothers in the lobby at seven so they could meet Mitch and his friend, Lionel.

Paul was not really anxious about them going on a date, but he *was* cautious. The kind of madness that happened—shootings at schools, random violence—made most any sane person wary of the next.

As they got dressed for dinner, Paul stopped what he was doing and walked over to his wife. She looked up at him.

"You're beautiful," he said. "And before you say, 'You haven't said that to me in years,' let me say I apologize. I love you."

They kissed and hugged each other tightly. "We should tell Helena to come home next weekend," Ginger said. "We shouldn't wait any longer. I don't want this hanging over us. I want us to get past it so I can totally enjoy being pregnant and my family."

Paul said, "OK." He agreed with Ginger, but he wondered how she would respond when he told her of his winnings. He was amazed that he had not told anyone but Big Al of his millions. Well, he did tell his father, too; he knew he was not going on the trip and would not blurt it out, as his mother might.

After a restful few hours talking, nodding off and watching *Law*

& *Order*, they prepared for the evening. Paul got in the shower first. "So I can get out of your way and let you take over the bathroom," he said. "This dinner is going to be special."

"I hope so. I'm starving," Ginger said as she applied makeup. "Thanksgiving dinner was good, but not great. Last night, I couldn't eat anything after you left. So I'm ready for a great dinner."

Paul was not speaking of the meal, but he said, "Me, too."

He found the David Yurman diamond ring he purchased for her and slipped it in his jacket pocket. He poured the last of the wine he had remaining into a glass and enjoyed it and watched *SportsCenter* as he waited on Ginger.

Several minutes later, she emerged from the bathroom looking lovely. "You're having a boy," Paul said.

"Wishful thinking," Ginger said.

"I can tell," he added. "You're glowing. Your skin is glowing."

"That's called lotion, Paul," Ginger said. "You didn't say I was glowing yesterday."

"Yesterday I didn't realize you were pregnant," he said.

"I heard people say that if you're pregnant with a boy your skin will glow," Ginger said. "It's too early for that with me. But that raises a question: Do you want to hear the gender of the baby in advance or when the baby is born?"

"I want to wait. I like surprises," he said.

"I do, too. So it's a deal; we will not learn the gender of our baby until *she* is born," Ginger said.

"Agreed—until *he* is born," Paul cracked.

Ginger participated in the little game, but she did not care if it was a boy or a girl. If anything, she leaned toward a boy because she had the experience of raising a girl—and she knew Paul was serious about wanting a boy.

They debated the issue from the room to the lobby, where they were to ask their parents of their preference. But then they got to the lobby, Madeline and Brenda were not there. Ginger went to check the bathroom and they were not there. Before they could call the room, Paul's cell phone rang. It was his mother.

"Paul, we're in a taxi," she said. "Mitch and Madeline got things mixed up. He thought we were meeting there. She thought he was coming to pick us up. The restaurant does not seat unless all parties are present—and we couldn't move the reservation back. So we jumped in a taxi so you and Ginger can go on with your night."

"Ma, we could have taken you to the restaurant," Paul said. "Which one is it? Maybe we can meet you there for drinks after dinner."

"OK, good. It's called Tra Vigne," Brenda said.

"That's close to where we're going. We passed it twice today," Paul said. "OK, keep your phone on. I will call you after our meal. Or you call me before you all leave the place."

Tra Vigne was an Italian restaurant with vine covering the building with green and white awning just beyond a railroad track. It looked like something carved out of Italy.

Mitch and Lionel waited at the bar for Madeline and Brenda, who were looking elegant and younger than their sixty-plus years. Both wore dresses and heels, but not too high. "You'll never catch me falling on my butt," Brenda said.

Mitch, tall and distinguished with gray hair and a mustache, noticed Madeline immediately, and he and Lionel met them at the reception area. He and Madeline hugged while Lionel—who was not as tall as Mitch but was handsome with a wide, engaging smile—introduced himself to Brenda.

Madeline and Lionel and Brenda and Mitch exchanged handshakes and pleasantries and they were escorted to their table.

The restaurant was alive and noisy, full of people. It was an ideal setting for a double/blind date: nice, but not overly romantic.

Mitch said, "To eat good food is to be close to God. It's an Italian saying. And I agree with that. Eating is one of my true pleasures."

"Mine, too, Madeline said. "This place is supposed to have good food."

Madeline sat at the square table to Mitch's left, with Brenda next to her and across from Mitch and Lionel to Brenda's left. Madeline and Brenda strategized on this arrangement. They wanted it so that if Mitch desired to engage in private conversation with Madeline, he would be able to do so without talking across the table. And the same with Lionel, who was an interesting man.

He spent the latter part of his life running a foundation for underprivileged boys, after retiring from the military. He played the saxophone. He seemed genuine. And he had an edge about him.

"Our foundation was legit; I can see how you're looking at me," Lionel said. "You're thinking about that Jerry Sandusky fool from Penn State who molested all those boys. Don't get any ideas."

The ladies laughed.

The evening flowed nicely. The food was delicious and hearty. The wine was nice and flowed like water. The conversations ranged from raising kids to travel to the Presidential election to the awkwardness of blind dates.

"Funny, but I never felt uncomfortable tonight," Lionel said. "This has been great. My man Mitch took care of me, introduced me to a couple of nice women."

Something in those words forced Brenda to focus more on Mitch. She found herself looking across the able at him, as if drawn to him. She could not understand it—until then. She was not just looking at him anymore; she was staring.

Her heartbeat increased and she excused herself to go to the bathroom. "Want me to go with you?" Madeline asked.

Brenda sipped some water. "No, it's fine. I'll be right back," she said.

She collected herself and made it to the restroom. She was glad it was empty. She looked at herself in the mirror. She was shocked. But she was sure: Madeline's friend, Mitch, was the young love of her life, Mitchell English.

Brenda had not seen him in more than forty years. When last she did, he walked away with tears in his eyes after she refused to marry him. She was pregnant by her eventual husband, James, but he still wanted her to be his wife.

Now there he was, sitting across the table from her. How could it be? How small *is* the world? More importantly, what would she do? Should she tell Madeline first? Should she pull Mitchell to the side? Should she do it at the table? And did he realize who she was?

The more she thought about it, the more she realized that every time she looked at him, he was looking at her. He *did* know, she thought. *At the very least he was studying me, trying to figure out how I'd look more than forty years later*, she thought.

Brenda did not know what to do, how to handle it, but she washed her hands, took a deep breath and went back to the table. Both of the men stood up to greet her. Lionel held her chair for her.

"Gentlemen," Brenda said. "Thought they went out with bell bottoms. Thank you."

She got settled in her seat and refused to look up at Mitch. She immediately started talking about a bad blind date experience.

"My friend, Celeste, set me up with this man about three months ago," Brenda began. "And, look at me, I'm five-foot-five. This man she introduced me to was the same height as me. Now,

I don't have anything against short men. Just keep them away from me."

Everyone laughed. She glanced at Mitchell and her heart fluttered. That smile was the one that owned her heart when she was twenty. She knew for sure then. And she was panicked.

She also knew then that he knew because he stared at her as if he was sending a message.

"Mitchell," she said to him. Just hearing her say his name made him sit up in his seat.

"Mitch," Madeline corrected Brenda. "Not Mitchell."

"Actually," he said, "Mitchell is my given name. Only a few people in the world still call me that."

He stared at Brenda as he spoke. "But most people call me 'Mitch,'" he added. Then he said, "You were going to ask me a question."

"I was," Brenda said. "I was going to ask how did you pick Lionel to bring with you for me to meet?"

"Good question," Madeline said.

Mitchell smiled and looked away. Then he said, "From the way Madeline described you, I figured you deserved to meet a man who is a good man, committed, smart…someone you'd be comfortable with. Did I do you justice?"

Brenda glanced at Lionel and looked back at Mitchell. "Let me put it to you this way: I am really glad I am sitting here right now," she said.

Everyone smiled as Brenda reached for her wine. Then she remembered that Madeline called Mitchell from Brenda's phone because Madeline's battery was weak. She had his cell number and thought of texting him to meet her near the bathrooms. Her mind was consumed with how to broach the subject and how to get a few minutes alone with him.

She did her best to learn more about him while not seeming as if she was prying.

"So how is it that two fine men like you are single?" Brenda asked, while grinning with Madeline.

"Yes, I'd like to know the same thing," Madeline said.

"Unfortunately," Lionel said, "I am a widower. My wife passed a few years ago now. Kidney failure… And I have not found that one woman since. Didn't even know how to begin to start my life again, really. So…"

"Sorry to hear that, Lionel," Madeline said. "I can relate to losing a spouse. My husband died about a year ago, suddenly."

"I understand what you're going through," Lionel said. "Be patient. Somehow, you'll find your way."

"And you, Mitchell?" Brenda asked. She was not in a mood to hear Madeline's story.

"Well, I have been divorced for a while now," he answered. "I think there could be just one person really meant for you. And she was not it."

She knew Mitchell was speaking to her in code. She was so excited and amazed and scared that she did not know what to do.

"Lionel, so where did you meet Mitchell?" she asked.

"We actually met in the Army many years ago in North Carolina and stayed in touch. Then we ran into each other years later in Korea. I'm from out here, Oakland. Always felt I'd come back this way when I retired. So I have been back on the West Coast for a long time now. When he told me he was moving to San Diego, it was great because we could get together regularly."

"And you and Madeline met in Atlanta, right, Mitchell?" Brenda asked.

"We did," Mitch said. "I was visiting a few months ago."

"That's it?" Madeline asked. "There's more to it than that.

Lionel gave a better answer about meeting you than you gave about meeting me."

She smiled as she said it, but Madeline was a little perturbed by his answer. "Oh, I wasn't trying to bore folks with the details," he said. "I was just getting to the point."

"Why would anyone be bored by how we met?" Madeline asked.

"Excuse me; wrong use of words," he said. "Brenda, I was visiting your fair city to play golf before the weather broke and visiting with my sister, who I hadn't seen in a long time. She and Madeline here happen to go to the same church. And at the end of service we were introduced by a friend of my sister's and have been sort of pals since then."

"Now that story was sounding good until the 'pals' part," Madeline said.

"Everything is a process," he said. "Gotta be pals to get anywhere else."

"Pals sounds a little too buddy-buddy for me," Madeline said.

"It's really just semantics," Mitchell said. "I came all the way up here from San Diego and then drove ninety minutes because I wanted to see you. And I'm glad I did."

He looked at Brenda as he said that last sentence. And she knew he was trying to say to her that Madeline meant nothing to him. But to draw his attention back to her, Madeline leaned into Mitchell's ear and whispered into it. It was if she sensed his interest in Brenda or Brenda's in him—or just felt that she was not getting enough attention.

The last thing Brenda wanted to do was upset Madeline. They had spent the better part of three days together and had overcome some hang-ups in order to, for the first time, feel like friends, like family. Their kids were elated about it, and so she did not want to upset that which was just built.

At the same time, she had told the group on Thanksgiving that she remained in love or "the idea of love" with Mitchell after more than four decades. Now, miraculously, he was sitting across from her. How could she simply let him drive off, even if she did have his phone number? She was headed back across country the next evening.

Then a small miracle happened: Lionel excused himself to take a call from his son and Madeline spilled a little Shiraz on her dress and excused herself to tend to it. This happened at the same time.

Brenda took a deep breath as Madeline rose from the table. Mitch helped her out of her chair and he did not sit back down. Rather, he stood across from Brenda, staring down on her. So, she rose from her chair, all the while looking into his eyes, the same eyes that were so hurt many years before.

He moved Madeline's chair out of the way and approached Brenda, who was defenseless. Mitchell delicately placed his hands on her shoulders.

"Brenda," he said.

"Mitchell," she said. "I can't believe this. It's really you."

He shook his head. "This is amazing," he said. "I have thought about you so often over all these years."

"I have never stopped thinking about you," Brenda said. "I even got on my daughter's Facebook page and put your name in there to see if I could find you."

"That's funny," Mitchell said. "I remember the last time I saw you."

"I remember it, too," Brenda said. "I remember it well."

"You look fantastic," Mitchell said, smiling. "When I saw you, I felt something. Just through seeing you, I felt something."

"You felt familiar to me," Brenda explained. "And then suddenly, I knew it. And my heart started beating so fast."

They stood there for a few seconds, looking into each other's eyes just as Lionel was returning from his phone call and as Madeline emerged from the bathroom. They stopped side-by-side in their tracks, stunned by what they witnessed.

"How could this happen?" Mitchell said.

"I don't know," Brenda said. "I guess it was meant to happen. What else could it be? I mean—"

Mitchell leaned in and kissed her in midsentence. She kissed him back and Lionel and Madeline looked at each other. "What is going on?" she asked.

"Hell if I know," Lionel said. "But let's go find out."

He let her pass and they headed to the table, where Brenda and Mitchell stood in loving embrace.

"Ahem," Madeline said as she returned. "Y'all been busy since we left."

"Oh, please, sit down," Brenda said. "You won't believe this."

"I already don't believe it," Madeline said.

Everyone got seated and Brenda said, "Madeline, do you remember on Thanksgiving I told you about the love of my life when I was twenty?"

"No way," Madeline said.

"Yes, it's him, Mitchell," Brenda said. "I'm so shocked I don't know what to think."

"Wait. The man you said went off to the Army when you were a kid? This is the guy?" Madeline said.

"You told her about me?" Mitchell asked.

"Just a few days ago I told her about you and about us," Brenda said.

"Wow," Lionel said. "So, I guess it's safe to say this is the woman you spoke of on our drive up here."

"Huh?" Brenda said. "What did he say?"

"He said his heart has only been broken once in his life—about forty years ago," Lionel recalled. "Said he never told anyone that he was practically in tears over this woman. Turns out *you're* the woman."

"I feel like I'm dreaming," Brenda said.

"Me, too," Madeline said with sarcasm. Then she gathered herself. She stood up and hugged Brenda. "I'm so happy for you. This is incredible, really. Of all the people in the world...Anyway, Lionel, would you like to join me at the bar for a drink?"

"I'd love to," he said, leaving the table to Brenda and Mitchell.

CHAPTER 21
JACKPOT

Ginger and Paul arrived at French Blue and were floating. The realization that they would have a child set in with each passing minute, and it injected their lives with a joy they simply had not had since Helena was declared theirs.

The restaurant was located on quaint Main Street, across from a chic boutique hotel, lined with specialty shops and restaurants. There was a coolness in the night air, a freshness, which was perfect for the occasion.

A white brick, lit fireplace greeted them outside the entrance of the destination, where people sat outside in light jackets and sweaters enjoying the climate. Inside was open and airy, with beautiful light hues and sparkling lighting. The huge windows stretched the entire width of the front of the place, and fresh flowers and tasteful art adorned the walls.

There was a wonderful vibe to the dining room, a wonderful smell. It felt like a celebration.

They were seated at a table near the front windows. Paul insisted Ginger take the seat with her back to the window so she could take in the entire restaurant.

This type of thoughtfulness had abandoned Paul many years before, and it had become so routine that Ginger forgot how special it felt to be treated like a priority. She could not pass on the opportunity to let him know that.

"It's very nice to be treated like you love me," she said.

"I do love you and I'm sorry it took all that we have gone through to get back to showing you that I do," Paul said. "But now that I'm here, I'm here for good."

"I believe you. I do," she said. "But we're going to have a baby pretty soon and definitely be wrapped up in her. I don't mean to spoil this great feeling we have, but we've got to figure out the financial part of this. A kid, as much as you love him, is costly."

Paul smiled. "What are you smiling about?" Ginger said.

"You're extra pretty when you're pregnant," he said.

Ginger smiled, but she was not thrown off course. "This is serious, Paul," she said. "We've got to get on a budget. You know how much stuff we have to get? Clothes, crib, bassinet, stroller—"

"Wait," he said, "I thought that's what the baby shower was for."

"I see you're in a silly mood so we can talk about it another time," Ginger said. "But keep in mind I have to get maternity clothes, too, as I get bigger and bigger."

"Hold that thought," Paul said as he addressed the server.

He ordered a glass of sparkling water for Ginger and a glass of champagne for himself. They perused the menu; everything read divinely, as menus do when you are especially hungry.

"I'm thinking fish," Ginger said.

"Good; fish has the Omega3 that everyone is saying we need in our diets now," Paul said.

"Yes, but not all fish, though," Ginger added. "It's wild salmon, tuna, trout, sardines and maybe one other that have the most benefits... And I see trout on the menu. That's what I'm having."

"I am so hungry," Paul said. "I'm going to start with a salad, the

Living Butter Lettuce with rosemary-buttermilk dressing and candied pecans. Then I want the Head-On Wild Gulf Shrimp with harissa butter, roasted garlic and something called levain. And for my entrée I'm going to have the Fisherman's Stew with sea scallops, red snapper, squid, tomato-fennel broth and pine nuts. And whatever they have for dessert."

"You act like you're the one pregnant," Ginger said.

"I *am* pregnant," he said. "I might not be carrying the baby, but I am so connected to you and this pregnancy."

Ginger smiled. She could not believe how her life had evolved in a matter of months. The same person who was distant and docile and eventually asked for a divorce was now caring and thoughtful and doing a nice job toward rebuilding their marriage.

She turned away to retrieve hand sanitizer from her purse and when she turned back toward Paul, there was a small jewelry box in front of her. Paul's sleight-of-hand was impressive; Ginger did not see him move at all.

"What's this?" Ginger asked.

"Looks like a box to me," Paul answered.

The surprise on her face was priceless as she slowly opened the small box, revealing a stunning diamond in platinum setting.

"Paul…"

"I hope you like it," he said.

"It's beautiful," she said. "But why? And how—"

Paul cut her off. "Why? Because I love you and because you're here with me, still here with me after all of my craziness," he said. "You deserve nice things and so much more."

"All I really want is for us to have a great family; that's it," she said.

"Well, let's do that," he said. "But there's one thing I have to tell you."

Ginger's face went from joyous to concerned. She did not want to hear anything that would take away from their jovial spirit. And she told him so.

"Maybe I should hear this at another time," she said. "We're in such a good place right now. Let's let it last a little longer."

Paul smiled. "You sure?" he said. "I can wait. But I think it's time you know this."

His smile helped Ginger; he wouldn't smile if it were bad news. *He got a job*, she thought. She wanted to say it, but didn't want to take away from his moment.

"Okay, go ahead," she said.

"Now, don't be mad I didn't tell you this before now," he started.

"See, you're making me nervous," she said.

"Don't be," Paul said. "All this time and I never really thought about how I would tell you this."

"Just say it," Ginger blurted out.

"We're rich," Paul said.

She was stumped. "What?"

"Baby, two months ago, I hit the lottery—eight million dollars!"

He pulled out and handed to her a copy of the check and a bank statement with their names on it that had two million dollars deposited in it and another that had another two-million plus in it.

"I...I... I'm...I'm....Brenda could not get out a sentence.

Paul sat back in his chair with his arms folded, smiling.

"Paul, what is this?" she finally said.

"Breathe," he told her. "Take it easy. I hit the lottery, baby. I couldn't believe it. I read those numbers over and over again at least ten times. I literally pinched myself to make sure I wasn't dreaming. It was real. Gin, it was a little more than four million after taxes. Pinch yourself so you know you're not dreaming."

Ginger closed her eyes for a few seconds, and then tears seeped from them and down the sides of her face. And then she let out a scream.

"Oh, my God," she said.

The people in the restaurant thought Paul had proposed to her because they saw the ring on the table. Those in adjacent tables clapped.

"Baby, can you believe this?" he said.

Ginger did not answer. She held her hand over her mouth. Paul went around the table and hugged her. "Our life is set up to be anything we want it to be now, Gin," he said. "Anything."

She still did not say a word. He helped her wipe away tears before going back to his seat.

"This is so crazy," Ginger finally said. "Paul…"

"I know," he interjected. "I still can't believe it."

"I can't believe you didn't tell me," Ginger said. "How could you not tell me? Why didn't you tell me?"

Paul's salad came before he could answer. "Congratulations," the server said. They said in unison: "Thank you."

He reached across the table for Ginger's hands and he blessed the food. "Dear Lord, we thank You for this food we are about to receive for the nourishment of our bodies. And we thank You for the amazing blessing You have delivered to us. Only You could be this gracious. Thank You, God. Amen."

Paul grabbed a small plate and shared his salad with Ginger. He bit into his third piece of bread with rosemary butter, which was so delicious that he asked the server if they sold the butter.

"Baby, I didn't tell you at first because I wasn't sure you still loved me," he said.

"What?"

"When I won, we were in hell. I was in hell," he explained. "I had said I wanted a divorce. I didn't mean it but I said it because you deserved better than what I was at that time. That's what I thought then in the state of mind I was in. So now here comes this miracle and it's like, 'I have a chance to fix all this.' But I needed to know that you would come back to me because of me and not because of money."

He braced himself for Ginger to snap. He knew it was insulting to her to think she would be motivated by money in a matter of the heart. And subconsciously it is a reason he did not tell her sooner. He was afraid of what she might think of him. But the longer he waited, the deeper his fear became.

"So, you think I'm a gold digger?" she asked calmly. She took a sip of the sparkling water. "You think I would stay with you because of money? That's what you think of me."

"What I thought was I love you and I want you to love me," Paul answered. "That's it. I didn't want any outside influences playing a role. So, I said, 'Let's go on a trip and see if we can find the magic.' But I knew we would because I was a different person from the last eleven months. I was out of my funk and, even though we had fallen into a rut, at the core of everything was that we had a true love for each other—and for family."

"Still, you put me through a test," Ginger said. She wasn't mad; almost nothing could make her mad at that point. There was too much to be joyous about in her life.

"I don't think it was the right thing to do, looking back on it," Paul said. "So I'm sorry. But for a man, it's important to know that his woman loves him for who he is, not money. I needed to know that for my psyche."

"The fact that I even agreed to go should have told you where my heart was," she said.

"That's true," Paul responded. "And the fact that I bought that ring should tell you what I believed would happen."

They smiled at each other.

"Don't be mad, Gin. Please," Paul said. "We have too much to be thankful for, too much to look forward to. Plus, being mad ain't good for the baby."

Ginger smiled a big smile then, just as the food arrived. Her grilled rainbow trout with Yukon golds, bacon, Gravenstein apples and grain mustard was delicious. And Paul devoured his seafood stew.

She let go of her concern and wanted to scream again, but suppressed it. "What are we going to do with all this money?" she asked.

"Save it, a lot of it, for Helena and our new baby," he said. "Donate some of it. Get a reputable financial adviser. Don't you think?"

"No doubt about it," Ginger said. "There are so many people we can help—women who have been in abusive relationships, cancer research, homeless shelters, foster kids, disadvantaged youths. I am so glad you said that.

"See, this is the Paul I fell in love with. You could have answered that question by saying what you were going to buy for yourself and where we would travel and so on. But your first thoughts were to provide for our children and to help other people. Those are the qualities I fell in love with a long time ago."

"Thank you, Ginger," he said. "And you're the same way, which makes us a good match. I can look back on it now and be honest: A man tying his success or who he is to a job is too much. I put my whole stock in a job, in what I did for work. I'm not saying it's not important. I know it is. But to lose my job—and lose it the unjust way I did—messed me up. And it almost messed up my life.

"Big Al was helping me come around, telling me to 'man up' and do what I needed to be a good husband. Crazy as he can be, he knew how much you meant to me."

"Wait until you tell him you won the lottery; he's going to go off," Ginger said.

"Well, actually, he already knows," Paul revealed.

"What? You told Al, but you didn't tell me?" Ginger said, disgusted.

"I wasn't trying to stay married to Big Al," he said. "And I had to tell *somebody*. My head would have exploded if I hadn't."

"You didn't tell your mother? Does she know, Paul?" Ginger asked.

"No. But I did tell my father," he said.

Ginger shook her head. "So we have a *third* important thing to tell Helena," she said.

"Yes," Paul said. "Maybe we should tell her about the money first. That'll keep her little butt under control."

They laughed. The more they ate, the farther away they got from Paul not telling Ginger about the money. They were a couple in love, pulled together by love, not money.

CHAPTER 21
NEW FRIENDS, OLD FRIENDS

P aul called his mom after their meal to see where they were. He still wanted to meet Mitchell and Lionel—and he wanted to tell her about the lottery.

She answered on the first ring. "What are y'all doing?" she said into the phone. "OK. We're here."

"That was my son, Paul," she said to Mitchell. "He and his wife will be here in about ten, fifteen minutes."

Brenda and Mitchell caught up on each other's lives and essentially fell in love all over again.

When Madeline and Lionel left them alone at the table, they reverted to their youth almost instantly.

"You broke my heart," Mitchell said. "I'm not ashamed to say it."

"It's a little late, but please let me fix it," Brenda said. "I can honestly say that I never forgot you. I never forgot how I felt about you. I never forgot how you felt about me, offering to marry me although I was carrying another man's child."

"I look back on that time of my life as something that was special, but it also scarred me," Mitchell said. "It scarred me in the sense that I spent the rest of my relationship life trying to feel like I did with you, about you, and I couldn't. I actually had two marriages. I hardly even count the first one because it was less than a year after I last saw you. Classic rebound. And it only lasted fourteen months."

"I married Paul's father when he was two, almost three, and stayed married to him until about a year ago," Ginger said. "Nice man... But he wasn't...you."

They were working on their second bottle of Pinot Noir.

"What are we going to do, Mitchell?" Brenda asked. "You live in California. I live in Atlanta. But I really don't want to let you walk away from me again. This wine has made me super aggressive, but it's the truth."

"And the truth is, I don't want to walk away from you,' Mitchell said. "Twice in one lifetime? No. That can't happen. I'm not such a spiritual person, but I believe this was fate. It *had* to be."

"It *had* to be," Brenda agreed. "When we met at the front, I said to myself that you looked familiar. But it was more than that. I felt something...I never envisioned you at sixty-three years old. But then, I never envisioned seeing you ever again, either."

"I will come to Atlanta as often as I can and I would love for you to come to San Diego," Mitchell said. "It's beautiful. Laid-back. The perfect weather."

"Can't wait to experience it," she said.

"So, what do we do about Madeline and Lionel?" Mitchell said.

"Forty-something years ago, I was concerned about other people's feelings and thoughts about me," Brenda said. "I'm too old and too smart to worry about them now. I don't mean to sound cold, but it's the truth."

"I don't think they are that concerned," Mitchell said. "I met with Madeline two times. Nothing was happening there. She's a nice woman. But you...I have held you in my heart all my life."

Brenda looked up and Paul and Ginger were approaching. "Oh, here's Paul, my son. They got here fast."

Paul hugged his mom and turned to Mitchell. "So, you must be Lionel. Nice to meet you," he said, extending his hand.

"Actually, I'm Mitch," he said. "Nice to meet you. Lionel is over there at the bar with Madeline."

"Huh?" Ginger said, puzzled. "Madeline is my mother."

"Nice to meet you," Mitch said.

"Nice to meet you, too. But I thought my mom met you at church in Atlanta."

"She did," he said. "It's a long story."

"Actually, it's a short story," Brenda said. "Remember when I told you about the love of my life when I was twenty years old? The man I really wanted to be with but I was pregnant by your father?"

"Yeah," Paul and Ginger said.

"Well, incredibly, this is the man. Madeline met Mitchell in Atlanta," she said. "And when we saw each other, it all came together."

"*What?*" Paul said.

"How's my mom?" Ginger asked.

"I need a glass of wine," Paul said. "What's this? Pinot?"

"How could you tell that by looking at it?" Mitchell asked.

"I just know," Paul said. "The color. The density. But wait. Ma."

"I know, Paul, it's crazy," Brenda said. "It's a miracle."

Ginger bolted over to her mother and Lionel. "I guess you heard?" Madeline said. "Small world. God is working on this family.

"This is my daughter, Ginger. This is Lionel."

"How did this happen?" Ginger asked. "I want to know all the details because this is something else."

Madeline and Lionel shared the details as they saw it.

"Looking back, I did notice that they were making a lot of eye contact," Madeline said. "But I didn't think anything of it. I thought they were just being good communicators, looking those in the eye you're speaking to."

"I noticed that, but I also noticed that Mitch was a little more quiet than normal. Somewhere at the table he figured it out and when he did, his mind was churning on how to say something instead of talking to us," Lionel said.

"But guess what, honey?" Madeline said. "It has worked out great. Lionel and I have a lot in common. And we're going to keep in touch."

"That's nice," Ginger said.

It was so surprising that Paul and Ginger forgot to share the news of the lottery money—until Paul told Brenda at the table. She had told Paul that she would have to save money to travel back and forth to California to see Mitchell. That's when it registered to Paul that he had not shared the news.

When he did, she screamed. That's how Ginger, standing at the bar, knew Paul had told her.

"Wow," Madeline said. "Did you hear that scream? What was that about?"

"Well, mother, it was probably because Paul told her that he hit the lottery for eight million dollars," Ginger said.

And then Madeline screamed—and Paul knew his wife had told her mother.

The three of them left the bar and went over to the table. Hugs were shared. Lionel said to Paul: "I guess I'm meeting you at the right time," and they laughed.

Paul called over the server and they ordered another bottle of Pinot—and a glass of sparkling apple cider.

Lionel pulled up two more chairs and the six of them talked and laughed and marveled at the stunning developments until long after the last diner left.

When the bill came, Paul picked it up.

"This one is on me," he said.

No one argued with him.

CHAPTER 23
MUDDY
WATERS

They had an evening flight back to Atlanta the next day, and Paul had one more surprise for Ginger.

"A mud bath?" she asked.

"Yes. We cannot come all the way out here and not experience a mud bath. Calistoga is the mud bath capital," he explained. "We have a noon appointment. It's like a spa treatment. But there are these crazy minerals in the water and the mud that reinvigorates your body. And my back hasn't been right since that long flight.

"And you said you feel a little achy, too, right?"

"I do, but you sure about this?" she said.

"I already told our moms what we were doing. They're having lunch with Lionel and Mitchell," he said. "When we get back, we can head straight to the airport."

And so they took the drive to Golden Haven Hot Springs spa in Calistoga. Along the way, Paul talked to Big Al and Ginger called Serena, who were ecstatic about all the developments.

Paul called Helena right before they got to the destination. "Been an amazing trip, honey," he said.

"So you and mom are doing better?" Helena asked.

"Better?" Paul said. "Who said we weren't doing well?"

"Daddy, I'm not a kid," she said. "I lived in the house with you. You hardly talked to each other."

He was surprised. He thought she was so caught up in her own life that she did not notice theirs.

Paul repeated what Helena said so Ginger could hear it. "You noticed we weren't talking to each other?"

Ginger told her girlfriend, "I'll call you back."

Paul then put Helena on the speakerphone. "Honey, Mom can hear you. I have you on speaker."

"Hi, Mom. Dad still thinks I'm a kid. He didn't know I knew you and he were having issues."

"Well, to be truthful, I didn't know you knew, either."

"You don't remember what I said to you right before you left me in my room at college? I said, 'Mommy, take care of Daddy. He loves you.' That was my way of saying I understood what was going on. You didn't get it?"

"I didn't but you're even smarter than we thought," Ginger said.

They pulled up to the spa, which looked like a motel. "Helena, we're about to take a mud bath before we head back to Atlanta. But we're going to call you later. There's a lot we have to talk about."

"A mud bath?" she said. "You old people… Anyway, okay. Call me. Have fun. Love you!"

They checked in at the desk and were taken to the room for their couples' mud bath. Immediately, the smell of the mud was jarring. "Stinks in here," Ginger said under her breath.

The young man gave them instructions on how to enter the tub that was virtually spilling over in hot mud. There was a hot tub to the right that did not look inviting. And there were showers to the left.

"OK, enjoy," the man said. "I will check on you later."

Paul and Ginger got undressed and approached their side-by-side tubs of mud. Paul was eager to get in. His back bothered him and his neck was a little stiff, too, from sleeping awkwardly and lying on that thin jail mattress. He went in butt-first, as instructed, and was almost immediately soothed by the mud and the heat.

"Oh, baby, it feels weird the more you submerge yourself, but it's hot and it's like you're floating," he said.

Ginger took her time but finally eased her way into the tub. Her facial expression didn't convey that she was happy. But as she got more comfortable, she relaxed.

"It's hot," she said. "And sand is in the crack of my butt."

They laughed and in a minute or so she was in and covered and totally relaxed. The guy came in to check on them, put a smoother version of the mud on their faces and a cold towel across their foreheads.

"You should stay in about twenty-five minutes and then you can shower and get in the hot tub or get a warm body wrap," he said. "Enjoy."

They settled into the mud and found a comfort zone. Paul was so relaxed that he almost fell asleep. Ginger was not as comfortable, but she enjoyed the experience.

They talked for a short time, but then drifted into a totally relaxed place. Paul actually fell asleep for a few minutes. Ginger lay in it, but her mind was so filled with emotions and thoughts that she could not doze off. Plus, the heat bothered her.

She did feel better about it when she got out and the aches in her lower back she felt were gone. Just like that. Paul said, "I feel like playing basketball. I cannot believe how fresh I feel. Amazing."

They showered and took their time cleaning themselves off— they passed on the hot tub and warm body wrap—before heading back to Napa to pick up the luggage and their parents.

"That probably was a little messy and stinky to you, Gin," Paul said on the drive back. "But I'm glad we went for two reasons:

One, I wanted us to experience something together neither of us had. That's one way to keep things fresh in a marriage. Do different stuff."

"I like that way of thinking," she said. "What's the other reason?"

"I didn't know it at the time I planned it, but that mud was symbolic of what our marriage had been like," he said. "We were stuck in the mud. Just lying there, floating. If we didn't do something, we were going to sink deeper and deeper until we drowned.

"But on this trip, we pulled ourselves out of the mud. And just like our bodies feel now, coming out of that mud bath, our relationship has been reinvigorated."

Madeline reached over and held Paul's hand. They listened to music and enjoyed the beautiful countryside the rest of the ride back to the hotel, where their parents were in the lobby.

Mitchell and Lionel had said their goodbyes. The ladies were ready to head home. Paul loaded up the car and they were on their way. They decided they would eat at the airport.

"The mud bath was great," Ginger said. "I feel totally refreshed."

"Really? I probably could have used one after all that wine last night. My goodness," Brenda said.

"Brenda, I am so happy for you—Mitch, I mean, Mitchell, is a nice man," Madeline said.

"Thank you. He is," Brenda said. "And it seemed like Lionel was really into you."

"I like him. We got along great. Who would have guessed this?" Madeline said. "But I'm trying to figure out why we aren't in a limousine, Mr. Millionaire."

Paul laughed. "Next time," he said.

His phone rang. It was Helena. "Hi, honey. I'm gonna put you on speaker so you can say hi to your grandparents, too."

Everyone greeted her.

"So, Dad, what is it you want to talk to me about?" Helena asked.

"Well, there are three things, but the one I want to speak with you about first is very sensitive and we should talk about it in person," he said. He looked around the car and the ladies nodded their heads in agreement.

"Dad, it can't be that serious? Is anyone dying?"

"No, no one's dying, Helena."

"Then tell me now. I don't want to wait."

Paul looked around the car for a consensus and everyone shook their heads "no."

"Baby, come home this weekend so we can sit down as a family."

"Dad, what is it? That I'm adopted?"

Paul nearly veered off the road. "What?"

"Dad, come on. I'm eighteen. You told me this two years ago."

"What? What are you talking about?"

He looked around the car and was greeted by puzzled faces.

"Daddy, you and I stayed home one weekend when Mommy went on that bus trip with Grandma Madeline to Savannah," Helena said. "You and I cooked dinner and then I went to the movies with my friends. You said you were going to stay home and drink some wine that you ordered. Malbec, I think it was.

"When I got home that night, you were watching TV and I asked you how the wine was. You said it was so good you were into the second bottle. I didn't think that was a lot at the time, so I sat down with you and you just told me."

"I…I can't believe this. What did I say?"

"You said you and Mommy love me very much and that you had to tell me something very important and that I had to listen really carefully. You said, 'You are your mom's and my daughter. We raised you from the first days you were born. But you did not come out of your mother's stomach. We adopted you.'

"I didn't say anything. Then you said, 'Listen, you are our child.'

"I asked you whose stomach I came out of and you said, 'Her name is Rita.' You said if I wanted to meet her and the man who got her pregnant—you were so cute; you wouldn't call him my 'dad' or 'father'—that you and Mommy would make it happen. I said, 'No. You are my parents.'

"I was trying to let it go but that wine had taken over. You said, 'They are probably good people but they did some bad things, so they are in prison.' You told me their story. Then you started crying, Dad. You said you were sorry that you made Mommy not tell me before then. I said it was 'OK because we are a family and I love you both, no matter what a birth certificate says.'"

Ginger wept, again. "Did I say anything else? I can't believe this," Paul said.

"You said, 'Your mother and I love you with everything we have.' And we hugged and you passed out. And I just laid there in your arms and fell asleep, too."

"Oh, my God," Paul said. "Why didn't you say anything after that?"

"Because it didn't matter," she said. "You are my parents."

"I'm so sorry we didn't tell you the right way," Ginger said.

"Mom, it's OK, it's fine," Helena said. "I love you."

"Still," Ginger said, "we want you to come home so we can talk about it together."

"OK," Helena said. "What are the other two things?"

Paul was so emotional he couldn't talk. Ginger wiped her face and said, "Well, your daddy told me something last night that was shocking."

"That he hit the lottery?" Helena said.

"*What*? How could you know that?" Ginger said. "Did you tell her, Paul?'

"No," he said.

"Daddy didn't tell me," Helena said. "Grandpa did."

"That damn James," Brenda said. "He knew?"

"Yeah, I told Dad about a month ago," Paul said.

"You told him but not me?" Brenda asked.

Paul said, "I told him because I knew—or I thought—he could keep a secret. I know you can't, Ma."

"Well, I'll be damned. What secret haven't I told?" Brenda inquired.

"Do I really need to list them, Ma?" Paul said.

Brenda thought about it and said, "Never mind."

"So you know about the money? Why did he tell you?" Ginger said.

"Well, I call Grandpa probably every two weeks," Helena said. "We had our 'pop' call — that's what he calls it. And I asked him: 'So, Grandpa, what's really going on with the family?' And he said, 'You're my little angel and I cannot lie to you.' And he told me. He said you would tell me when the time was right and to not say anything until he said it was OK. Last night he said it was OK."

"So how do you feel about it?" Madeline asked.

"I feel good because now I can finish college without my parents having to spend all their money," she said. "I felt kinda guilty about that."

"What a sweetheart you are, Helena," Brenda said.

"My goodness," Paul said. "OK, so we have that to talk about to and how we're going to manage it and not let it manage us."

"OK," Helena said. "So I guess that means the third thing to talk about is the baby."

"*Huh?*" Paul shrieked. "This is crazy. Who told you about the baby?"

"Grandma Madeline and Grandma Brenda called me this morning," Helena said.

Paul and Ginger turned around to look at their parents.

"See what I mean, Ma?" Paul said.

"I'm sorry," they said in unison. "We were too excited. The girl needed to know she's going to be a big sister. That's a big thing. She has to prepare for that," Madeline said.

"I totally agree," Brenda said, smiling.

"But we talked about this last night," Ginger said. "She should not have gotten the news from you."

"It's OK, Mommy," Helena said.

"Soooo, how you feel about that, Helena?" Paul asked his daughter.

"I'm so happy," she said. "I can't wait. I hope it's a girl. Then I can dress her and show her the ropes. But then again, if it's a boy I can teach him about girls and when he gets old enough he can beat up boys that get on my nerves."

"I can do that for you," Paul said. "Gladly… Anyway, I guess that's it. You're all caught up."

"Nobody gonna mention that Grandma Brenda is in love?" Helena said.

"Ah, what did you say?" Brenda said.

"Mommy told me that you met your childhood sweetheart last night and you're still in love with him," she answered.

Everyone looked at Ginger in astonishment.

"Helena, we're going to call you later, when we get home," Ginger said.

"OK, have a safe trip," Helena said, laughing. "I love you all. And have a drink for me."

ABOUT THE AUTHOR

Curtis Bunn is a national award-winning sports journalist and author of six critically acclaimed novels that explore compelling relationship dynamics. His debut book, *Baggage Check*, ascended to No. 1 on the *Essence* magazine bestsellers list.

His most recent books, *A Cold Piece of Work* and *Homecoming Weekend* have been lauded for their authenticity and gripping storylines.

Bunn spent twenty-five years writing sports at *The Washington Times*, *New York Newsday*, *New York Daily News* and *The Atlanta Journal-Constitution*. Over that time he wrote about every major sporting event, including the NBA Finals, Olympic Games in Seoul, Korea and Sydney, Australia, Super Bowls, NCAA Final Fours, World Series, boxing championships and so much more. He now serves as Deputy Editor of www.AtlantaBlackStar.com, a leading online news organization.

In 2003, Bunn, who also taught journalism for four years at Morehouse College, created the National Book Club Conference, an annual event that brings together some of the top African-American authors and readers from across the country.

You can find him at www.curtisbunn.com. He also has a presence on Facebook and Twitter @curtisbunn.

READER DISCUSSION GUIDE

Questions to help facilitate a book club or group discussion
(Don't cheat and read these questions before reading the book. :-)) :

1. Have you experienced getting a loose tongue under the power of
   alcohol? What was the occasion(s)? What secret or truth did you
   reveal?

2. Was it acceptable for Paul to keep his incredibly good news a
   secret from his wife until he learned that she wanted to make the
   marriage work?

3. Considering Ginger's emotional state at the time, do you
   understand her drastic decision she revealed in California that
   really upset Paul?

4. What is your position on telling a child he/she is adopted?
   Should you reveal it or keep it concealed? Why?

5. How would you accept learning your father had killed or
   contributed to someone's death in protecting you?

6. Would you, as Ginger did, have tried to make the marriage work
   after your husband (or wife) told you he/she wanted a divorce?

7. What did you think of Paul's jail experience?

8. What did you think of the main characters telling funny stories that they had not shared with anyone?

9. Were you surprised by the twist with Mitchell and Brenda? What did you think of it?

10. How would a trip with you, your mother, mother-in-law and spouse turn out?

THE CRAFT
WRITING *The Truth Is In The Wine*

I typed the final words of this book at exactly 1:59 p.m. on Friday, February 1, 2013. I let out a sigh of relief, closed my laptop and placed it on the hotel bed. I then retrieved a bottle of Fairview Mourvèdre, a red wine that traveled with me from Atlanta to Chesapeake, Virginia, where a book party was to be held for me that evening for my previous release, *Homecoming Weekend*.

I saved the wine, purchased six months before in Cape Town, South Africa, just for this occasion. And it was *good*.

In the past, I celebrated completing books by cooking, which is one of my favorite pastimes, along with golf and more golf and movies and making cocktails. In this case, considering the title of the work and the relief that came with finishing it, wine was the appropriate way to mark the occasion.

It was appropriate the way you might need a libation at the end of a long day, to, at once, steady the nerves and to reward yourself for surviving the challenge. That's how I felt: accomplished and like I had endured in the face of significant odds.

The truth is, staring at an empty computer screen with the idea of filling it with eighty thousand words is quite a daunting thing. Even after having written five other novels, it remains intimidating. But it is an amazing thing when the characters you create grow and live inside you. You take their journey together, making it kind of strange when you are done and it is time to discard these "people" that have resided in you and become a part of you for so long.

The good news is that Paul, Ginger, Madeline and Brenda will never leave me; they will hover in the recesses of my mind, and probably emerge again and demand that I write a sequel.

They were fun characters because they were honest. They said things they wanted to say, things that were on their heart. Many times it was the influence of the wine that released those reservations, but at least they cleared their conscience. Some of us cannot say that.

To get to their place, I had go to Napa and indulge in the wine, take in the country, breathe the spirit of the place. And it was a wonderful experience. For someone who has gained a strong interest in wines, it was great research.

Strange, but I find myself still "researching," even though the book is done! That's how much I enjoyed learning about wines and ingesting them. Now, wine is very much a part of my life.

I sipped wine as I read back on this book, and I was reminded of the deadline pressure I put on myself. In the last forty-five days I had to write about fifty-five thousand words. I was doing more research (if you know what I mean) than writing.

But in that last month and a half, the book took life, as I crafted storylines that challenged love and piqued curiosities. The characters became more clear to me—and more complex. The themes of the dilemmas strengthen as characters' inhibitions weakened.

For an author, it is a beautiful place to be—in command of your imagination and story, knowing where you are going and how you're going to get there. I found myself writing wherever I was—the couch, bed, coffee shop, airplane, airport, dining room table. When you feel like you must write to feel good about yourself, well, that's where you want to be.

"Truth" was no more difficult or easy to write than any other book. But it is always a challenge to create interesting characters with interesting stories. It is in the complexities of each that make a book thought provoking. I had fun doing that.

So I partook of the wine when I was done, and I have not failed to think of this book each time I have poured a glass since then. It's like each sip represents a celebration of the work.

CURTIS BUNN'S FAVORITE WINES

I am hardly a wine connoisseur, but I have grown to really appreciate it, how it is made and cultivated. And I enjoy it. I make sure some wine is consumed on most days, especially reds because of the health benefits. *(Wink, wink.)* Here are my ten favorite wines. If you try any of them, I hope you enjoy.

—Curtis

REDS

TOBIN JAMES FAT BOY ZINFANDEL 2008: *"Sex in a bottle,"* it was described to me by Frank Ski of Frank Ski Restaurant in Atlanta. And I get his point. 16.2 percent alcohol. Need I say more?

THE PRISONER ZINFANDEL: *"Subtle hints of berries and spice. The more you consume, the more you want."*

FAIRVIEW PINOTAGE 2010 (SOUTH AFRICA): *"Distinct flavor and taste. Perhaps my favorite wine of all. Good for celebrating."*

PHEBUS (MENDOZA) MALBEC: *"Spicy and flavorful. Good to drink while in bed watching a good movie."*

STERLING 2007 RESERVE CABERNET SAUVIGNON: *"Elegant wine that makes you want to close your eyes with every sip."*

WHITES

OYA RIESLING: *"Flavorful and delicate. Delicious. My favorite white wine of all. Order it at www.oyawines.com."*

ST. SUPERY CHARDONNAY 2009: *"There's a sexiness to this wine, first consumed at The Lamb's Club in New York—or maybe it was just the woman drinking it…"*

STERLING VIOGNIER 2011: *"First of all, it looks great in the glass—light and bright and ready to take in. It's refreshing and fruity, but not too sweet."*

ZOLO SAUVIGNON-BLANC: *"Crisp and light, ideal for a summer day while wearing sunglasses, sitting out on a patio. Cool and refreshing."*

VEUVE CLIQUOT PONSARDIN (champagne): *"The ultimate celebratory drink. I'll take this over any other champagne. It is refreshing with fruit flavors bursting in every sip. Just look for the orange label. Want to impress? This is the one for every toast."*